Jeanne

To understanding it.
JazakAllah for being
part of this process,

Kn.

Jalaffa

o Kaw ou Gaza

L

S

ufch

H Aylah

A

Bahr Akaba

Habir-Akaba

A R

J O R H E

E J

A

Z

al Medinah

MER

R O U G E

ou G O L F E

Yambou

M E

Djiddah

omol

ydhàb

Farate

Mekka

Fuhaa

Dradab

Ahwaz

Korna

Basrah

Endian

Bandar Dilem

Bandar Rik

Kargo

Karak

C. Rokle

I. Relecke

Bandar

Zesarin

Anger

GOLF

C.

Ch

C. Nabon

I Lar

van

GOLF

PEK

I. Bahrayn

P

Perl

E

Al Katif

Bank

B.

Kutara

Goda

A

H

B

R

A

Y

Tropicus

Cancri

I

A

A Qur'aanic Odyssey

Towards Juz Amma
by Umm Muhemmed

Bismillahir Rahmanir Raheem

First published in Great Britain in 2012 by Greenbird Books
Text © 2012 by Umm Muhemmed
Illustrations © 2012 by Anna Rammis
This book has been typeset in Palatino Linotype
Printed in USA

British Library Cataloguing in Publication Data:
A catalogue record for this book is available from the
British Library.

ISBN: 978-0-9562141-5-7

www.greenbirdbooks.com

For Shah Bano who is light incarnate.
Thank you for lighting the way.

Praise for A QUR'AANIC ODYSSEY

'Children's literature classically contains stories about life as a journey or quest. This exquisite narrative of a spiritual Odyssey is a sublime evocation of this theme and I am eager, as one who reads regularly to children at various stages of development, to offer them this inspiring and inspired tale.'

Dennis Dalton, Professor Emeritus of Political Science, Columbia University

'A wonderful inspiration! Umm Muhemmed reminds one of the ultimate reason for studying Qur'aan: to understand and reflect on the message. Her narrations are reflections of how Islam should be taught, not moments of forcing religious texts, but rather seeing opportunities and taking lessons from the Qur'aan and Sunnah.'

Umm Aasiyah Muhammad, author of *A Muslim Princess*

'An insightful story that highlights challenges and victories which a Muslim family in the West experiences. Essential reading for anyone wanting to understand the phenomenon of Qur'aanic memorization, Muslim & non-Muslim alike.'

Hafidha Rayhaanah Omar, Founder of Fee Qalbee

'As commendable as the pursuit of hifdh can be, it can easily become an academic exercise of the mind rather than a spiritual journey of the heart. This book is a bridge between learning the Qur'aan and living the Qur'aan, between memorizing the sacred texts and understanding them. The examples that Umm Muhemmed gives – of drawing a straight line to illustrate Siraatul Mustaqeem, of using a space such as a garage to learn Surah Takathur to illustrate the abundance of our stored properties – bring home the message that the Qur'aan is relevant and that its lessons are accessible to old and young. It is also a book about conscious and conscientious parenting, about being aware and in tune with your child's development and about the sincerity of intention. I plan to use these lessons for my own reflection and for my children's journeys with the Qur'aan, and pray that Allah blesses the writer in her pursuit of hifdh so that we may see subsequent additions to 'A Qur'aanic Odyssey.'

Umm Zakariyya Gardee, Freelance Writer and Editor

'An intimate and eloquent portrait of one mother's journey to instruct her children in the basis of Islam. This lovely book reminds us of the importance of giving our children a spiritual berth, while nurturing their adventurous, naturally inquisitive spirits. With humor, grace, and insight, Umm Muhemmed shows how our children have as much (if not more) to teach us than we have to teach them.'

Jerusha O. Conner Ph.D, Assistant Professor of Education, Villanova University

'A Qur'aanic Odyssey is a vibrantly written book about the everyday joys and challenges of parenting but with the added dimension of how parents can provide spiritual guidance to their children. While the Qur'aan is a source of guidance for over 1 billion Muslims, too often, the ethos of the Qur'aan is overlooked. Just as Prophet Muhammed was described as a "living Qur'aan" this book brings to life how this family has chosen to "live the Qur'aan", through the journey of hifdh, thus making this sacred book a means of guidance, discovery, and moral and spiritual development through our everyday adventures.'

Zuhaira Razzack, Pricipal, ILM Academy

'A Qur'aanic Odyssey will resonate with mothers everywhere – regardless of backgrounds and beliefs – as a portrait of the early years in our children's lives during which we aim to guide them - from the depths of our hearts - while learning so much from them along the way. The book's format makes it a pleasure to read: meaningful snapshots from the lives of a delightful family whom we feel we know in person by the end, followed by practical and spiritual advice based on the teachings of Islam. While interesting and informative in regards to its religious basis, this book transcends cultures and geography as well, getting at the very heart of a mother's dedication to her children.'

Jenny Curtis Fee, author of *Pancakes at Midnight – Jet Lag and the Young Traveler*, and mother of three multi-cultural children, Geneva, Switzerland

DISCLAIMER:

It should be noted that the author is not an Islamic scholar, but rather a junior student of Qur'aan. The text does not purport to be an instruction book for those departing on a *hifdh* journey, but rather a companion text to help inspire and animate part of the journey. Anyone who is considering undertaking *hifdh* should seek instruction from a recognized scholar.

Contents

As stories from Ibrahim and Amna's lives are recounted, generally one *surah* and/or one element from one *surah* is highlighted. The chapters do not, however, provide comprehensive coverage of each of the *surahs*. As is common with *hifdh* studies, the children are starting from the back *surahs*, which are also the shortest, and making their way through the 30th *juz* (part) of the Qur'aan.

ACKNOWLEDGEMENTS

Thank you to Humaira for always having an open home and keeping life rooted in the ground, albeit with some transcendental talk too. Thank you to Aasiyah and Carimah for inspiring. Thank you to Hafidha Rayhaanah for the infinite lessons. Thank you to Jameela for being a font of knowledge, and friendship. Thank you to Niaz for doing more than his share and accompanying me on a never ending adventure. Thank you to the Lauras in my life, for being such dedicated readers. Laura A deserves special recognition, as being the most committed reader I know; I have often simply written for your audience, of one. Thank you to Joel and Becky for listening, despite language barriers. Thank you to Dennis and Sarah for believing in dreams. Thank you to Lauren and Jerusha for 20 years of literary criticism and religious 'real talk'. Thank you to Aisha and Zuhaira for helping to make it relevant to today, and to Greenbird Books for publishing it. Thank you to Ali and Hasbi for the companionship, the teaching and the endless learning. You keep me humble, but also help me to strive, always. Thank you to Shah Bano for being the guiding light. *Inshaa Allah* this work will be accepted, and these efforts will help those who seek to understand Qur'aan amidst life's lessons.

PREFACE

This is a story about Ibrahim and Amna. They are two rapidly growing children, brother and sister, who, at the start of our story, are aged two and five and a half, and who are both embarking on learning the Qur'aan. Their Ammi (Khadija), who is originally from Karachi, Pakistan, narrates the story, alternately leading and following in the children's adventures. She has taken a break in her own career to shepherd them through their Qur'aanic study as well as to undertake her own *hifdh* (Qur'aanic memorization/preservation), under the guidance of Hafidha Rabia, who hails from Jakarta. Born and bred in Brooklyn, New York, Papa (Abdurrahman) is very close to the heart of the story as well. He commenced his own Qur'aanic study six and a half years ago after converting to Islam, and, together with Khadija, is guiding the children in their study, albeit while still continuing his own study as well as working as a financial analyst.

Not far from these pairs are the children's Nani (maternal grandmother, who stays with them much of the time) and their Nonna (paternal grandmother, who is always 'virtually' present and also visits often), both of whom are retired journalists. Other main characters include Uncle Geo, a mechanical engineer, who has lots of old cars. There is Sabir, a best friend, presently living in Cape Town (from where Ibrahim and Amna have just moved), and their cousins in Houston (where they have just arrived), namely Yasmeen and Yaseen, aged seven and eight respectively, and who have between them a butterfly collection and an ant farm. There are also cousins and twins, David and Alexandra, hailing from Cambridge, Massachusetts, who the children see at Thanksgiving, and who have just celebrated their 14th birthday.

This story will take us around the world and back again (including Brooklyn, Doha, Dubai, Jakarta, and Karachi, not to mention the Houston Zoo) as we adventure along with these two children, who are learning and aspiring to live the Qur'aan, day in and day out, amidst all life's episodes. In this story, the children are working toward completing the 30th section of the Qur'aan, also known as *Juz Amma*.

BASED ON...

This story is based on real life, but all characters and events have been fictionalized, with the exception to footnotes.[1] Many ideas incorporated in this narrative are inspired and informed by Fee Qalbee. The author is grateful for the *hifdh* mentorship provided by the founder of Fee Qalbee, Hafidha

---

[1] For any information contained in the footnotes that is not cited, the sources are material widely available in the public domain, which have been fact checked and paraphrased.

Rayhaanah Omar. The author is also indebted to Kinza Academy for its wealth of homeschooling resources.

Who is it for? *A Qur'aanic Odyssey* is for all who are interested, including parents who are helping to coach their children in learning and memorizing Qur'aan or more general Qur'aanic study. The author also hopes to reach out to non-Muslims, especially any who may be linked to cross-cultural families, trying to navigate and understand some of the intricacies of the 'culture' of Islam, especially with regard to the Qur'aan. In addition, the text may be used in a classroom environment including by teachers, of any faith or conviction, who seek to present Islam and more specifically the Qur'aan in a positive 'real-life' 'Western' environment. Through her storytelling, the author aspires to demonstrate that the 'culture' of the Qur'aan and Islam may be complementary to the West.

MORE ABOUT THE AUTHOR...

Umm Muhemmed is an American born development economist, who recently commenced her own *hifdh* pursuit and hopes that this small effort of writing will help her, as a parent, student, and fellow human being *inshaa Allah*. She has most in common with the character Abdurrahman; however, she has a French, not an Italian, connection. Her hope and prayer is that the story will be a vehicle of learning and peace for parents and children, and the teachers who read it as well.

MORE ABOUT HIFDH/QUR'AANIC MEMORIZATION...

In South Africa, where the author has moved from (together with her fictitious characters, Ibrahim and Amna) there may be approximately 300 *hifdh* programs, as nearly every locality and mosque has one (Omar 2011). In Houston, Texas, where the author is presently living, there are countless such dedicated programs as well. Some children commence as early as 4-5 years old; however, there is no fixed age, with *hifdh* largely depending on the interest and maturity of the child. Quite apart from any dedicated institutions, the teaching of Qur'aan, including memorization, is undertaken in mosques and Muslim homes worldwide. And it is not uncommon for children to begin learning short *surahs* (chapters) from the Qur'aan at the age of 3. "The Holy Qur'an has been memorised [in its entirety] for over fourteen centuries. People of various ages and nations have managed to complete this... task... It is [also] a matter of honour to have memorized even a small part of the Holy Qur'an... Those who dedicate their lives to the study and preservation of the entire Holy Book are known as [Allah's] special servants." (Londt 2008, p.3).

CAST OF CHARACTERS

A Qur'aanic Odyssey includes a vast array of characters, hailing from around the world. The cast grows as the story unfolds. Characters are introduced below, chronologically and not alphabetically.

Ibrahim: aged five at the start of our story, recently moved to Houston, Texas from Cape Town, South Africa. He also plays the part of 'Captain Kashif' in a make believe game created by the family, during their trek to Aransas National Wildlife Refuge

Amna: aged two at the start of our story and fellow traveler, she also plays the part of 'Sergeant Faith' (see above under Ibrahim)

Ammi/Khadija: mother of Ibrahim and Amna and the narrator of the story, development economist, and aspiring *hafidha*, she also plays the part of 'Lieutenant Laila'

Papa/Abdurrahman/Nico: father of Ibrahim and Amna, financial analyst, amateur poet, and aspiring *hafidh*, he also plays the part of 'Private Nouman'

Hafidha Rabia: accomplished Islamic scholar, based in Jakarta, who is also a *hafidha* in her own right and mentors *hifdh* students, including Khadija (via telephone); in addition, she has a weekly *hifdh* and *tajweed* session with Ibrahim, which are supplemented by daily lessons, primarily with Ibrahim's mother

Nonna/Carmen: meaning grandmother in Italian, Ibrahim and Amna's paternal grandmother, retired international journalist, based in Brooklyn, New York

Nani/Nasheeta: meaning maternal grandmother in Urdu, the children's maternal grandmother, retired community journalist, living primarily in Houston, she also plays the part of 'Officer Ayesha'

Ms Suzy: Ibrahim and Amna's first teacher (outside the home) in Houston

Abdullah Mamoo: Ibrahim and Amna's uncle and Ammi's younger brother (Mamoo being the term for mother's brother in Urdu), computer engineer, presently living in Houston

Najma Mumani: Ibrahim and Amna's aunt, presently completing her medical studies, specializing in cardiology

Yaseen: Ibrahim and Amna's cousin and Abdullah and Najma's first born

Yasmeen: Ibrahim and Amna's cousin and Abdullah and Najma's second born

Uncle Geo: Ibrahim and Amna's uncle and Abdurrahman's older brother, presently living in Boston, Massachusetts, professor of mechanical engineering

Aunt Margaret: Geo's wife, librarian

Alexandra: Ibrahim and Amna's cousin and Geo and Margaret's first born

David: Ibrahim and Amna's cousin and Geo and Margaret's second born

John Henry: among Ibrahim and Amna's friends at their half day Montessori program

Sabir: a best friend to both Ibrahim and Amna, living in South Africa

Taleem: one of Abdurrahman's closest friends, presently living and working in Abu Dhabi

Uncle Bill: Ibrahim and Amna's downstairs neighbour, in Houston, retired entomologist

Aunt Beatrice: Uncle Bill's wife

Hamza: Ibrahim and Amna's uncle and Ammi's elder brother, who lives together with his family in Doha, Qatar, petroleum engineer

Mary: Hamza's wife and Ibrahim and Amna's aunt, botanist

Naeem: Hamza and Mary's 10 year old son

THE AUTHOR RECOMMENDS

The Meaning of the Holy Qur'an by Abdullah Yusuf Ali
(Amana Publications) as a good companion to this story.
In addition, the glossary (pp.165-169) may also help
considerably with reading and understanding the text.
A Cast of Characters list is provided (p. vi) to help navigate
the many characters and terms. Also included is a 'date/
place' description at the start of every chapter to help situate
the story, together with a cast of characters for that specific
chapter.

1

THE OPENING:
WHAT'S YOUR NAME?

Date/place: early October, 2010, new school, Houston, early morning

Cast of characters: Ms Suzy, Ibrahim, Khadija, Amna

"What's your name?" I hear the teacher ask. It's a new day, in a new place, and a very new teacher for all of us. The question, however, is a familiar one.

My son, who keeps reminding me that he will be five and a half in a matter of weeks, responds, "'My name is… …Ibrahim… Well, actually, it's longer, Muhemmed Ibrahim Shaban, but call me Ibrahim for short. I jumped off Signal Hill right before we left Cape Town. I wore a helmet and had sort of… umm… a net and a pair of wings. Do you want to see my picture? You can also see the World Cup Stadium if you look carefully, but, you know, Spain won, not South Africa."

The teacher is taken aback. I can imagine her asking herself the following questions silently: He jumped off a hill with wings? Near the World Cup Stadium?[2] And what exactly was that name? Even the short name doesn't seem very short or familiar. "Well," she finally says, "welcome Ib… ra… him." Slowly, the name comes out from her mouth and, although tentative, its pronunciation is followed by a smile.

As a mother, on the sidelines, I can't help but interject, "Thank you Ms Suzy; Ibrahim went tandem paragliding right before we moved, and just one month after the World Cup. It all left quite an impact. And his name is Arabic for Abraham, like the Prophet Abraham, peace be upon him, or Abraham Lincoln, if you will. This is my daughter; her name is Amna, A-m-n-a, almost like 'Amy'. I am Khajida. Mine is more of a mouthful, but once you've said it once or twice and maybe even seen it in writing, it will all seem quite natural." I start to take out a piece of paper, but before I can, Ibrahim has already finished writing out his name and hands it over to Ms Suzy, together with his photograph, taken in flight.

"It all sounds and looks good. Yes, very good, provided we have a little more introduction. Welcome, again. I hope you will enjoy our school, and we'll all learn together, including about all those soccer teams.[3] And yes, maybe you can write out the other two names, especially your daughter's. That would help."

Once again, before I can respond, Ibrahim in his excitement and ever-forthright manner adds, "Do you know my father actually has at least three names; I call him 'Papa' and my mother calls him 'Abdurrahman' and my Nonna calls him 'Nico'. I'm sure some of his coll… eag… ues at the office call him 'Sir', too. Now isn't that interesting?"

Ms Suzy nods. She seems to be taken aback again, a bit, but maintains a smile. Perhaps she is getting used to us all, or perhaps we are actually not that unusual.

Yes, so here we are, at least some of us, for now. Papa, also known as Abdurrahman, Nico and Sir, will be coming home from work, in the evening, and probably want to go out to watch the sunset. And Nonna, my mother-in-law and the children's grandmother, has just come to stay, together with a pledge to start learning Spanish, which she claims is not so different from Italian, her mother tongue. Meanwhile, if all goes according to plan, I start my *hifdh* lessons with Hafidha Rabia, tomorrow morning after dropping the children.[4] Then, Nani, my mother, will be with us again, next week *inshaa Allah*. She's been trying to teach me how to cook and start the children on Urdu. It's been a busy first month in Houston, but the hot spell is breaking, and today we found a new school. Today we also started reading, with the children, the first chapter of the Qur'aan, *Al Fatihah* ('The Opening'), which seems auspicious and fitting. This afternoon, we'll begin working on the translation, and, if Ibrahim is up to it (and Amna occupied), we may even try to write out an *ayah* or two in Arabic *inshaa Allah*.

Al Fatihah (1)[5]

1. In the name of Allah, Most Gracious, Most Merciful

2. Praise be to Allah,

The Cherisher and Sustainer of the Worlds;

3. Most Gracious, Most Merciful;

4. Master of the Day of Judgment.

5. Thee do we worship,

And Thine aid we seek.

6. Show us the straight way,

7. The way of those on whom

Thou has bestowed Thy Grace,

Those whose (portion) is not wrath,

And who go not astray.

HIFDH TEACHING NOTE

Khadija chose to start reading *Al Fatihah*, the first chapter of the Holy Qur'aan, with her children on their first day of school, albeit after extensive preparatory work of reading and understanding the Arabic alphabet, as is alluded to later in the text. Starting school and Qur'aan on the same day may seem like an ambitious task, but it also is a way to integrate Qur'aanic work into our lives. The two projects (school and Qur'aan) reinforce each other in the larger continuum of learning, and hence Khadija's characterization of 'auspicious and fitting'. When would you (or did you) introduce the Qur'aan? How would you make it exciting, relevant and a date to remember? Apart from reading the translation and potentially writing out the text, what would you do with your young ones to help the text come alive? Would you consider sharing a recording of your favorite reciter with them? What about going to a special place in the house or neighborhood to read *Al Fatihah*, also considered the 'mother of the Qur'aan' due to the way in which it lays out essential elements of creation and faith?

---

[2] Between June and July 2010, South Africa hosted the 19th FIFA World Cup, which was the first time for any African nation to hold the event (only the Ghana national soccer team, however, made it to the quarter finals). The event prompted extensive infrastructure additions and enhancements, including the construction of the Green Point Stadium in Cape Town.

[3] As excerpted from the author's note of the children's book *Goal!* "To this day, in the face of poverty, bully rulers, and unsafe alleys, people play soccer. Through war, revolution, and hardship, people play soccer. In South Africa, East Asia, North America, the West Indies, and in all corners of the world, people play soccer. Soccer bonds. Soccer makes both young and old feel that they belong, that they matter, and that they can win," (Javaherbin 2010).

[4] *Hafidha* is the honorary title given to a woman who has memorized the Qur'aan (the male designation is *'hafidh'* also spelled 'hafiz'). The name 'Rabia' means 'spring' in Arabic. Among the most renowned personages to hold the name 'Rabia' in Islamic history is 'Rabia al Basri', the 8th century, Sufi mystic.

[5] Excerpted from *The Meaning of The Holy Qur'an* (Abdullah Yusuf Ali 1989, pp.14-15).

2

The Gun

Date/place: October, 2010, Houston, Ibrahim and Amna's living room, weekday afternoon

Cast of characters: Ibrahim, Khadija, Nonna, Amna

"I want a gun," says Ibrahim.

"What?" I respond, slightly flabbergasted. We were just involved in a virtual *thikr Allah* with countless iterations of the *Tasmia* and Ibrahim's comment seems to come from way out in the left field.[1]

"Geo had guns," pipes in Nonna, who has just entered the kitchen where we were all reciting. I turn around to look at her. She's been staying with us now for six days, all of which have been good (I generally feel that everyone behaves better when my mother-in-law is staying with us), but I wonder about the timing of this particular comment.

"What?" I say, again.

"Geo had guns growing up. I don't remember about Nico, your Papa," she says, looking directly at Ibrahim. "I think he had one, but maybe it got lost or maybe Geo 'borrowed' it. Why do you want a gun?"

"I want to shoot the baddies."

"What baddies?" I say. I feel the need to redirect this conversation, before learning more about what kind of guns Geo had when he was a young man in Brooklyn, New York. Meanwhile Amna seems to like the sound of the word 'baddies' and starts repeating it over and over.

"You know all the bad people," Ibrahim responds.

"No, I don't know." Whenever kids talk about guns, I can't help but think of Columbine and a film we saw shortly after arriving in Cape Town, entitled *The Wooden Camera,*[2] and Mahatma Gandhi, but I can't explain this all to five-year-old Ibrahim. He'll think I'm dodging the question or simply being overly sensitive.

"So Papa had a gun, and Uncle Geo had a gun, and my cousin Yaseen has a gun," Ibrahim says, now standing up from his chair and walking right over to me, so that he is taller than me (as I am still sitting). "And Sabir has a gun. Even

Christopher Robin has a gun. Why can't I, Ammi? Come on. Please."

"What about basketball?" It's all I can think of at the moment. Maybe I can redirect the conversation with another game.

"Ammi, we played basketball yesterday." Ibrahim is not giving up, but that's pretty normal.

"Ok, let me think; just give me some time to think about this. When your Papa comes home tonight, we'll talk about it *inshaa Allah*." I feel like I am being bullied by a little boy. But, then again, maybe I should have simply taken Nonna's more nonchalant approach. Her boys had guns and grew up to be good people. Perhaps there's something natural in giving a toy gun to a kid, but intuitively it just doesn't yet seem right for my son. I've got a couple of hours to work out a response and gear up my arguments for Papa (and more importantly, for Ibrahim). Thankfully, it's *Asr* time, and I may exit without looking like I am actually dodging the issue. I beckon to the children to join me.

A couple of minutes later, on my prayer mat (post-*Asr*), I see an answer, which should be viable. And I don't think I need any more hours to work out a response or engage Abdurrahman (Nonna's 'Nico', short for 'Nicholas'). I head to my desk, with Amna in tow, while Ibrahim goes back to Nonna who's taking the lead in tonight's dinner. I sit down and take out a piece of paper. Amna also wants one (actually she wants three pieces of paper), and her own pencil and eraser. So the exercise doubles in length, but at least there are no (terrible two) tears, right now.

"Dear Ibrahim," I write. "Let's get a water gun for *Eid* (one for you and one for Amna), let's look into archery, and let's keep talking about all the goodies and the baddies. I love you a lot. Your Ammi."

I head back to the kitchen and place the note near Nonna (who has her hands deep in meatball preparation), and ask her to help Ibrahim decipher all the words. I don't quite know yet what I'm getting into with archery, but I sense the Robin Hood connection and of course that with Prophet Muhemmed, *Salla Allahu 'alayhi wa sallam* and hope we're all on the right track *inshaa Allah*. Now it's back to working on the *Tasmia* and other tasks.

HIFDH TEACHING NOTE

Although the children have already started with *Al Fatihah*, in this evening's scene, there is repeated emphasis solely on the *Tasmia*, amidst a larger discussion of guns and appropriate toys. Khadija is reluctant to buy a gun, which may appear to be a potentially over-protective response to her five-year-old's yearnings. Still, one is led to question how *hifdh al Qur'aan* ultimately integrates with toys and which are the best or better amusements for young children embarking on a *hifdh* journey. Should they have any/all toys at their disposal or should the *thikr* of Allah (including via the simple iteration of the *Tasmia*), as referenced in the text, also inform the selection of toys, without ultimately being too restrictive on the child?

---

[1] The *'Tasmia'* is *'Bismillahir Rahmanir Raheem'*, which is translated as 'in the name of Allah, Most Gracious, Most Merciful'. It is recited before every *surah* in the Qur'aan, except *Surah At Tawbah*. It is also recited before the inception of virtually any activity.

[2] *The Wooden Camera*, released in 2003, directed by Ntshaveni Wa Luruli, tells the story of two boys, living in a township near Cape Town, who find two very different instruments (a camera and a gun) and subsequently lead very different lives.

3

SIRAT AL MUSTAQEEM

Date/place: October, 2010, Houston, Ibrahim and Amna's home, Sunday morning

Cast of characters: Abdurrahman, Ibrahim, Khadija, Amna, Nonna

It is Sunday morning. There is no race to or from work or school; no lunchboxes to be prepared; nothing special to iron or iron out. Yes, it is Sunday morning, a truly sacred space, when time feels like it stops, and there is simply life in an uncalculated and natural form.

Of course, both Amna and Ibrahim need breakfast (very soon), and Nonna will be flying out tomorrow, and we do have a date with Nani at Memorial Park in an hour, and then a lesson for Ibrahim with Hafidha Rabia in the evening,[1] but still there is a real suspension of time, for now.

Abdurrahman has taken the lead in this morning's short recitation and lesson, following a glass of milk with honey to get our hearts and minds going. He is correcting our *tajweed*, after receiving more than two years of instruction himself, and he has also asked the children to draw a picture of how they see *'Sirat al Mustaqeem'*.[2]

"That's simple," says Ibrahim. "It's straight, like you told us Papa. All I have to do is draw a line from this apartment to my school and back, with no stops and no errands and no fights with Amna."

"Ok, so draw it. I want to see it, *bambino*," says Abdurrahman.

Ibrahim takes out a green marker and then leafs through his pencil case. "Ammi, where's that ruler that Abdullah Mamoo gave me? You know the one with the American Presidents?"

"*Baita*, I don't know. Why don't you just try to make a straight line, without a ruler? Or maybe you could use the edge of another piece of paper or a book. Look." I start to demonstrate, but Amna interrupts.

"Pool, pool," she calls out, racing past me with her swimming suit in her hand. Her vocabulary is growing, and there is a constant word association activity playing itself out in her mind. Perhaps she heard me say the word 'ruler' and mistook it for 'pool(er)'? I actually can't understand this one.

"Are we going swimming?" Asks Nonna, who hears Amna's declaration and is just emerging from her room. "I thought we were going to meet Nani at the park?"

"Yes, Mama, we are," responds Abdurrahman. "Amna may be a bit confused. *Come stai?*"

"*Bene,* very well. It's a beautiful morning." Mother and son move in and out of Italian,[3] here and there, enough for us to understand a little, but rarely making us feel excluded. "I'm looking forward to seeing my journalist friend, and walking those pathways again with you Ibrahim, and weren't we going to bury anger too?" Nonna looks first at me and then over at Ibrahim.

"Yes. Do you have your spade? And are you going to run this time or are you going to walk?" asks Ibrahim.

"Let's see," says Nonna, never missing a beat or a chance to interact with her grandson. "Depends whether you make me run. And yes, my spade is ready and waiting. Are you planning to play 'mission possible?'"

"I don't know. I'm still waiting for Ammi to figure out archery; we may just have to pretend. But I think if Nani comes you are going to get distracted and forget me for a while. It seems like whenever you two meet you just want to talk to each other." Ibrahim turns his head down and starts walking away, pouting.

"Pool, pool," is Amna's refrain for now. Perhaps she thinks that her brother is getting up to join her.

"Oh Ibrahim, don't be a jealous *bambino.* You should be happy. What if your Nani and I had nothing to say to each other? Isn't it a blessing that we're friends? Now, come back and stop reacting. It's early; it's my last day, and I don't want to see any of that attitude today *amore mio.*"

Ibrahim turns around and runs toward Nonna, leaping up into her arms. They've staged this sort of reconciliation before. I always fear that Ibrahim is going to push his 5 foot tall grandmother over, but she's a stalwart in more ways than one, and, as far as I have seen, has never fallen.

"Ok, you can talk to Nani," Ibrahim says, now in his grandmother's arms, "but you have to talk to me too, and you have to help me bury anger, together with my Ammi and Amna and you also have to pretend to play archery with me." Then, looking over at his Papa, Ibrahim says, "I know what I'm going to draw for my *Sirat al Mustaqeem*: walking a straight path, holding Nonna's hand, and doing my *thikr Allah*. What do you think?"

Abdurrahman doesn't respond, but a smile spreads across his face, as if it were emanating from his heart.

HIFDH TEACHING NOTE

In this chapter, *Al Fatihah* is the backdrop again. However, the focus is specifically on *'Sirat al Mustaqeem'* or the straight path, as discussed in detail in footnote 2. Khadija and Abdurrahman are deliberately taking their time with the children and the memorization of this *surah*. Abdurrahman has asked Ibrahim to draw how he envisions the straight path: we learn that Ibrahim ultimately links the path to his grandmother. How would you introduce the straight path? How would you reinforce it? Would you consider drawing? Walking? Holding your child's hand? In your estimation, why might it be important to spend time on this *surah* and the fundamental concepts that *Al Fatihah* lays out?

---

[1] The relationship between parent and child in the *hifdh* activities described above is central to the story; however, in addition, the characters of Khadija and Abdurrahman are each involved in serious study with well recognized *huffadh* (plural for *hafidh*), alluded to in the introduction and throughout the text. The children, particularly Ibrahim, is also being coached in elements of *hifdh* and *tajweed* by these experts, as will be mentioned, albeit briefly, later. Although this book does not purport to be a manual for how to memorize the Qur'aan, such expert guidance is largely considered a critical piece in any *hifdh* undertaking, as noted in the introductory 'disclaimer'.

[2] In his/her obligatory (*fard*) daily prayers, a Muslim utters *Surah Al Fatihah*, which includes the phrase *'Sirat al Mustaqeem'* (straight path), and more precisely calls on *Allah Subhanahu wa-ta'ala* to guide him/her to the straight path, seventeen times. If we add the recommended (*sunnah*) prayers, this number comes to 31. By adding the optional (*nafl*) prayers, a Muslim will utter the phrase approximately 40 times, over the course of the day. Furthermore, this total does not take into consideration the mention of *'Sirat al Mustaqeem'* in *surahs* other than *Al Fatihah*. The focus on the straight path and seeking guidance toward the straight path is a cornerstone of Islamic prayer and overall belief.

[3] Towards the end of the 19th century and early 20th century, approximately 4 million Italians emigrated to the United States, with a total immigration flow amounting to about 5 million. The majority of the immigrants came from southern Italy, including Sicily. Italian was largely preserved as a first/mother tongue in the first several generations after immigration.

4

BURYING ANGER

Date/place: October, 2010, Memorial Park, Houston, Sunday morning

Cast of characters: Nonna, Nani, Ibrahim, Amna, Abdullah, Abdurrahman, Khadija

They've swapped greetings. "*Assalaamu 'alaykum,*" calls out Nonna, as she sees Nani approach, and Nani in turn says a warm "Hello". Suffice it to say, whether it is explicit or not, peace has definitely been conveyed by both parties.

"*Assalaamu 'alaykum Nani* jaan," Ibrahim exclaims, running up to his other favorite grandmother. For a moment, Nonna, not to mention my brother Abdullah, who has also come out, is upstaged by Ibrahim who in his vigorous, loving and customary way has jumped into my mother's arms.

"*Wa alaykum salaam baita* jaan. *Kiya haal hein?*" She says, kissing him on the forehead.

Amna in *her* customary way seeks to emulate her brother and squirms out of my arms and also runs over to Nani. "Me up, me up," she says.

"*Jee, jee, jee, baita.*" Nani bends over and hugs her granddaughter rather than trying to pick up the two children. There are precious lessons that come from rearing four children, as my mother has done, and this is one of them.

"*Salaam,*" my brother finally says, as the children quiet down. He's just dropped his own little brood, Yasmeen and Yaseen, at Sunday school and so is solo today, with the exception, of course, of my doting mother, as Najma is still working around the clock.

"*Wa alaykum salaam* Abdullah," responds Abdurrahman, giving Abdullah a big hug (which even after six years of being kin still always catches my brother off guard). "You're looking good today. I think you've already been running, no?"

"Yup, I like this weather," says Abdullah. "It makes me feel young, again. What about you guys? What have you been up to?"

"We're getting ready to bury anger," Ibrahim volunteers.

"Bury anger?" Abdullah inquires.

"Yes, you see, sometimes Ammi gets mad, and sometimes Amna gets mad. Nonna doesn't get mad very much. And Papa, well, hardly ever, but those of us who do, yes, me too, we have our spades, and so we're going to go dig a hole and put all our anger energy in and bury it. Do you want to join?"[1]

"It sounds too easy." There is a little trace of cynicism in Abdullah's voice.

"No, not easy. We buried anger in Cape Town too, at a park. In fact, we went at sunset because Ammi thought someone might be suspicious." The way Ibrahim is describing it, it actually does seem a little suspicious. I can't help but think of corpses, but yes, he is correct. We did attempt to bury anger in Cape Town, and we are trying to do so again here in Houston, at Memorial Park (provided we can be discreet). Ultimately, we'd like to bury it altogether, but we all seem to have our own version of temper tantrums every so often and so, apart from *wudu* and *thikr*, we also resort to this sort of pseudo burial process. In addition, Ibrahim relishes any chance to use a spade, and Amna well, for her, dirt is simply fun, anytime of the day.

"Interesting concept. I think I would have a lot of holes in my backyard, and I don't think your Najma Mumani would be very pleased," says Abdullah.

"That's ok," responds Ibrahim, as if to console his uncle. "We're all trying. And every effort counts. Remember He's *Ar-Rahman Ar-Raheem*." Then turning to me, Ibrahim says, "Ammi, I think I got it. Did you hear my pronunciation?"

I nod my head in affirmation, but I hear a lot more than the correct pronunciation. I hear a little boy who is actually trying to integrate his *deen* in a way that makes sense.

Nonna breaks the momentary silence. "Well, are we going to walk or just smile at each other all day? My grandson has big ambitions this morning, and I want to talk to Nani too." I find it interesting that Nonna has started calling my mother 'Nani', which means maternal grandmother in Urdu. Then again, one of Nonna's most fundamental relationships is with her grandson, and so she has, on some level, adopted his relationships.

"Let's walk and talk," my mother suggests and heads out, together with Nonna, in the lead. The two have a lot to say, or at least that's what we hear. And yes, at times, Ibrahim does get jealous. Abdurrahman and I are always stunned by the parallels of our two journalist mothers who share a love of reporting, good stories and a pursuit of truth.

"Did you see the *Sunday Times*," Nani starts the conversation, still within earshot.

"No, the kids didn't get the paper, and I got distracted online. A lot of trip logistics. Tell me the headlines?"

"Well, Pakistan was there, unfortunately. How I wish, just for once, we'd get some good news. Unrest in Baluchistan. Serious strife in NWFP."[2]

"Little changes," Nonna responds.

"I know," laments Nani. "Do you know that I reported on some of these same stories, albeit with slightly different narratives, 30 years ago? I simply feel as though we are replaying the same old, bad news story."

"Perhaps if we had teamed up earlier, we could have done something. Now we're just a bunch of retirees, melancholy about the state of the world, but look at Amna. She owns the world. I think it's time for us to learn from her. What about that good news press idea again? What if we start small?"

"Carmen, I don't have your drive now, not to mention the focus and time. I'm a stay at home grandmom. I think we needed to meet 30 years ago. No good news now."

"Stop it. You've got all the vigor of Ibrahim. And I maintain that we did meet, in Karachi, when *The Times* first sent me over there."

"No, it wasn't me. I was never such a high flyer as you. I wouldn't have been in your crowd."

"How is it that we also have the same conversation every time we meet, and you always insist that we didn't meet in our youthful thirties and you further offend me by insinuating that I flew in high crowds, above you." Nonna punches back with her words, but I suspect that she will also easily call my mother 'Amore mio'.

"Ok. This is not fun now," shouts Ibrahim. "And you are all straying from the path," he says, admonishing them. In the brief time that Nani and Nonna have been conversing in front of us (and Abdurrahman with Amna on his shoulders has been taking up the rear with Abdullah), I have been walking alongside Ibrahim and reviewing *surahs* with him. Ibrahim and I have gone through *Al Fatihah*, and we've started back at *Surah An Nas* as well.[3] Nothing was said of the translation during our brief review and yet his comment about straying from the path couldn't be more apt.

"I want to see the gorillas," Ibrahim insists.

"I thought we came here to bury anger and play imaginary archery. Anyway there are no gorillas here. You must be thinking of Kirstenbosch."[4] Responds Nonna. Nonna had visited us often in Cape Town and as was equally if not more familiar than all of us with the layout of that great garden.

"Oh yeah, sometimes, man, I just get it all mixed up."

"Sweetheart, please don't call your grandmother 'man'," I add. And then, "Yes, I want to see the gorillas too, but let's look for small snakes instead and how about some squirrels? And I also agree with Nonna, we need to put our spades to good work. Here I am wearing my gardening gloves for the last hour, just waiting for the next project. Mission possible, no?"

"Ok, Ammi, how about right here?"

"Here, here, here," Amna mimics. She's ready to dig.

Just then one of the mountain bikers, for which Memorial Park is now known, whizzes by.[5]

"How about some place a little less public?" suggests Abdullah.

12

"I agree," says Abdurrahman.

Nani and Nonna go off trail a bit trying to stake out a small piece of turf under which we may all lay down our anger. I can't help but see the metaphor taking real life proportions. I wonder how long it will take all of us to find an appropriate spot.

"Here, here, here," Amna calls out again. She's identified the spot. There are a dozen pine cones and some soft pine needles, as well as several birds overhead. For a moment there is no sign of bicycles. Without speaking, each one of us picks up a spade (we have three that Ibrahim has collected over the last week) and then a piece of dirt. I shift between watching Abdullah's face and Ibrahim's, trying to figure out what might be going on in their minds. But, then it is time to look inward and focus on my own self. Yes, *inshaa Allah,* may we bury anger, and may we all grow up to be good.

HIFDH TEACHING NOTE

Burying anger does not feature explicitly in either *Al Fatihah* or *Surah An Nas*, as highlighted in this chapter. However, it is the chosen activity, during a Sunday family walk in Memorial Park. While there is no direct link to the *surah* themes, Ibrahim and his mother have taken time out to review while walking, thereby integrating their *hifdh* routine into the (active) activities of the day. *Hifdh al Qur'aan* need not be restricted to a place or a day, but, as the family is attempting to show, is part and parcel of their daily lives. Furthermore, one could argue that (while not spelled out in the above noted *surahs*) learning to restrain and overcome one's anger and emotion is paramount in the practice of Islam. How do you teach good behavior alongside *hifdh al Qur'aan*? How can we memorize with our hearts and minds so that the text ultimately impacts and improves our behavior? When was the last time you took a walk and recited with a child, restrained anger and let the text convey its inherent wisdom and peace?

---

[1] "Abu Hurairah *[Radiallahu Anhu] RA* narrated that a man asked the Messenger of Allah *[Salla Allahu 'alayhi wa sallam] SAW* to give him a piece of advice. He *SAW* said, 'Do not be angry.' The man repeated his question several times, and each time the Prophet *SAW* replied, 'Do not be angry," (Sahih Bukhari as cited in Beshir, p.115 (2004)). The aforementioned text also provides four excellent strategies to dealing with anger, as based on the Qur'aan and Sunnah (pp.116-7). Another potentially valuable (Muslim children's) resource related to this subject, is the 'Home Sweet Home' film in the Adam's World Series, produced by Sound Vision (2004).

[2] NWFP, meaning North West Frontier Province, was renamed to Khyber-Pakhtunkhwa, in 2010, by President of Pakistan Asif Ali Zardari, which the National newspaper *Dawn* alleges will cost upwards of US$92 million (*Dawn*, April 10, 2010). Figure based on author's conversion (US$1=86.147 PKR, May 28, 2011).

[3] *Surah An Nas* (114), "Mankind, 1. Say: I seek refuge with the Lord and Cherisher of Mankind, 2. The King (or Ruler) of Mankind, 3. The God (or Judge) of Mankind—4. From the mischief of the Whisperer (of Evil), who withdraws (after his whisper)—5. (The same) who whispers into the hearts of Mankind—6. Among Jinns and among Men," (Abdullah Yusuf Ali 1989, p.1718).

[4] Kirstenbosch National Botanical Gardens was founded in 1913 to ensure the preservation of rare flora, unique to the Western Cape of South Africa. It is recognized as a natural World Heritage site.

[5] Memorial Park, located in Houston, spans approximately 1500 acres. Initially the land was used for a training camp during World War I. By 1925, the area was gifted to the City of Houston and identified as park land. It is estimated that about 4 million people visit the park each year.

5

TV

Date/place: October, 2010, Houston, Ibrahim and Amna's living room, Saturday evening

Cast of characters: Abdurrahman, Ibrahim, Nani, Amna, Khadija

"Why do you like it?" asks Abdurrahman.

"It's fun," responds Ibrahim.

"That's a fair answer. So what else is fun?"

"Well, hide and seek is fun, and cooking meatballs with Nonna is fun, and learning Urdu with Nani is fun." Ibrahim pauses for a moment and smiles at his grandmother, who has come to stay for a couple of days, following the departure of Nonna. Sitting very near to Ibrahim, Nani appears to be reading a new travelogue about Kashmir (but is easily distracted by her grandson). She smiles back at him and adds *"Zabardust"*.

Then taking in a big breath of air, Ibrahim says, "Ammi makes Qur'aan fun and so do you, most of the time. Yaseen is a lot of fun when he shares. Amna can be fun, but it's also a challenge having her imitate me all the time and break things and spill things, but I think pretty soon she'll be more fun, when she's three. School can be fun with Ms Suzy when she's not too busy with the other children. Legos are fun, but not when Amna is eating them. Oh yes, singing in Spanish in the car with Ammi is really fun. And yesterday she did cartwheels with us and that was a lot of fun."

The list is long, and I can't quite believe Ibrahim still has so much energy after a full Saturday of play, followed by revision of *Al Fatihah* and *An Nas*, writing (of the *surahs*) and a collage of our next/new *surah*. But I also wonder where exactly we are going, and how we're going to get back on subject. Cartwheels? I thought we were going to discuss our home TV policy, after Ibrahim announced in detail over dinner what John Henry, one of his new classmates, gets to watch every night at his house.[1]

"Ibrahim, what's the most fun?" Abdurrahman says as if sensing my concern that we are straying from the topic.

"The most fun? Hmm, I need to think about that one. No, wait, I know, I know. What I'm doing right now." Ibrahim insists pointing down at a very intricate lego car he is building, while Amna chews on the extra lego wheels. "And I also think Ammi's translation of *Surah Al Falaq* was fun, just now, but it was also a little scary, how she mentioned mischief and blowing on knots."[2]

"*Buono.* I also think legos and translation are a lot of fun. So why is TV such fun?"

"Tee, tee," says Amna, spitting out the legos in her mouth and pointing to the television in our living room, as if picking up on Abdurrahman's cue.

"Well," Ibrahim finally utters, giving his sister time to express herself. "Sometimes there are some really silly cha… ra… cters." He says the final word slowly as if it is new to his mouth.

"Yup, silly characters, I agree. They can be fun, but why do you think your mother, your Nani and I don't want you to watch a lot of a TV?"

"I don't know. No, no, wait. I know, I know. I've got a lot to learn. And TV isn't always really *thikr Allah*, or at least that's what Ammi says. I kind of understand it, but I still think TV is fun."

"Me too, Ibrahim, but you're right, we've all got a lot to learn and sometimes TV can be a little bit of a distraction, from *Allah Subhanahu wa-ta'ala* and our work. Do you know what Nonna and my own Papa used to do with me growing up?"

"No, what?" Abdurrahman now has Ibrahim's full attention, who adores hearing stories from when we were young. Nani has also put down her book to listen to this one.

"Well, my Papa and I had a date every week."

"Sort of like the date I have with Ammi every day, playing outside after my school work?"

"Yes, you know you're lucky to have a play date with her every day (and have Qur'aan, and extra English and Math with her), but back to *my* Papa. Once a week, quite apart from baseball and playing with our printing press and all our other favorite fun activities, he and I would watch a show together. We'd find something that both of us really enjoyed. And we'd watch it and then we'd talk about it and then we'd plan for the next one. It was still TV, but what you'd call very in… ter… active. We'd interact with each other, not just with the TV. And so we'd always learn something, about the world and about each other too. Sometimes we even went to the movie theater."

"Hmm, I wish I knew your Papa," Ibrahim says. "He always sounds cool."

"He taught me how to be a papa," says Abdurrahman.

"You're lucky. I wish I had one."

"You do, and now *you're* the one being silly," Abdurrahman says, reaching over, pulling Ibrahim into his lap, and giving him a big kiss.

"So are we going to have a TV date, Papa?"

"Well, I think maybe one of us in this room (me or your Nani or your Ammi)

16

could alternate each week. And yes, we could have a TV date. We could even keep a record of who watched what and how it was. Maybe we could even dip into that cool stack of DVDs there. We need to make sure Amna also has something constructive to do."

"Don't worry Papa, she'll watch with us," says Ibrahim with assurance. Despite any sibling rivalry, he generally seems to understand Amna better than all of us. Ibrahim then puts his hands around his father's head in an affectionate way and says, "Papa, maybe you and Ammi can even go out and watch a movie once and then talk about it, like you said you did, before Amna and I were born, and let us stay home with Nani and have fun." Continuing, he then adds, "And maybe we can play video games and…"

"How about we see how our TV date goes first and then we'll talk about it, ok? And just remember that thing your mother said about not getting too distracted and finishing our work. She's a wise woman, just like your Nani here, and your Nonna, back in Brooklyn."

I smile, on the sidelines, happy that Abdurrahman led this conversation about TV and happy that we might have come to a compromise. The video game conversation is on the horizon and surely there will be many more about television; but, here in our living room, bedtime nears, the last pieces from our collages of *Surah Al Falaq* dry, and our work, for the day, seems to be mostly done, *alhumdulilah*.

HIFDH TEACHING NOTE

Is there any educator or parent who does not grapple with TV (and other electronic media)? How much? When? Where? What? With whom? Good programs abound, but so too do not such good programs. And, even if 'the good' are in our midst, should we really be idle in front of the television for hours on end? Is that level of passivity good for us and our children? Each parent and educator will *inshaa Allah* make the right decision; however, surely it is a decision that needs to be re-evaluated, as the media evolves, and as our children mature. Furthermore, how we communicate our home rules may be as important as the rules themselves so that the children come to appreciate how the home operates and how, hopefully, it represents to them a fun, engaging and loving environment, which promotes profound and lasting life lessons. In the scene above, apart from discussing TV, Khadija references collages that she has just completed with the children to aid their understanding of *Surah Al Falaq*. If you ask a child to turn off the television, you may be faced with resistance, but if you ask that same child whether s/he would like to imagine 'daybreak' (*Al Falaq*), then cut and glue and color, you will probably be able to entice and engage. Help the *surah* to come alive by reading the translation, or, if they are able, by having the children read out the translation. As you are working, introduce (in the background) a recording of a beautiful *qira'at* of *Surah Al Falaq*. Space the activity over two or more sessions so they may work toward a real masterpiece. Compile the masterpiece(s) in a small booklet that they may refer to for fun, and to help reinforce the themes of the *surah*, and possibly even share it with visiting friends and relatives. Television is not inherently pro or anti *hifdh*, but it is up to us as parent-educators to assign what role we want it to play and to continuously engage and stimulate our *amanahs* (or responsibilities, referring here to our children).

---

[1] According to a study released by the Kaiser Family Foundation in 2010, "8-18 year-olds devote an average of 7 hours and 38 minutes (7:38) to using entertainment media across a typical day... because they spend so much of that time 'media multitasking' (using more than one medium at a time), they actually manage to pack a total of 10 hours and 45 minutes (10:45) worth of media content into those 7½ hours," (Generation M2 2010).

[2] As excerpted from Abdullah Yusuf Ali, *Surah Al Falaq* (The Daybreak) "In the name of Allah, Most Gracious, Most Merciful. 1. Say: I seek refuge with the Lord of the Dawn, 2. From the mischief of created things; 3. From the mischief of darkness as it overspreads; 4. From the mischief of those who practise Secret Arts; 5. And from the mischief of the envious one as he practices envy," (p.1716).

6

SPACE

Date/place: end October, outside NASA, Webster, Texas, mid-day, family picnic, under a shady tree

Cast of characters: Ibrahim, Abdurrahman, Amna and Khadija

"I want to be an astronaut."

"I thought you were dressing up as Salahuddin, and becoming a gallant knight, at school and in general," says Abdurrahman, smiling at his son.[1]

"I'm astro… lot," says Amna, taking the cue from her brother.

"No, you're not Amna, and anyway, there's no such thing as 'astrolot'," says Ibrahim, then continues. "Papa, I don't mean for the school party. I mean, for always. Like when I'm old, like you. That's what I want to be. You go to the office in the morning, and I want go to the moon, or maybe Mars."

"Really, I thought you wanted to go to my office during the day, and then recite at the mosque at *magreb,* and then head to the fire station for some evening community service; at least that's what your mother told me last week," Abdurrahman responds, nodding at me.

"Well, he is growing and evolving, by the day," I add.

"Yup, just look at my shoes, Papa. Ammi says I might need to get some new ones way before *Eid,*" says Ibrahim, holding up one shoe in the air, which reveals the sole rubbed away.

"I don't think that's exactly what I said Ibrahim. I think I asked you not to use your shoes as bicycle breaks and to make them last until *Eid,*" I counter.

"Oh, yeah, now I remember," says Ibrahim. "But I am still growing, and I might need some new sneakers, and also an astronaut suit so I can start training."

"Me too," says Amna, nodding at her brother. "I'm astro… tot."

"Amna, you're not an astrotot, and this is my turn at talking. You were talking all the time inside, including in the film and when that woman was telling us about the spaceship," says Ibrahim, with increasing irritation in his voice. I move in between the two children to try to defuse any tension as well as avoid any spills. Our somewhat precariously placed picnic mat is sloping on a small hill, and my mother packed grape juice, among other items, which is now in three plastic cups (and one sippy cup), on the mat.

"I am astro… tot," repeats Amna, not heeding her brother's warning.

"You are not," Ibrahim shouts, as though she has seriously offended him.

"Wait a minute, *bambino,*" says Abdurrahman, patting Ibrahim gently on the back. "Let her be an 'astrotot' or 'the atrotot' for that matter; it's fine. It won't interfere with any career path you choose; in fact, it could even help you."

"How?" queries Ibrahim.

"She might also join you in space and help you in your training," I say, not knowing quite where Abdurrahman was going with his line of argument but trying to play along nonetheless.

"I don't think so," says a much more contemplative Ibrahim now, shaking his head. "I really don't think Amna is going to help me in space."

"Listen, before we decide on everyone's future utility, why don't we say *dhur salah,* and maybe we can even practice *Surah Al Ikhlas,*" suggests Abdurrahman.[2]

"After the grape juice is done, please," I caution. "But yes, that's a great idea; and then we can head back in and maybe even out on the tour to see the Mission Control Center?"

"I'm ready," says Ibrahim.

"For what?" asks Abdurrahman.

"Well, everything that Ammi suggested, and you too Papa, but I need some help with the last *ayah* before we recite," says Ibrahim.

"*Baita,* don't worry, we don't say *dhur* out loud," I say.[3]

"But Allah still hears us," responds Ibrahim.

"Yes," affirms Amna.

"Yes," says Abdurrahman nodding.

"You're right, future astronauts," I say, slowly retrieving my *mushaf* from my purse, opening up to *Surah Al Ikhlas.*[4] "Now, with what exactly were you having difficulty?"

"The last *ayah,* and the second to last *ayah,* and a little bit with the third to last *ayah* too," says Ibrahim.

"But Ibrahim, there are only four *ayaat,*" Abdurrahman says.

"I know Papa, but they're not easy. Remember I don't go to the office yet," says Ibrahim sounding a bit defensive.

"And from the sound of it, you may never be going since you're bound for Mars. Listen, don't get me wrong, I never said they were easy, neither the pronunciation nor the meaning. I actually think some of the shorter *surahs* are the most packed."

"What do you mean?" says Ibrahim, looking at his father.

"Well, this one, *Surah Al Ikhlas*, practically tells it all. It has the answer to the whole universe inside," responds Abdurrahman.

"Like NASA?" questions Ibrahim, pointing to the buildings around him.[5]

"Not quite. NASA is looking for the answers. *Surah Al Ikhlas* actually tells us from where the universe originates," says Abdurrahman.

"I'm not NASA," Amna says, following along in her customary way.

"No, you're not, *bambino* and neither am I, but I am here at NASA and I am trying to finish up my lunch and offer my prayers, give a short clarifying lesson to your brother and head back inside," says Abdurrahman, not realizing that Amna is not always able to absorb more than one concept at a time.

"I eat lunch," is Amna's response.

"Me too," says Ibrahim. "And after lunch, I am going to eat astronaut's ice cream," he adds, looking at both his father and me as though we hold the key to his happiness. "I was also thinking we could even take a picture of it and send it to Hafidha Rabia."

"What?" I query.

"To share our treat," says Ibrahim, who's had four successful weekend lessons with her in the last month.

"How?" says Abdurrahman.

"Well, it could be a treat for her too. You know how she's always sending me stars on the computer during the lesson. I was thinking that it would be nice if we sent her a picture of the ice cream, and then told her about all of this, I mean, all the universe stuff you said Papa," says Ibrahim.

"Sticky," says Amna, perhaps remembering the last time she ate ice cream.

"Well, that sounds very sweet Ibrahim, but do you really think she would enjoy it?" I ask.

"Yes, she told me during our last lesson that she likes chocolate, so I think she'd love a picture of a chocolate ice cream. But maybe Papa could write out the explanation since I'm a little slow at typing," says Ibrahim.

"I'm ready," says Abdurrahman.

"For the ice cream?" asks Ibrahim.

"For *dhur salah* and then the ice cream and that tour your mother mentioned," Abdurrahman says.

"Yummy," says Amna, and we start to pack up the picnic lunch and move on to the next chapter of the afternoon.

HIFDH TEACHING NOTE

Using new (and old) *surahs* in *salah* may be one of the most effective ways to reinforce *hifdh*. Encourage the children (and yourselves) to make *salah* an expression of *hifdh*. Within reason, also consider giving treats for new *surahs* learned (and old ones retained), such as the astronaut ice cream proposed by Ibrahim in the scene above. And wherever possible, make the connection between where you are with the children (i.e. NASA) and where you are with your *surahs* (i.e. *Surah Al Ikhlas*). Here, unlike in some of the earlier scenes, the parallel is striking, as highlighted by Abdurrahman, namely how NASA and *Ikhas* seek to address the origins of the universe.

---

[1] Salahuddin was born in Tikrit, Iraq in the 12th century AD, and is accredited with recapturing Palestine during the Crusades. He was renowned for his chivalry among Muslims and non-Muslims alike, including by Richard the Lionheart.

[2] *Surah Al Ikhlas (112th surah)*, "In the name of God, Most Gracious, Most Merciful, 1. Say: He is God, the One and Only; 2. God, the Eternal, Absolute; 3. He begetteth not, Nor is He begotten; 4. And there is none comparable to Him," (Abdullah Yusuf Ali 1989, p.1714).

[3] *Congregational dhur* and *asr salah* (mid-day and afternoon prayers) are said quietly, in contrast to the other three *fard* (obligatory) prayers, which, when said in congregation, are audible.

[4] *Mushaf:* "scholars make a distinction between the printed text of the Qur'an and the recited text. The printed text is referred to as the *Mus-haf* which means 'bound pages'. The orally transferred, untainted and untouched, mentally preserved, recited text is what all refer to as 'the Qur'an'," (I. Londt , p. 23).

[5] "NASA's vision: To reach for new heights and reveal the unknown so that what we do and learn will benefit all humankind… President Dwight D. Eisenhower established the National Aeronautics and Space Administration (NASA) in 1958, partially in response to the Soviet Union's launch of the first artificial satellite the previous year (excerpted from NASA www.nasa.gov, June 12, 2011)".

7

QUR'AAN CONTRACT

Date/place: early November, 2010, Houston, Ibrahim and Amna's living room, Sunday evening

Cast of characters: Abdurrahman, Ibrahim, Nani, Khadija, Amna

"I just couldn't get it; there must have been some sort of mental block between me and it."

"What's a mental block, Papa?"

Abdurrahman, who is holding a *mushaf* in his right hand, moves the Holy Book away from himself as if creating more distance and demonstrating the 'block'. Ibrahim and Amna listen on attentively, watching their father's movements and trying to understand what motivated him to take up his own *hifdh* work six years ago.[1] We've all taken a brief break from the evening's lesson on *Surah Al Lahab* to talk about it.

"And then it dawned on me. No matter how much I wanted to memorize to commemorate the *Hajj*, I wasn't going to get it until I could actually understand what *Allah Subhanahu wa-ta'ala* was trying to teach me."[2] Abdurrahman then moves the *mushaf* back to him and holds it closely to his chest. The children are still quiet, and both Nani and I also listen in.

"But that's not all. There was something more, and it had to do with you two." Abdurrahman says pointing to his two children and then putting his free arm around both of them.

"I couldn't imagine becoming a father and trying to explain the Qur'aan without first understanding it myself. Your mother was three months pregnant with you Ibrahim, and I was so nervous that I wasn't actually ready to be your father. What had I done to prepare? I remember feeling spiritually very small. And so, I made a Qur'aan contract with myself, pledging to read and learn by heart the whole Qur'aan *inshaa Allah*. And that's where I was, and still am today, reading and learning and reading and learning, together with you."

"I'm spiritually small," says Ibrahim. "I only finished the orange book last month," he adds.[3]

"Oh no you're not small, *bambino*; you're growing a lot faster than me *masha'Allah*. You may be lean, but you're getting tall, and just think how far

23

you've come," responds Abdurrahman.

"I feel very spiritually small," Nani adds. "And I don't think I've read the orange book yet."

"Oh Ammi, come on, we're all learning together here, *alhumdulilah*. Just think what you just taught us about Abu Lahab's wife and what the firewood may represent?" I respond.

"I know, but sometimes when I hear Abdurrahman speak, I am very humbled, by who he is and what he has done," Nani says looking at her son-in-law.

"Now, Ammi, don't speak that way," says Abdurrahman, adopting my term of endearment for my mother. "Your daughter is right; we're all learning from each other here, *alhumdulilah*. Ibrahim is teaching me, and Amna (now, don't get mad Ibrahim), yes Amna is teaching Ibrahim. And well you're certainly teaching all of us and vice versa."

"*Es verdad*," Nani nods, surprising us all with one of her new Spanish phrases that she may have learned from Nonna, "but I am still humbled."

"So how are we going to comrate the *Hajj*?" asks Ibrahim, bringing us back on topic.

"Commemorate? Yes, well, we could start by trying to imagine ourselves completing it; just imagining *Hajj* is quite a big undertaking. We can greet some of the *hajjis* on their return *inshaa Allah*. And in the meantime, we could also try to learn this new *surah* we're working on tonight, together with *Surah An Nasr*, our next one, which seems particularly appropriate to tonight's discussion since it's about people entering Allah's religion, which is what I did. And I am sure your Nani has some special *Eid* recipes to teach us as well."

"Nani, will you please teach Ammi how to make *Sheer Qorma* for us this year?" asks an excited Ibrahim, who has only ever eaten it at other people's houses.

"*Bilcul, baita*," responds my mother, then adds, "that is, if she's game. Remember, Ibrahim, as I've told you in some of my lessons, there's no coercion in love or cooking."

"I'm up to it Ammi. And maybe you can also tell us other things you used to do, growing up?" I say turning back to my mother.

"I think I'd like to tell Ibrahim and Amna about my first *Hajj*," says my mother slowly, looking at both children.

"You've been on *Hajj*, Nani?" says Ibrahim.

"Yes, twice, *alhumdulilah*. Once when I was first married and then a second time, with your Abdullah Mamoo and Najma Mumani, shortly after their marriage."

"They've been too?" inquires an increasingly astounded Ibrahim.

"Yes, and I'm sure they'd also tell you, about their stories," responds my mother.

"Can I call them, tonight?" says Ibrahim, getting up, as though he can't quite contain all the new information.

"Well, I don't see why not," responds Abdurrahman. "And perhaps we can also ask them what Yasmeen and Yaseen are doing?"

And so the evening ends, as we dig back into the past, for the lessons, and the reconsideration of our own Qur'aan contracts, and our pilgrimages.

HIFDH TEACHING NOTE

Consider putting the pause button on, for a moment (even though you may be hard at work on *Surah Al Masad* (also known as *Surah Al Lahab*) including some challenging *tajweed* lessons). Consider your own Qur'aan contract. Do you have one? Is it time to renew it? What is the goal? How will you reach it? Have you shared your Qur'aan contract with the children? Have they made any such contracts? This could be done in one evening or it could be done over the course of several days. The main goal is to keep Qur'aanic learning at the heart of your learning and to teach by example. Extra credit given for understanding the meaning.

---

[1] See introductory note about *hifdh* (More about *hifdh*, p.v).

[2] *Hajj* is one of the five pillars of Islam, and among the largest pilgrimages performed in the world. In 2010, approximately 2.8 million pilgrims performed the *Hajj*, in Saudi Arabia (The Week Online, 2010). Although the *Hajj* is directly connected to the life of Prophet Muhemmed [*Salla Allahu 'alayhi wa sallam*] SAW, there is evidence of pilgrimages to Mecca dating back to the time of Prophet Adam, peace be upon him.

[3] The orange book to which Ibrahim refers is *Towards Reading the Qur'an: Part Two*, a pre-Qur'aanic primer, used in South Africa and abroad that illustrates basic pronunciation and *tajweed* rules (Lenasia Muslim Association).

8

HAJJ & MENTAL NOTES

Date/place: early November, 2010, driving to Ibrahim and Amna's school, Houston, early morning

Cast of characters: Ibrahim, Amna, Khadija

"Are the birds going on *Hajj*?" asks Ibrahim.

"Bird, bird, bird," mimics Amna.

"Ammi, are the birds going to be *hajjis*?" Ibrahim repeats.

I am smiling, trying to figure out how to answer this one. Generally I have to think, hard, before answering any of Ibrahim's questions. We are on our way to school, and I am still wondering whether I managed to get all the snack box tops on. "I suppose they have been invited, yes. But some of them may simply be flying south, now, for the winter. You know the birds are in constant prayer, unlike, us, who get distracted and need constant reminders."[1]

"Are the birds in *wudu*?" Ibrahim probes.

"I suspect they are, but I may need to ask a *mullah baita*. Animals are pure at heart and follow their Maker. We have pure hearts *alhumdulilah* but also the potential to deviate."

"Davate?" Ibrahim asks.

"Almost, d-e-v-i-a-t-e, meaning, we get off track, we get angry, we get distracted. *Hajj* is a reminder and a rebirth if you will; it's our chance to reset all our programs."

"I'm not going on *Hajj* this year because Amna is too small, but I'm going to try to reset my program Ammi. Papa and I are learning *Surah An Nasr* this week, and then we're getting ready for our *Eid* party with Yaseen, and maybe I can even dress up like an astronaut."

"*Inshaa Allah*. It sounds like a very good plan, except you may want to run the astronaut dress-up by Nani. I think she'd like to see you in *kameez shalwar* on Eid. As for *Hajj*, I was actually thinking we might map out some parts and create a mini *Hajj* at home. Remember last week what Papa said?"

"Can we sleep in a tent?"

"Tent, dent, sent," sounds out Amna who has been quietly playing with her car seat straps, but obviously listening in on the conversation.

"Well, that's an idea. Let me look into it. Maybe we could make a tent and sleep in it. And perhaps you could do a half-day fast on the *Day of Arafat* with me, like you did in *Ramadan*."

"*Jee, jee* Ammi, I'm ready. I told Papa I was ready for a full day too, but…"

"But let's wait a little longer," I suggest.

"Yes, I can wait, but Ammi, I really want to sleep in a tent. I need a sleeping bag though. Remember Nonna said I could get one for my fifth birthday, but then we were packing up in South Africa and you said 'no more objects'. Ammi, please can I get my sleeping bag now before *Eid* and sleep in a tent?"

The tent seems pivotal together with the sleeping bag. "*Baita*, give me a day, and *inshaa Allah* I will come up with a plan. It might just be the right time for that sleeping bag now. I was also thinking of mapping out some of our friends and relatives and their *surahs*."

"What?" says Ibrahim.

"What, what?" repeats Amna.

"Well, last week you told me that Yasmeen is working on *Surah Az-Zalzalah*? And Yaseen has already finished one whole Qur'aan. And so I was thinking of putting all our friends and relatives on a map with little indications of where they are with their Qur'aan study."

"It sounds complicated Ammi, and what about Nonna? She wouldn't be on the map since she's not working on a *surah*?"

"Very good thought, maybe we'll just focus on the tent for now and then maybe I'll just keep a mental note of your relatives who are working on *surahs* to help encourage us."

"I wonder what David and Alex are working on?" Ibrahim inquires.

"Hmm, I don't know, but *inshaa Allah* we'll soon find out at Thanksgiving. I bet they are very busy. Ok, do you realize we've been sitting outside your school for 10 minutes now talking about birds and tents and Nonna? I think Ms Suzy is waiting for you two. And I've got to get back to my *hifdh* work too. One kiss, two kiss, three kiss, four, and now you're out the door, for 3 whole hours."

Amna starts blowing kisses and we all manage to organize ourselves and our snack boxes and get out of the car. Standing up, carrying Amna, and holding Ibrahim's hand, I marvel at how much I've learned in just 15 minutes.

HIFDH TEACHING NOTE

What are you doing for *Hajj* this year? If you are not en route to Mecca, could you still attempt a re-enactment with children (perhaps your own and those of any interested friends/relatives), and could you also make a goal of completing one *surah* (or part of one *surah*) for the days of *Hajj*, to help commemorate it? Ibrahim mentions *Surah An Nasr* above as being the *surah* on which they are working, which seems fitting, not only because, as Abdurrahman says in the previous scene, it speaks of people entering Allah's religion (one may almost imagine the masses entering into *Masjid Al Haram*), but also because of the fact that the *surah* speaks of victory. *Hajj* may be among the greatest reminders of our origins and our ultimate destination, and also reinforces that all victory comes from and with the help (*nasr*) of *AllahSWT*.

---

[1] "Seest thou not that it is Allah Whose praises are celebrated by all beings in the heavens and on Earth do celebrate, and the birds (of the air) with wings outspread? Each one knows its own (mode of) prayer and praise. And Allah Knows well all that they do." (Abdullah Yusuf Ali 1989, p.879, excerpted from *Surah Al Nur, ayah* 41).

9

GETTING READY
FOR THANKSGIVING

Date/place: November, 2010, on the sidewalk, walking back from a public park, Houston, late afternoon, a week-day

Cast of characters: Ibrahim, Khadija, Amna

"Ammi, what is stuffing?"

"What?"

"I heard Papa talking to Uncle Geo about stuffing last night on the telephone. Papa asked him what kind of stuffing he was going to make, and then I think he said something about being extra careful about it being *halal* and having no wine, and then Papa seemed a little upset or Uncle Geo sounded mad or... I don't quite know."[1]

"Upset stuffing?" I say, smiling and pausing for a moment. "Hmm *baita*, I may be the wrong person to ask, but let me give it a try. As far as I know stuffing is what they put in the turkey or the chicken. And it's different from what we talked about with *The Velveteen Rabbit*. Normally it's made out of bread crumbs."

"Like in *Hansel and Gretel*?"

"Yes, if you wish, breadcrumbs like the ones Hansel and Gretel used, but mixed in with other spices and sometimes other things. If I remember correctly, your father once told me that Uncle Geo used kumquats in his stuffing."

"Robots?" Ibrahim asks, turning back to me. He's been walking up ahead just calling out his questions, but here he finally stops and turns back to Amna and me (or me carrying Amna and all our other paraphernalia). We're on our way back from the public tennis courts where we went for our first impromptu game with our new rackets, which Ibrahim chose for his *Eid* gift instead of a set of water guns. The water guns somehow lost their appeal in the last couple of weeks; but then again, the weather is also colder these days.

"No, kumquats. They're a smallish orange-ish type of fruit. You know your Uncle Geo, he's a gourmet cook. As for anyone being upset, I wouldn't worry about it. They're brothers, and most of the time they get along like you and Amna, but they also have some differences. I think what's hard for the two of them is that certain things have changed, like, for instance, your father..."

"Converting to Islam," Ibrahim is quicker than me and more direct.

"Well yes, Abdurrahman's reversion. For Uncle Geo, Papa is 'Nico', his kid brother, and I don't think he always appreciates being instructed on how and what to cook."

"Cook. Cook. Cook," Amna intones. Her mouth is pursed and her eyes are focusing on my mouth as if to ascertain the correction formation and pronunciation.

"But Uncle Geo invited us for Thanksgiving."

"*Bilcul, baita.* Uncle Geo invited all of us *masha'Allah,* and of course he wants us to share a wonderful meal with us to commemorate the pilgrims' Thanksgiving meal with the Native Americans, but there are still certain differences and ironing them out takes time and effort. Just think, Uncle Geo has never had to prepare a *halal* meal before, and he is going out of his way to ensure that we may all eat together. I think he is really looking forward to hosting us, but it takes some time and effort, and I don't think he likes receiving cooking instructions from his younger brother."

"I would listen to Amna."

"Would you? I've seen the two of you argue making brownies before."

"That's because she makes a mess. Maybe it might be a little difficult if she wanted me to make a turkey and stuffing in a certain way."

"You see, and you're both Muslim; imagine if you had to learn a different religious recipe?"

"Well, if we were all vegetarians, there wouldn't be any issue," Ibrahim outsmarts me yet again; I think he's getting the point.

"By the way, did you have a chance to speak to David or Alexandra last night or was it just Papa and Uncle Geo who spoke?"

"Yup, I spoke to Alex; she's going to make an apple pie, and she wants me to cut the apples."

"Cut them?"

"Yes, she said I could. I told her that Nonna taught me how to use a knife."

"Oh, I see, and David?"

"He just wants to play cricket with us."

"Cricket? On Thanksgiving?"[2]

"Yup, remember when they visited us in South Africa, and he saw me and Sabir play, and he really liked it; well, he said that we can play cricket together, after the turkey and the stuffing."

"Does he have a bat?" I ask.

"I don't know; maybe we can just make it up?"

Amna has been unusually quiet, but her eyes light up with the words 'cricket' and she so starts her characteristic chorus of "cricket, cricket, cricket".

"Ammi, what do you think about Thanksgiving?" Ibrahim asks, now sitting down on the sidewalk as if preparing for a longer discussion. I sit too. Amna is starting to get a little heavy, and I'm also feeling the weight of her (not so baby) baby bag and the tennis rackets.

"Well, it's new to me," I respond. "But I'm glad to be sharing a meal with different family members and friends. I also think that it's nice that it falls so close to *Eid* this year when we share the sacrifice as well. And, it's a good reminder of so many of the *surahs* we've been learning lately, including *Surah Al Kafiroon*, namely respecting and also accepting differences."

"Do you think Nani would also agree?"

"I do. I think that Nani and Nonna would both agree."

"But Ammi, I think *Surah Al Kafiroon* is hard."

"I do too, and do you know that until I met Hafidha Rabia and you, I couldn't say it correctly? I always used to invert the different *ayaat*."

"Ammi, you didn't meet me. I'm your son, and I'm also your part-time Qur'aan coach and that's what we're supposed to do: help each other. So will you help me?"

"Only if you promise me you'll let Alexandra do most of the cutting and you won't worry about your uncle and father."

"Ok, it's a deal. Now, let's get *Kafiroon* down before Thanksgiving and then... Amna, stop it." I have to hold Ibrahim's arm as he is ready to strike his sister who is now beginning to irritate him with her incessant chorus of 'cricket'.

"Ibrahim, please don't hurt your sister; remember we're getting ready for Thanksgiving. I suppose in a certain way we're all taking out our old stuffing and putting new stuffing in and making sure that it is all good and wholesome."

"Like during *Hajj*."

"Yes, sort of, like on *Hajj*. Your father may be able to help us connect all these dots, but it's starting to make sense to me. Ok, I'm ready to listen to you; give me the third *ayah* of *Surah Al Kafiroon* and then the fifth one and let's see just how hard it really is. I know you can do this."

"Ok, Ammi, here I go. *Bismillah*..."

HIFDH TEACHING NOTE

This scene showcases the joyous but at times challenging aspect of partaking in meals and festivities with non-Muslim friends and family. *Halal* issues inevitably crop up. At the same time, there are almost always ways to work around areas of potential conflict, namely through open dialogue and mutual respect — an area that *Surah Al Kafiroon* stresses. *Dawah* is a central tenet of Islam, and sharing and partaking in Thanksgiving (or similar such festivities) provides an excellent opportunity for us to learn from others and showcase the beauty of Islam. Are you ready? Are you preparing your children for such an encounter? Could not *hifdh*, taught in the spirit of love and understanding, be compatible with Thanksgiving?

---

[1] In Arabic, the word *halal* means permitted or lawful. *Halal* food excludes the following: pork or pork by-products, animals that were dead prior to butchering, animals not slaughtered properly or not slaughtered in the name of Allah, blood and blood by-products and alcohol. The recent debate over the quality of meat and poultry in the United States, including coverage in the documentary film, Food Inc. (2009), as well as in The Omnivore's Dilemma (Pollan 2006), raises critical questions about the integrity of food, which ultimately has a bearing on 'halal' as well.

[2] Although no longer known for cricket, the United States was involved in the first international cricket match, which was played against Canada in 1844.

10

LEARNING HOW TO DRIVE

Date/place: Thanksgiving week and weekend 2010, Uncle Geo's home, Cambridge, Massachusetts[1]

Cast of characters: Amna, Abdurrahman, Uncle Geo, Ibrahim, Khadija, David

"My car! My car!" cries out Amna, speeding towards Uncle Geo's miniatures. He has a series of Model A and Model T Fords lined up along the windowsill in his study.[2] I hesitate for a minute, wondering how old the miniatures may be. Abdurrahman's reaction time is, however, nil. He immediately races past Amna and takes his brother's cars and replaces them instead with a chocolate toffee.

"Uncle Geo's cars," Abdurrahman then asserts. "But don't you worry, you'll get 'your car' in just a bit." Then turning to his brother, Abdurrahman asks, "Hey, Geo, where did you pick these up? They're not the same one's Papa gave you in high school are they?"

"They sure are Nico. I had them in a glass case for a while but then when Alex and David were seven, right after you headed overseas, they broke the glass. I never got the full story, but the glass certainly made them more enticing. I just haven't got around to putting them back. Maybe it's time, or maybe Amna here is going to show us all who's boss."

"Oh, Amna's the boss," chimes in Ibrahim, "but soon she'll learn about the Big Boss."

"And who might that be?" asks Uncle Geo.

I sense that Ibrahim might be on the cusp of a theology lesson, particularly since we spent much of our plane ride working on *Surah Al Kauthur* and trying to explain abundance given from *Allah Subhanahu wa-ta'ala*. But it's our first time at Geo and Margaret's house, ever, and both Abdurrahman and I are trying to tread lightly. I think that any discussion about the 'Big Boss' could be potentially divisive and so opt to change the subject.

"It's a beautiful room, Geo. Do you work in here?"

"Margaret and I share and of course both Alex and David like using it too, as does Mama, so let's just say there are many proprietors."

"I totally understand. Somehow my home office belongs to at least four people," I respond, gently, patting Ibrahim on the head. Amna is out of reach, in

Abdurrahman's arms now, but I look at her as well.

"So, what about that cricket game?" Ibrahim interjects, looking at his cousin, David, who has been standing at his father's side and seems to have grown more than a foot since we last saw him a year and a half ago in Cape Town.

"I thought that was only after the turkey. We haven't even seen the house, or greeted Alexandra *baita*. And did you see Nonna yet?" I ask Ibrahim who is ready to run again after all his sedentary traveling time.

"Nonna? Where's Nonna?" And then, "Alexandra," Ibrahim calls out, as if he's been in the house all his life. Amna follows suit and is soon calling, "Nonna, Nonna, Nonna."

"*Baita*, please, inside voices."

"Don't worry Khadija, it's not so formal here. David has quite a set of lungs and so does his twin. And remember, we're Italian, not English. How about we start with the garage? I think Ibrahim and David might have something to teach me out there. Alexandra is coming back in an hour, and Mama, your Nonna…" he says looking down at Ibrahim, "…is busy with the cranberry sauce. She's trying to do her own thing this year, from scratch. It's so interesting what retirement has done to my mother… let's head out, ok Amna?" Geo says putting his arm around Abdurrahman's shoulder and indirectly around Amna as well.

"I'm ready," says Ibrahim.

"I know you are. And I also heard you might be ready for the Boston Tea Party Ship and the Aquarium, together with your cousins.[3] Nonna reports that you're all ready to take on the world."

"Hmm, I don't know about that. The world is a big place," responds Ibrahim in his serious tone. "But I think Nonna could take on the world after all her traveling. Do you know that she went to Pakistan right after my father was born?"

"Yes, I do. I think I was two at the time, and my Nonna was taking care of me. I got to see the pictures afterwards."

"I'd like to see the pictures," Ibrahim responds.

Amna is honing in on the conversation and adds, "too" or perhaps it is "two". I can't quite tell. Meanwhile, we've reached the garage and Uncle Geo is starting to undo the padlock on what looks like a very old garage door.

"Is there treasure inside?" asks Ibrahim.

David nods and smiles but then lets his father respond. "Well, sort of. My cars are sort of like my treasures. Your Papa may have told you about that. Did you Nico?"

"I showed him the pictures, and remember, in South Africa, you brought that old Ford decal? Ibrahim still has it. I think it's in his bookshelf. Isn't it Ibrahim?"

"Yup, and… wwwoow, is that really your car Uncle Geo?" Ibrahim is awed. I don't think I've seen him look so impressed since his Signal Hill jump, months ago. "Ammi, can we go in?"

"*Baita*, this is not my car. I think you should be talking to Uncle Geo."

"Of course, climb right in. Then as soon as Alex returns, I'm going to take everyone out. And then maybe later this evening the boys can all have a ride to the Aquarium."

"What?" I say, sounding a little too surprised and concerned.

"Don't worry, it's not a Houston highway; we'll just putter around the neighborhood. I'm not one to drive too far at night with this one, but I thought Ibrahim might get a kick out of it, at least imagining driving back over the bridge."

"Oh, I'm sure he would, but yes, puttering sounds good. Don't you think Ibrahim?"

Ibrahim has disappeared behind the back of the car. He's mesmerized. Amna seems to like the wheels and I am concerned that she actually might try to bite them.

"Ammi, this is the best car I have ever seen. Can I get one?"

Abdurrahman comes to my rescue, again. "Let's wait for that first pay check, *bambino*. Now how about finding your Nonna and her cranberry sauce? I think we have a special meal to start."

"I want to eat my meal in the car Papa. What about you David?"

Neither Abdurrahman nor I respond to this one, letting Ibrahim daydream a little about his new infatuation. My mind is also busy, racing with ideas. I'm trying to think how I could stage our next Qur'aan lesson in this car and help connect some of the points in the children's universe. Or maybe back in Houston I can find a car museum? Perhaps by tomorrow Ibrahim will have moved on to ships? The speed at which both children move never ceases to amaze me; then again, the car has definitely made a mark, as has Uncle Geo. I sense that I have a lot to learn, and that by the end of this weekend, we might all be changed, for the better.

HIFDH TEACHING NOTE

The fact that the children are learning *Surah Al Kauthar* over Thanksgiving seems a wonderful coincidence. Thanksgiving is a time when many share a meal with family and friends; although largely secular, the meal itself has the potential to be a spiritual act as well. One way to convey this aspect is to recite the *surah* and then speak specifically about food. Where does our food come from? How? Who ultimately created the food? And to whom ultimately do we owe our thanks? This is a practice that may be adopted at Thanksgiving, but it could also be done throughout the year, to help remind ourselves and our children of life's (infinite) daily blessings. Another possible activity is to encourage children to consider doing some act of charity when they recite this *surah*, to help them learn and remember that the abundance we have is not ours, but rather, all thanks to *AllahSWT*.

---

[1] In 1863, during the Civil War, President Abraham Lincoln established a national Thanksgiving Day to be celebrated every November. Prior to that 'thanksgiving' celebrations had taken place on a regional basis, with both religious and secular roots. Many historians trace the first Thanksgiving celebration to a meal shared between the Wampanoag Indians and the Plymouth colonists in 1621.

[2] Model Ts, dating from 1908, designed and manufactured by Ford, are largely considered the first affordable (middle class) car. The cars were produced on an assembly line, rather than individually made. Henry Ford said the following about the Model T: "I will build a car for the great multitude. It will be large enough for the family, but small enough for the individual to run and care for. It will be constructed of the best materials, by the best men to be hired, after the simplest designs that modern engineering can devise. But it will be so low in price that no man making a good salary will be unable to own one—and enjoy with his family the blessing of hours of pleasure in God's great open spaces," (Ford 1922).

[3] The Boston Tea Party is a pivotal event leading up to the American Revolution, related to the issue of 'taxation without representation', namely tax levied on American colonists including on tea by Britain. The Boston Tea Party involved American colonists destroying tea by throwing it overboard in Boston harbor.

11

YOUR QUR'AAN CLUB

Date/place: late November, 2010, Houston, at Abdullah Mamoo's house, a late Sunday afternoon

Cast of characters: Yaseen, Khadija

"What are you doing Phuppi jaan?"

"What do you think?"

"I really don't know. It just looks like you're busy with a lot of papers and pens and more papers."

"Well, I'm trying. Do you know *Surah Al Ma'un*?"

"*Bilcul*. I presented it at my *Qur'aan khatm* earlier this year.[1] But you and Uncle Abdurrahman were still in Cape Town, so you missed it."

"Yes, I know, Yaseen *baita*, but *masha'Allah* what I heard from your *Abbu* was wonderful. Do you still remember it?"

"*Surah Al Ma'un*? Is this a test?"

"No, I'm just curious."

"I think I could recite the first couple of *ayaat*, but I forget what it's all about."

"Agreed. It's hard to remember everything. You know Yaseen, Ibrahim and I were talking on the plane, on the way back from Thanksgiving at his other uncle's house, about starting up something called 'Your Qur'aan Club' to help us all remember. What we were thinking is that club members would get points by helping others to learn the meaning. With people who aren't Muslim, it would be particularly nice if you could learn something about their beliefs as well so it becomes a real exchange. It would be a way to open up the Qur'aan to a broader audience and also help us with our *hifdh* work."

"Phuppi jaan, I'm not doing *hifdh*. That's *your* work."

"*Baita*, I know, but you're still trying to understand the Qur'aan. Just think of all the work you do at Sunday school with your teachers. Anyway, Ibrahim and I thought it would be helpful if we tried together."

"Are his cousins in Cambridge joining the club?"

"Maybe. For now, though, it's just me and Ibrahim and Amna of course. I think your sister also expressed some interest when I spoke to her yesterday. She and Ibrahim started working on this sketch of *Surah Al Ma'un*. That's Yasmeen's depiction of an orphan. And here is Ibrahim's rendering of someone showing off but not responding to neighborly needs."

"Hmm, I didn't know Yasmeen could draw like that. And Ibrahim's work is not bad. I'm in. What's my job? And by the way, how do you keep track of all the points?"

"Welcome to the club *baita*. As for keeping track of the points, it's an individual thing; you keep track yourself, and *inshaa Allah* all your work will be pleasing to *Allah Subhanahu wa-ta'ala*, the real point keeper. Your first assignment is to add your piece to this collage, and then I am going to make membership cards for everyone based on the collage. Next week we may do a life-saving mission."

"Life-saving, for real? Do I get to keep my own membership card?"

"Pretend, but I promise it will be fun. And, yes you can keep your card. Maybe you can help me cover them all with plastic to make them a little more durable. I'm concerned that Amna will chew on hers."

"Is she still teething?"

"Teething? No. She speaks as you know. She runs and mimics, and she loves saying '*Alaq*', but yes she still senses most things with her mouth.[2] I suspect we're in this phase for at least a couple more months."

"That's ok. We can cover the cards for Amna. Yasmeen also spills a lot so it will probably be good for her too. Phuppi jaan, did you have a Qur'aan club when you were growing up?"

"I guess we have all had our own sorts over the years, but this is different for me, now. I think my heart is in a very different space now. Before my Qur'aan work was mostly about getting through, getting done, moving on. Now, it's more about trying to understand the lessons and see if I can transform myself, for the better."

"Sounds good. Me too. Can I start drawing now?"

I nod and Yaseen is off, drawing his rendition of *Surah Al Ma'un*, as though it has all come back to him.

HIFDH TEACHING NOTE

Whether we acknowledge it or not, as Muslims, we are almost all engaged in some form of *hifdh*, namely preservation of the words and teachings of the Holy Qur'aan. We may be a *hafidh* of an *ayah*, or a *surah*, or a *juz*, or of the Qur'aan in its entirety. What distinguishes us, however, is not necessarily how much we learn, but how we take care of what we have learned. Are we truly preserving and protecting it? Are we seeking to understand, and, perhaps most importantly, apply it, in our daily lives? *Surah Ma'un*, as cited above, offers a wonderful opportunity to teach about the true principles of *deen*, namely exhibiting small kindnesses, and not showing off. It is these small kindnesses that pave the way to *jannah*, day after day, act after act, *inshaAllah*. After listening to and reciting the *surah*, you could suggest a drawing, as done with Yaseen above, in the context of the Qur'aan Club, or you could ask the children to make a list of all the 'small kindnesses' they can imagine, and then encourage them to try to incorporate at least two such acts into every day.

---

[1] It is customary for many young Muslims to complete a reading of the Qur'aan in Arabic (*Qur'aan Khatm*, also known as *'Ameen'*), which is often a celebrated event. In addition, during the month of Ramadan, every year, Muslims often strive to complete at least one reading of the entire Qur'aan. Furthermore, throughout the year, some Muslim will complete the Qur'aan multiple times. Most *huffadh* are perpetually reviewing and reciting Qur'aan, according to different systems, including in their daily prayers, and in groups.

[2] *Alaq* is the title of the 96th *surah* in the Qur'aan; *'alaq'* means congealed blood and refers to how humankind is created from a clot of blood; it was also the first *surah* revealed to Prophet Muhemmed [*Salla Allahu 'alayhi wa sallam*] SAW.

12

THE WHOOPING CRANES

Date/place: early December, southern Texas, inside Aransas National Wildlife Refuge, late Saturday afternoon

Cast of characters: Khadija (Lieutenant Laila), Ibrahim (Captain Kashif), Abdurrahman (Private Nouman), Amna (Sergeant Faith)

"What is Captain Kashif going to do about it?"

"About what?"

"About the whooping cranes? They are having a difficult time this fall, with their migration. Didn't you hear the field guide just now? So what is Captain Kashif going to do about it?"

"I need to think about it a little, Lieutenant Laila. I'll come back to you after lunch with a plan."

I can't help but smile with Ibrahim's proposal. We've taken the weekend off to explore the Aransas National Wildlife Refuge. We hope to spot the majestic but endangered whooping cranes that make their migration from the Northwest Territories in Canada to southern Texas every fall. During our drive south, we have devised a new make believe game. Ibrahim is Captain Kashif. I am Lieutenant Laila. Amna is Sergeant Faith and Abdurrahman is Private Nouman. Nani has opted not to join in our outdoor weekend getaway but she will surely want a role upon our return. I am thinking that Officer Ayesha might suit her well as a title.

"I got it."

"Got what?" Abdurrahman inquires, slowing the car, and then pulling off to the side of the road for fear that something is happening in the backseat.

"I know what to do about the crane," Ibrahim exclaims.

"I thought you wanted to report back after lunch with your plan," I say.

"No, it's clear. I have a plan now. I'm ready to do it. Who's coming?"

"Ibrahim… sorry, I mean, Captain Kashif, can we first hear the plan before action-ing it? I don't mean to sound insubordinate but isn't it prudent to review as a group first?"

"Lieutenant Laila, there is no reason to fear. I am serious, and I am ready, and I think I have a very good plan. But, if you really want to talk about it first, then here it is." Ibrahim gestures widely almost batting Amna in the face in her nearby car seat. We are all ears, and Abdurrahman nods to signal that his son, the Captain, should continue.

"I am going to use *Surah Quraysh inshaa Allah.*"

"What?" I ask, a little bit in disbelief.

"I said, I am going to recite *Surah Quraysh*; I think it will be just the right solution to bring the whooping cranes to safety."[1]

Sometimes art imitates life and sometimes, vice versa. Here we are, having just reviewed *Surah Quraysh*, which seemed particularly fitting given our southern-bound journey, and now Ibrahim, as Captain Kashif, intends to use the *surah* to bring the birds back from extinction. Abdurrahman and I look at each other and share a rare moment of profound parenting joy.

"That sounds interesting *masha'Allah*. How exactly do you plan on reciting?" queries Abdurrahman.

"Well, Private Nouman," Ibrahim addresses his father in all seriousness, "first I suggest we get out of the car and recite the *surah* in Arabic; then, just in case the whooping cranes can't hear us or don't understand, I suggest we recite in English as well. You don't know the Italian translation do you Papa, I mean, Private Nouman?"

"May I get back to you about the Italian translation, and the Spanish one as well? Maybe Lieutenant Laila here can enlighten us with the Urdu? And what about Sergeant Faith, Captain? She's been a little neglected in the action plan?"

"Don't worry she can say 'good job' at the end."

"Good job?" both Abdurrahman and I respond.

"Yes, that's her new thing. Whenever I recite these days she says 'good job' and then smiles. It's like she's sealing the *surah*. So I think that's what she should do, seal the *surah*, at the end and help make sure that the whooping cranes hear us and travel safely to their winter home. It might even earn her a point in the Qur'aan Club. What do you think?"

"Good job," says Amna almost right on cue. As for the rest of us, we are ready for this adventure, and probably a dozen more before the weekend is through. Meanwhile, Ibrahim has already unbelted and is finding a spot for his recitation, ready to begin the 106th *surah* of the Qur'aan. In an instant, we hear, "*Authu Billahi Minishaytonir Rajeem, Bismillahir Rahmanir Raheem, Li-eelafi Quraish...*"

In the name of Allah, Most Gracious, Most Merciful [2]

1. For the covenants

(Of security and safeguard

Enjoyed) by the Quraysh

2. Their covenants (covering) journeys

By winter and summer

3. Let them adore the Lord

Of this House,

4. Who provides them

With food against hunger, And with security

Against fear (of danger).

HIFDH TEACHING NOTE

Neither life nor *hifdh* exists in a vacuum. How did you live your *hifdh* today? Where did you take your *surahs*? What did you do with them? Did you recite them to a whooping crane in distress? Like most imaginative five-year-olds, Ibrahim has found an instant application for how to 'use' his *surah*. This could be done with *Surah Al Quraysh*, which helps remind us that *AllahSWT* is the ultimate protector, amidst all of life's trials, or it could be done with any number of other *surahs*. The name of the game is to inculcate respect (and love) for the *surah*, the teacher, and the student, and of course to have fun simultaneously.

---

[1] In 1941, there were approximately 15 whooping cranes left in North America; a range of conservation efforts have helped to revitalize the birds, whose numbers now total approximately 450 (U.S. Fish & Wildlife Service 2010).

[2] *Surah* 106 (Abdullah Yusuf Ali 1989, p.1702).

13

ASHURA

Date/place: December 2010, Houston, Ibrahim and Amna's living room, Monday evening

Cast of characters: Nani, Abdurrahman, Ibrahim, Amna, Khadija

"What's the matter?" Nani asks, as Abdurrahman enters the kitchen. His face is down, which is rare, and he seems not altogether present. My Ammi's intuition is also strong and her connection with Abdurrahman, at times, is like that of his own mother.

"*Kuch nahin,*" he responds, in her mother tongue.

But, she is not convinced. "*Sahih?*" she probes, again.

"Papa, what's wrong? Hard day at the office?" Ibrahim follows up with his own inquiries.

"Wrong," repeats Amna.

"*Niente, niente,*" Abdurrahman insists in his own mother tongue, but then stops and looks up, sensing that this audience will not back down. "Ok, ok, well, I just received a note from Taleem about *Ashura.*" Then, turning directly to me, he says, "do you realize Khadija, I'd actually forgotten it."

"Well, you've been very busy; we're nearing year-end and there's some pressure riding on you," I say, trying to assuage him.

"I don't think that's ever really an excuse," responds Abdurrahman. "Taleem asked what I've taught Ibrahim and Amna about *Ashura* and what we will do on the day. And then I realized that the only thing I had planned was three meetings at work. The night before, you know, we have that holiday party as well. At present, I'm doing nothing for *Ashura,* and I haven't learned anything new, let alone teach anyone anything. I'm feeling pretty caught up in my own little life." Abdurrahman sits down next to us and picks up one the sheets of paper on the table. He sketches a small cube and then a stick figure inside of it.

"Hey Papa, that looks like Ammi's *Kaaba.* Do you see Ammi?"

"Well, it is a cube, *baita,* but I don't think your Papa intended to draw the *Kaaba,* did you Abdurrahman?"

"No, not exactly….Ibrahim, I might be a little off subject here, but did you draw this elephant?"

"Yup, that's mine. I actually traced Nonna's gingerbread cookie elephant. And this is Amna's. She doesn't really understand, yet. Ammi and Nani have been reading the translation of *Surah Al Fil*, and I really liked the elephants – not what they were sent to do, but how they were stopped. It all reminded me of South Africa, too."

"You and your mother and your Nani have a real gift *masha'Allah*. And don't underestimate Amna, here."

"Abdurrahman," my mother says, "you should be glad you received the note from Taleem before *Ashura* and not afterwards. That's a blessing. You've still got two days. Will you fast?"

"*Inshaa Allah*, it will help me reset my compass."

"Me fast," interjects Amna. My mother, Abdurrahman and I look at each other and smile.

"But that doesn't really seem like enough," continues Abdurrahman.

"Do you want to do a re... en... act... ment Papa?" asks Ibrahim, sounding out the word slowly. "Ammi and I started doing act... ments of *surahs* last week and it really helped me with my Qur'aan work."

"That's an interesting suggestion *bambino*; you know that Taleem has probably been one of my best teachers in Islam. He taught me how the Prophets, peace be upon all of them, were relieved of many of their struggles on that day. One of the best known examples is how God parted the Red Sea for Prophet Musa, peace be upon him, so he could escape from Pharaoh. I need to review some of the other stories, as well as what happened at *Karbala*.[1] What do you think Nani, a little review and then maybe some Red Sea re-enactment, followed by some prayers at the mosque?"

"*Theek hae*," my mother says, nodding. "How about we all open our history books?"

"Papa, what's *Karbala*, and where did you meet Taleem?"

"*Karbala*? I am going to let your Ammi and Nani explain a little bit later, *bambino*, and Taleem, I first met in the UAE.[2] Now, I think it's back to the books we go. I'm also thinking it's about time to take up the pen again and start writing some poetry."

"Ok Papa, as you wish, but how about I, I mean," Ibrahim coughs lightly and then changes his tone. "How about Captain Kashif presents *Surah Al Fil* to you as a gift so you can smile again, like you normally do. I know you'll like the elephants and the *ababeel* and all the animals and how good wins in the end. And *inshaa Allah* you'll be happy with my memorization."

"Bambino, your *hifdh* is not for me, it's for *Allah Subhanahu wa-ta'ala*; and don't think that you have to memorize a *surah* just to make me happy. But of course it would be a real gift to hear *Surah Al Fil* from you. I'm ready and waiting. I've also been thinking that Nonna might appreciate hearing you recite again. You know it was very special how you recited to her over Thanksgiving. We also need to thank her for the gingerbread animals she sent, and maybe, when we call her, just before bedtime she could hear you too?"

"I like the gingerbread Papa," says Ibrahim.

"Me, bread," Amna says and then looks over toward the counter at the plate of cookies that is lying there, from the afternoon snacks. I don't know how exactly my mother-in-law did it but she managed to bake 5 dozen cookies, package and send them out to all her relatives just before the 13th of December, 12 days before the celebration of Christmas. My mother was equally awed and the kids were very happy with the special treat.

"Me, bread, too, like," says Abdurrahman, kissing his daughter on her forehead. "Ok, let's listen to Ibrahim and then let's call Nonna and then maybe we can all put our thinking caps and our reading glasses on and start to reflect on *Ashura*. Two days is not a lot, but *inshaa Allah* we'll be ready. And yes, I may just put pen to paper again."

HIFDH TEACHING NOTE

Surah Al Fil is often a favorite for young *hifdh* students. They are drawn to the imagery of the elephant and the miracle of the *'ababeel'*. In this scene, *Surah Al Fil* is being learned in the context of *Ashura*, the 10th day of the month of *Muharram* (1st month of the Islamic year). As explained by Abdurrahman, many Prophets, peace be upon them, were relieved of their struggles on this day. *Surah Al Fil* is inherently exciting; however, imagine making it even more exciting by connecting the moral of the tale to another event in history (which may be being commemorated, such as *Ashura*), and using it to highlight *AllahSWT's* glory. When we start to use our daily lives and history to reinforce our *hifdh* lessons, the possibilities are truly endless and the learning becomes both palpable and profound.

---

[1] *Karbala* refers largely to the Battle of Karbala, which was fought in 680 AD in the city of Karbala (in Iraq); after Mecca, Medina and Najaf (also in Iraq), Karbala ranks among the holiest sites for Shi'ah Muslims.

[2] UAE, United Arab Emirates, which includes among the highest rates of immigrant communities in the world, with less than 20 percent of the total population being Emirati nationals (CIA World Fact book Online 2011).

14

SABR & CACTI

Date/place: mid-December, Ibrahim and Amna's apartment, Houston, mid-morning

Cast of characters: Yasmeen, Khadija, Ibrahim, Yaseen, Amna

"My cactus isn't growing. Do you think if I added Christmas lights it would grow better, Phuppi jaan?"

"Yasmeen, they're very pretty, but no, I don't think Christmas lights will do the trick. I think there's another vital ingredient that we require."

"And what would that be?" she asks. Yasmeen and Yaseen are with us for the first day of school holidays. Yaseen and Ibrahim are on the porch, playing their version of Robin Hood; Amna is busy (momentarily) with her legos, which has allowed Yasmeen and me to address her plant issue. About three months ago, just after we arrived in Houston, I gave all the cousins cacti on *Eid ul Fitr*, thinking they would be a fun gift. Yasmeen has brought her cactus along for the day as she is concerned that it is not growing.

"Ok, so you have been watering it, every couple of weeks?" I ask.

"*Jee haan*. And I even gave it some plant food. I talked to it and placed it near my butterfly collection, for company. I smiled at it, but still, look. It looks exactly how it looked the day you gave it me it. What should I do now?"

"*Sabr*," I say, slowly.

"Sorry Phuppi jaan. I don't quite understand. *Sabr*?"

Just then Ibrahim pops his head in. "Ammi, is Sabir calling from Cape Town?" Last week Ibrahim and Amna's best friend, Sabir, had called, which may have prompted him to ask the question.

"No *baita*, it's not Sabir, but it is something important. Why don't you and Yaseen come in for a moment? Which one is Robin Hood by the way?"

"We both are Phuppi jaan," responds Yaseen, "or at least that's the way Ibrahim wanted to play. He's Robin, and I'm Hood, and together we're Robin Hood and we're very, very good."

"You're also rhyming. Ok, come one, come all, you too Amna. I want to talk about *sabr*."

"Excuse me," says Amna, or more audibly 'skus me', as she hiccups, and then stands up and walks over to the group. She finds a seat in my lap as the three other children take up the small chairs in our kitchen.

"So what's the issue?" says Ibrahim, who is quite accustomed to our impromptu lessons.

"Ibrahim, your cousin is concerned that her plant is not growing. Here it is, exhibit A." I hold up the plant as if we are embarking on a detective story. "She's done everything she could: food, water, air, entertainment. She's even considered dressing it up in Christmas lights for the season, right Yasmeen?"

"I never actually considered that. Maybe the cactus is cold. I suppose I could put some cloth around it."

"Yasmeen, your house is good and warm inside *alhumdulilah*. I don't think the cactus is cold," I respond.

"But why did you say '*sabr*' Ammi?" Ibrahim asks.

"Well, I think that's the missing ingredient. Ibrahim do you remember that song I made up when you were a baby?"

"Which one?"

"*Sabr, sabr*, patience, patience, God loves patience," I sing.

"*Sabr, sabr, intizar*, God loves patience," adds Ibrahim, finishing off the chorus.

Then Amna, adds, "Falling down, falling down," the refrain from her favorite song.

"Phuppi jaan, you've lost me, this time," says Yaseen.

"Look, Yasmeen's cactus may be growing, but we may not have noticed. The plant may be growing, slowly, in ways that only a microscope could pick up. We all want results, fast. In fact, to use an expression your father uses, Yaseen, 'we want results yesterday'. But life is actually not always that fast. Do you know, the word '*sabr*', or 'patience', is actually mentioned in the Qur'aan approximately 100 times? It is such an important quality, and yet something that is so hard to practice. I, myself, struggle with it all the time. For instance, sometimes I get frustrated with Amna being two and tipping everything over, drawing on the carpet, and hitting Ibrahim. But just think how much she has grown in the last year? And just think what she can do now? Did you all just hear her? She said 'excuse me'."

"I know, I know, Amna is growing, and she can say '*Alaq*' too, but, back on point Ammi; is 'sabr' in *Surah Al Humazah*?"

"You tell me? Isn't that what you're working on this week?"

Ibrahim starts to say the *surah* softly as if scanning for the word '*sabr*'. "I don't hear it Ammi."

"You're right Ibrahim," confirms his cousin. "*Sabr* is not in *Humazah*. In fact maybe that's one of the things that the people are missing in that *surah*?"[1]

47

"Nice point Yaseen. *Inshaa Allah* you'll earn some points in 'Your Qur'aan Club' for that one," I say, applauding my nephew for his insight.

"But Phuppi jaan, I thought we had school holidays now? Why are we doing this, again?"

"Doing what?" I inquire.

"You know, learning more Qur'aan. Aren't we on holiday?"

"Hmm, yes, you are on school break, but I don't think this work is too difficult, is it?"

"Yaseen, listen to my Ammi, she's older than you." Then Ibrahim adds, "You can read, can't you?"

"Yes, I can," says Yaseen confidently.

"Well then, read that," responds Ibrahim, pointing to a sign we made, which includes post it notes of the titles of our new, recent and old *surahs*, together with some motivating text. We decorated it and hung it in the kitchen to help us stay on track.

Cautiously, Yaseen reads out the following: *"The heart is soil, knowledge is a plant and revision is water. If no water is given to the soil, the plant will wither and die,"* Ja'far as-Sadiq.[2]

"Ok, so, we're still at school is what you're telling me Phuppi jaan, even if it's 'Club time'?" says Yaseen.

"If you want to think of it that way, but maybe we could also just consider life as one good, long lesson, punctuated by a lot of experiences. And the Qur'aan is one of the tools that helps us navigate our way through it all. However, whether or not you believe we're in school right now, it's time for a stretch. Which one of you is Robin and which one is Hood, again? And Amna and Yasmeen, how about joining the guys for a little game of pretend archery outside?"

"I'm in, but I'm still concerned about my cactus. Maybe I can leave it with you to practice *sabr* around it for a little while, while I wait. And then maybe after three more months I'll start to see results."

"It's a deal *baita*," I say, putting my arm around Yasmeen, picking up Amna and walking toward the door. And then, looking at Yaseen, "Lesson adjourned until tonight."

"Phuppi jaan, what does that mean?"

"How about we take up the meaning later? Remember you're done with school for now," I say, patting Yaseen on the head and opening the door for the eager children.

HIFDH TEACHING NOTE

"*Sabr* is not in *Humazah*. In fact maybe that's one of the things that the people are missing in that *surah*?" offers Yaseen to the group of children who are focused in part on Yasmeen's seemingly stunted plant. In teaching *Surah Al Humazah*, just as with the other *surahs*, one may adopt many different approaches. Like *Surah Al Masad*, the meaning is strong, focusing on punishment meted out to those who backbite and hoard their wealth. As teacher, one could focus on the backbiting and the associated punishment or, as in the case of cousin Yaseen, actually speak about the characteristics that the 'scandalmonger' (*Humazah*) is lacking, such as *sabr*, *taqwah* and other spiritually enlightened traits.

---

[1] *Surah Al Humazah* is translated as 'The Scandalmonger' (Abdullah Yusuf Ali 1989, p.1698).

[2] Cited in Londt (2008, p.41).

15

FROM MILK BOTTLES TO VASES, AT ASR

Date/place: December 2010, Ibrahim and Amna's kitchen, mid-afternoon

Cast of characters: Ibrahim, Nani, Amna, Khadija

"Ms Suzy doesn't like it."

"*Kiya?*"

"Ms Suzy, does not like it," Ibrahim repeats very slowly to his Nani.

"Not like it," repeats Amna, waving her index finger at her grandmother.

"*Jee baita*, I understood your English but not the sentiment. What is it exactly that you would like to convey?" My mother says equally slowly back to him, opening her hands in the gesture of a question to Amna.

"You are throwing out the milk bottle."

"Yes, and what would you like Officer Ayesha to do with it instead? Paint it and use it as a vase?" she says, using her new title as given by Ibrahim after our trip to see the whooping cranes.

"Well, that's an interesting idea, Officer. It might even be better than mine. But, first look, here, it's our new recycling center. We made it last week when you were at Mamoo's house. First Ms Suzy taught us how to do it at school, and then Ammi said we could take over this closet, and she re-read *The Queen of Green*, one of the books we brought from Cape Town.[1] And then last week, we went to a real recycling center, where they even recycle motor oil and telephone books. Can you believe that?"[2]

Amna moves into center stage and starts unpacking one of the bags filled with plastics (most recently the dish washing soap container). She starts to lift up the container to her mouth, saying slowly "Queen of clean."

"Whoa, stop, please," I call out to Amna just before she tastes the soap residue. Closing the recycling closet door gently, I then say, "*Bohaut shukria* Ibrahim. That's an excellent introduction. I'm sure your Nani has some things to teach us about recycling as well. Don't you Ammi?"

"Nani, have you ever had a recycling closet?"

"Well, not like this. It was different in Karachi. First we didn't have so much plastic. Everything was not wrapped up, like it is now. I can't recall having all these plastic drinking bottles either. And when I went out for shopping, I took my jute bags with me. I'm sure your Nonna had something similar. And with four growing children, there was hardly ever any food waste. Whatever was left over, we fed to the pigeons, up on the roof. Next time, you see your Abdullah Mamoo you can ask him about all those pigeons. You are the one who generally connects the links Khadija, but I find it interesting that you were just working on *Surah Al Asr* with Ibrahim and here we are talking about recycling and reusing through the ages. Did you already read the translation Ibrahim?"

"Me? No. I can't read that translation. Some of the words are too long."

"No, I mean, did your mother already read you the translation?"

"Yes, in the big green Abdullah Yusuf Ali Qur'aan, but then I sort of forgot it because I was too busy trying to recite *Surah Al Humazah* again. Ammi said I am forgetting my *mudood*."

"Oh no, forgetting your *mudood*... maybe you can teach me about that, along with the important lessons from Ms Suzy, but in the meantime, I just want to re-read the translation of *Surah Al Asr* for all of us," says my mother, moving over to the bookshelf and then settling herself at the kitchen table.

1. By (the Token of) Time (through the ages),

2. Verily Man is in loss,

3. Except such as have Faith,

And do righteous deeds,

And (join together)

In the mutual teaching

Of Truth, and of

Patience and Constancy.[3]

"*Asr* is nice and short," says Ibrahim.

"Yes, it is, and very potent too," I add.

"Are we doing righteous deeds when we recycle Nani?" inquires Ibrahim.

"Only Allah will be the judge of that *baita*," responds my mother. "But I think that generally treating the earth as a living being and trying to have less of an impact is a good thing, and as that kitchen magnet says here, 'we do not inherit the earth from our ancestors, we borrow it from our children.'"[4]

"I hope that Allah will be pleased with my recycling center... Ammi, did you hear Amna?"

"*Kiya?*" I say.

"She just said, 'patience, patience'. I guess she remembered it from our song. There's another '*sabr*' in *Surah Al Asr* isn't there?"

"Yes, Ibrahim, there is. And another '*haqqi*'."

"What do you mean Ammi?"

"I mean, I heard the word for 'truth' (*haq*) in *Surah Al Asr*. Haven't you seen that word in your first eleven *surahs*?"

"Ammi, is this a trick?"

"No, *baita*, I just thought we'd encountered it."

"I don't think so, but if you really want I can recite everything right now for you and see if I hear a '*haq*'."

"Please, I'll listen out for it." Ibrahim engages in an impromptu review of his first 11 *surahs* and we all listen in.

"Ammi, we haven't had a *haq* yet," Ibrahim finally says, just after he concludes *Surah An Nas*.

"No, not explicitly," I say, mostly to my mother.

"So was that a trick just to get me to review?"

"No, I honestly thought we had seen a '*haq*' before; but what I just alluded to with your grandmother is that while the word '*haq*' itself has not yet been mentioned, there is a lot of *haq* or truth in the first eleven *surahs*."

"All truth, Ammi," Ibrahim says, as if correcting me.

"Yes, *baita* you are right. All truth, and so much for me to learn. *Inshaa Allah* you'll be getting lots of points for that one. By the way, I really liked Nani's idea about the vase and the milk bottle. What do you think Amna?"

"Milk?" says Amna, smiling.

"Yes, milk. What if after *Asr* prayers, we undertake a little arts and crafts, and what if…"

"And what if we find a flower and then give it to Ms Suzy," says Ibrahim finishing the sentence.

"Better yet, why don't you plant a flower and then in two weeks when school resumes after holiday break you can give it to her, and *inshaa Allah* the plant will be alive, maybe even thriving," my mother says, one upping us all.

"Nice," says Ibrahim. "I'll keep it right next to Sabr, Yasmeen's cactus, which Ammi is trying to help grow up."

"Nice, nice," says Amna, in her characteristic repetitive way, which sounds now as though she is casting a double vote for the next activity and the cactus-plant collection.

"I might even write Ms Suzy a little note on the back of this recycled cereal box, thanking her for her contribution to our home," concludes my mother. And then looking over at me, "It looks like I have my New Year's resolution-orders, *sahih*?"

"*Sahih*," responds Ibrahim before me, as he heads off in the direction of our room, for *Asr*. Then calling back at me, "Ammi, do you remember those plants at Kirstenbosch, in plastic bottles; remember we saw them right before we left South Africa? I wonder whether everything is still growing there? Maybe Sabir will know, and maybe we can write him. I think it was in that special show called something like taming or tamed or untaming."

"Yes, *baita*. I can't quite believe your memory, *masha'Allah*. It's time to write Sabir and inquire about that exhibit at Kirstenbosch, and meanwhile maybe I can do a little research about it and share it with your school as well *inshaa Allah*."[5]

HIFDH TEACHING NOTE

Together with *Surah Al Ikhlas* and *Surah Al Fil*, as mentioned earlier, *Surah Al Asr* has many fans among young, aspiring *huffadh*. All three *surahs* are *short*, but they are also extremely powerful, especially *Ikhlas* and *Asr* in terms of the messages that they convey. It is easy to race through these short *surahs*, but instead consider devoting the same amount of time (if not more) to delve deep into the meaning. What is *AllahSWT* really trying to teach us, about "Truth, and […] Patience and Constancy"? Another important element, for *hifdh*, as showcased in this scene, is the review method. Rather than simply asking Ibrahim to recite all his *surahs*, Khadija asks him to look for a word (in this case '*haqqi*'). In this way, the review becomes a form of a detective game for the child, passing quickly, with a greater sense of urgency and fun — elements that are key for engaging young ones.

---

[1] See Taylor (2010).

[2] As of 2009, the United States of America ranked third worldwide with regard to per capital municipal solid waste (MSW), after Norway and Ireland (OECD 2009). Approximately one third of all MSW in the US is made up of packaging (Center for Sustainable Systems, Municipal Solid Waste, 2009).

[3] *Surah* 103 (Abdullah Yusuf Ali 1989, p.1693).

[4] Phrase attributed to environmentalist, David Brower.

[5] UNTAMED, exhibit at Kirstenbosch Botanical Garden, opened in June 2010, Cape Town, South Africa.

16

BOXING

Date/place: December 2010, the day after Christmas, Nonna's kitchen, Brooklyn, New York, early afternoon

Cast of characters: Nonna, Khadija, Ibrahim

"Khadija, after six years, I think I can speak to you candidly and you won't take offense," says my mother-in-law.

"Of course, what's the matter?"

"Dear, you're a professional. What are you still doing at home?"

"Carmen, I'm trying to set up a home in a new country; it takes time. And I'm also working towards some weighty *hifdh* goals. I'm aiming to have the last section of the Qur'aan within the next four months *inshaa Allah*."

"And then?"

"And then, *inshaa Allah* we'll move onto the next section. In the meantime, I'd like to follow your lead and pick up Spanish to help bridge some divides. It feels like there's such a cultural barrier in our new home-state."

"But what's happened to your career?"

"It's on hold for a little while."

"And are you really managing? Isn't there a piece of you that is a little unsettled? When Nico and Geo were growing up, I needed the outlet, and the extra income. I'd also attained a certain level where stepping down or scaling back wasn't really an option. The travel was tough for the kids, but they also learned a lot, even when 'mama' wasn't there. I just wonder when you're going to reconsider all this homemaking and return to your real roots. For goodness sake Khadija, you did a doctorate in your field, and have ten years under your belt. I think that you might serve humanity a bit better if you get back out there and start working. Your mother could help with the kids, and I am here for you as well."

"Ammi, are you going back to work?" asks Ibrahim, literally walking into our conversation. He takes up my hand in his and then continues. "Because if you go back to work now, then I'm going to have a really hard time with the next *surah*. And Amna will struggle as well. And you'll also disappoint Hafidha

Rabia. Remember she said we could celebrate the end by coming to visit her in Jakarta, in person, not on the phone. You might even lose some of your 'Qur'aan Club points'."

"*Baita*, please don't get upset. Your grandmother and I are just brainstorming here. It's an open discussion about what's the best course of life, for now. I loved my work, as you know, but at present, it's just a little incompatible with the *hifdh* goals, and all the homemaking."

"Papa said you were married to your work once, I remember that," says Ibrahim, causing me to blush a little.

"Maybe he did, *baita*. *Inshaa Allah* I will soon be married to my *hifdh* goals, or perhaps a better way of saying it would be, I'll be truly committed to them, but also create lots of time for you and Amna and your Papa and all the other important people in my life. And maybe then, we'll re-evaluate how to integrate the water sector work. By the way, did you finish cleaning the car? Or is it too cold for you out there? And is Amna really enduring the cold?"

"Amna is boxing," responds Ibrahim.

"What?" says Nonna, with surprise.

"Well, first we cleaned the car, but Nonna, it was *really* dirty; next time, you need to ask Uncle Geo to help you out, because I don't think you should have been driving such a dirty car on the highway. Or maybe, Ammi, we could come more often to Brooklyn to clean Nonna's car?" says Ibrahim looking at me.

"*Jee baita*, that sounds like a good idea. But why is Amna boxing, and do you think your father needs help with her?" I ask trying to get to the bottom of Ibrahim's story.

"No, no, Papa is fine and so is Amna. Just wait. Let me explain. After cleaning, Papa said I could recite *Surah At Takathur* in the driver's seat. Remember we did that at Uncle Geo's house over Thanksgiving and I think it helped me get *Kauthar*."

"Ibrahim, why is your sister boxing?" reiterates Nonna now, beginning to get a little concerned.

"Man, you don't have patience, do you?"

"Ibrahim, remember what I said about not calling your elders 'man'," I say, shooting a glance of 'not acceptable' in his direction. My expression is much stronger than my words.

"Yes, yes, sorry about that, but it's just I'm getting to my point and you are both being a little impatient."

"*Bambino*, tell us, we're waiting now," says Nonna, "but yes, try to always speak gently, especially to us old people."

"Ok, ok, where was I? Oh yes, I was reciting *At Takathur* behind the wheel. And, before that, Papa also reminded me of the translation about all the piling up of stuff. Nonna, you have a lot in your garage, even excluding all your new

Christmas gifts," he says, stopping briefly to look at his grandmother. "But now let me get to my point. As I was reciting, I saw a punching bag. Don't worry Ammi, I finished the *surah* without interrupting myself." Again he pauses, and this time looks at me. "But then I asked Papa whether I could play with it. He told me he used to use it in high school. He never buried anger before he met you Ammi, but he did get all of his agre… ss… ion out with the bag. Is that true, Nonna?"

"Yes, sir, your father even had some big black boxing gloves. Suffice it to say, Rocky was a hero for all of us. And of course Muhammad Ali was too."

"Ibrahim?" I say, also sounding concerned now.

"Yes, yes, anyway, Papa gave Amna and me a demonstration. It was really cool. And then he started to tell me about Boxing Day. Isn't that amazing? Today is Boxing Day!"[1]

"Yes, pretty amazing, and your sister, Ibrahim?" repeats Nonna.

"Well, she didn't really care much for Papa's history lesson about Boxing Day. She just liked hitting the punching bag. So she's still out there. I started to get a little cold, standing around watching her punch and so I decided to come in and have another gingerbread cookie. Can I Ammi-Nonna?" says Ibrahim looking at us both and smiling at himself.

Nonna and I look at each other. She starts to say 'yes' and I start to say 'no' but somehow I change in the middle and Ibrahim manages to get two 'yes's' out of us.

"*Grazie*," says Ibrahim, still smiling. "But Ammi, promise me, you're not going to leave me behind in my *surahs*. Remember Papa's Qur'aan contract?"

"Yes, *baita*, and no, no one is abandoning anyone or anything. By the way, I'd like to see that punching bag. I think it actually might come in handy in Houston. Will you take me out?" I say to Ibrahim and Nonna.

"Let's go," responds Ibrahim, grabbing two cookies from the kitchen counter and forgetting that he was cold in the garage. And off we go, again.

HIFDH TEACHING NOTE

Learning *Surah At Takathur* in a garage or an attic may be an effective way for some children to grasp part of the meaning. Garages and attics are often filled with lots of beautiful mementos, but often also with things that we actually may never use and we simply keep (and even hoard) because we think they are important. What is important to us? And what does the Qur'aan teach us about what is important to *AllahSWT*? Is it status? Wealth? Ask these questions before you start learning the *surah* to engage the children and their imaginations. Often, glossy magazines may provide good fodder for collages to help illustrate this *surah* as well, namely the endless piling up of things in this world that have the potential to distract us from our true purpose. Finally, try to connect the learning to an event in the children's life and/or history to make the experience of this *surah* even stronger.

---

[1] Boxing Day is a public holiday, generally celebrated the day after Christmas, in the UK and in many other English speaking countries, excluding the USA. The tradition may date back to the Middle Ages. The origin of the name appears to stem from 'box', namely the gift of a box from one's employer/benefactor on that day.

17

Surah Work, Leaf Blowing and Amna's Ikhlas

Date/place: January 2011, Ibrahim and Amna's living room, Houston, early afternoon

Cast of characters: Amna, Ibrahim, Khadija

"Can't hear," she says, putting her fingers in her ears.

"I can't hear either, Ammi," says Ibrahim, mimicking his sister, in a momentary role reversal.

"Well, I'm having difficulty too, but let's try to close the windows and doors. If that doesn't work, we may need to have another lesson in *la coche*," I say, winking at Ibrahim, who has enjoyed his two car Qur'aan lessons, first at Uncle Geo's and then more recently at Nonna's, and who is also starting to pick up some Spanish vocabulary with me.

It takes us about 5 minutes to run around our apartment and close up. Ibrahim and I have to keep Amna from reopening the porch door, but eventually she understands. The noise subsides, somewhat, but is definitely still audible.

"Ammi, why do they blow leaves?"

"*Baita*, it looks like the men are trying to gather them, and this may be their main tool. I didn't grow up with leaf blowers, and I never had them at work; in fact this is my first exposure to them in my whole life, just like you."

"But Ammi they make so much noise!"

"Noisy," says Amna, surprising us both with her turn of phrase.

"Yes, noisy indeed. Again, I'm no expert on the subject. I've only ever used rakes before, and my hands, but I also learned, long, long ago, in one of my Ecology courses at University that the leaves help nourish the soil, provided they are shredded and composted with equal amounts of green matter."

"What does that mean, Ammi?"

"As they decompose or they break down they actually serve as a natural fertilizer."

"So the leaves are like plant food?"

"Yum," says Amna, who seems now to be expecting a snack.

58

"Yes, yummy for the soil," I affirm, finding our new course of discussion very interesting, but also wondering how I will put us back on track for our lesson.

"But Ammi, the leaf blowing men put the leaves in bags and cart them away. Doesn't the soil get hungry then?"

"Yes and no, *baita*. Generally, they introduce their own type of fertilizer. But, I would rather we do a little more research before I make any great claims. Remember we were going to talk to the Management about recycling junk mail, rather than simply throwing it out. Maybe when we go to speak to them about the mail, we may also ask some questions about the leaves and the fertilizer?"

"Sounds like a plan, Ammi, but it's loud. It actually reminds me of that blowing on knots from *Surah Al Falaq* and now all your talk about *Al Qari'ah*," says Ibrahim, bringing us back to our lesson, without my intervention.[1]

"True, it is loud, and perhaps a little like the 'The (Day) of Noise and Clamour,'" I respond, reading out of the *Meaning of the Holy Qur'an* that I have in front of me. "But I don't yet see that the 'Mountains [are] like carded wool',[2] so I think we're ok for now *inshaa Allah*."

"I liked the part about the moths, but it's also a little scary."

"Agreed. Is that your picture of the scale?" I ask, looking now at the sheet of paper in front of Ibrahim. Amna's picture is equally eye catching as she has gone to town with a big blue marker and drawn many spirals. We have only just begun *Surah Al Qari'ah* and, as is customary with us, have started with a drawing, after reading the translation and listening to the *surah* several times.

"Yes, it is, and I think I get a point for helping to teach Amna *Surah Ikhlas* this morning. Did you hear her? She actually repeated almost all the words after me, Ammi? Isn't that amazing, even before you started her on the blue book?[3] Will it make my scale light on *Al Qari'ah*?"

Amna looks up, sensing she is the focus of discussion, and confidently utters "*Ikhlas*."[4]

"Yes *masha'Allah* it is amazing, and *inshaa Allah* your scale will be light, but remember what Nani said a couple weeks ago, when we were reviewing *Surah Al Asr*?"

"Ammi, are you testing my memory, again, or did *you* forget?"

"*Baita*, do you remember?"

"Ok, yes, she said, only Allah will be the judge of whether we are righteous."

"And so? Do you think that I can tell you if it will make your scale light?"

"Probably not, but I'm really happy Amna recited *Ikhlas*."

"So am I *baita*, and I am also proud of both of you, extremely proud, *masha'Allah*. I think we might even need to plan an ice cream treat for tonight."

"Ice cream," Amna mimics.

"Yes, ice cream Amna," repeats Ibrahim, jumping off his chair and jumping up and down. "We are going to have ice cream because you said *Ikhlas*."

"*Ikhlas*," says Amna again. I close my book, sensing that this lesson may be done and the next one will soon start.

HIFDH TEACHING NOTE

It is impossible for us to truly imagine what the Day of Judgment will be like, however, this *surah* provides some insights. Without damaging the children's ears, it could be helpful to expose them to a loud noise for a very limited time. In addition, while Ibrahim and Amna chose to draw images, using a real kitchen scale may also help bring this *surah* alive. Children could affix weights to good deeds and bad (with heavier associated with the good) and then see what may be the outcome. A key principal in the discussion, as highlighted by Khadija, for this *surah* and *Surah Al Asr*, is that although we must strive to increase our good deeds, we are not in a position to judge our ultimate fate (or that of others). Only *AllahSWT* knows, the Most Beneficent, the Most Merciful.

---

[1] As first discussed in footnote 2, Chapter 5, from the 'TV' Chapter. See also footnote 6305 (Abdullah Yusuf Ali 1989, p. 1716).

[2] *Surah Al Qariah* (Abdullah Yusuf Ali 1989, p.1687).

[3] As previously referenced, the character Ibrahim completed the pre-Qur'aanic primer *Towards Reading the Qur'an, Part Two*, just before he started in the Qur'aan (see Chapter 7). Part One of this two volume series *Towards Reading the Qur'an* has a blue cover and hence the mention of the 'blue book'. There are many such books in circulation. Generally students of Qur'aan may take between six months and one year to understand the Arabic alphabet and basic *tajweed* rules before starting on the Qur'aan, however, it depends largely on the aptitude and interest of the student.

[4] *Ikhlas* is translated as 'the Purity of Faith," (Abdullah Yousuf Ali, p.1714). *Surah Al Ikhlas* is also considered the essence of the Holy Qur'aan. See Chapter 6, 'Space' for a complete translation.

18

MLK Day

Date/place: January, 2011, the roof of a parking garage attached to the apartment building, that it is open and generally not filled with cars, Houston, sunset

Cast of characters: Uncle Bill, Ibrahim, Amna, Abdurrahman, Khadija

"Well, there you are, my little angels. I thought I'd find you up here," says Uncle Bill, calling out to Ibrahim and Amna.

Ibrahim waves back at the man approaching, who, although technically not his uncle, has been given this title by all of us, due to his age and his proximity. Uncle Bill lives, together with his wife, Beatrice, who is also an octogenarian, in the apartment below us, and has become part and parcel of our days since moving to Houston. We greet him in the morning, en route to school and again mid-day, upon our return. In the afternoon, rain or shine, when we head out for our excursions, he is also there, reading and observing, on his front porch. We give and receive baked goods and comic strips, as well as facts and figures about bugs, including the latest on Yasmeen's butterfly collection and Yaseen's ant farm, but mostly it is an exchange of smiles.

"Come," says Ibrahim, still waving.

"Come, Un... cle Bill," adds Amna, then, "bi... cycle."

Uncle Bill moves enthusiastically but slowly. While his age is apparent in his gait, it does not affect his smile, or affection. "I'm coming," he responds, and then adds in his customary way. "Any mosquitoes out tonight, or is it too cold for them?"

Abdurrahman, who is resting after having raced Ibrahim (on bicycle) by foot, stands up and greets Uncle Bill with a warm handshake. "Good evening. Yes, it's definitely too cold."

I smile and nod at him, then look back out. We are here because of the children and the sunset, which is starting to extend and give us a little more daylight. Tonight the colors are stronger than usual, or maybe I am simply able to see them with a little more clarity, not clouded by the normal evening routine.

"You know Khadija, tomorrow is Martin Luther King Day," Uncle Bill says addressing me. He knows that I am still adjusting and that my cultural and historical knowledge is still pretty limited.

"I do, or so I have learned recently. Ibrahim and Amna are off from school, and I'm trying to educate myself and then share whatever knowledge I may with them. I read one interesting comparison of Dr. King and Gandhi, and of course someone with whom they are both familiar… Nelson Mandela. I've been thinking about making a sort of non-violent activist map to help them see how universal the message is."[1]

"I like your message, Khadija," says Uncle Bill, still smiling. At times, he feels a little like my late father in his encouragement and affirmation.

"Ammi, what's taking you so long," shouts Ibrahim, who is eager for another race. "And why won't you let Uncle Bill play our game?" Responding on cue, Uncle Bill starts walking toward Ibrahim and Amna.

"*Baita*, we're all coming," I reassure him, and then quickly to Abdurrahman, "Will you remind me to print that article out later? I'd really like the kids to see the pictures of the men as well. They look so different and yet obviously are not."

"*Si, si*," responds Abdurrahman. "I also think we might finally be able to help them out if we can relate tonight's bicycle race to *Surah Al Adiyat*."[2]

"*Masha'Allah* Private Nouman, you're good," I say. "I think you get major points for that one. Did you think it up when you were recovering?"

"Your two children have a lot of energy in them, more than I could have ever imagined," Abdurrahman says winking at me, and then heading back to them, and Uncle Bill, who has reached the two now jubilant children.

HIFDH TEACHING NOTE

Earlier, in Chapter 4, we read about Ibrahim reciting in Memorial Park, while walking alongside Khadija. The children do have designated *hifdh* times, namely specific times throughout the day when they sit down and work, but in addition to these, *hifdh* is integrated over the course of the day. In this scene, Abdurrahman makes a passing reference to *Surah Al Aadiyaat* in the context of racing with the children. At the same time, throughout the scene Khadija is focusing on Martin Luther King, and themes of non-violence, employed by countless spiritual and political leaders. In teaching *Aadiyaat*, we may emphasize both themes, namely the physical running as epitomized by the "steeds that run with panting breath" and the spiritual, which is summarized at the outset by Abdullah Yusuf Ali as, "...the irresistible nature of spiritual power and knowledge, contrasted with unregenerate man's ingratitude, pettiness, helplessness, and ignorance," (p.1683). Consider reading the translation with your children (including some of the footnotes if you think they would be receptive) and ask them to tell you which is their favorite description of themes in the *surah* and why. Alternatively (or in addition), could they reenact any part of the *surah* with any toys that they have, including miniature horses? Meanwhile, try not to overlook the important events in your midst, such as Martin Luther King Day, which may embody critical lessons, such as truth, justice, equality and perseverance, and which ultimately reinforce many of the Qur'aan's lessons.

---

[1] Since the year 2000, all 50 American states have observed Martin Luther King Day, commemorating the civil rights leader, who was assassinated in 1968 for his resistance to racial and social inequality. Dr King was influenced by, among others, the work and writings of Mahatma Gandhi and was inspired by his non-violence resistance movement.

[2] *Surah Al Adiyat* (100), translated as 'Those That Run'. As excerpted from footnote 6241, "The whole conflict, fighting, and victory, may be applied to spiritual warfare against those who are caught up and overwhelmed by the camp of Evil," (Abdullah Yusuf Ali 1989, p.1684).

19

WHY IS MY NAME?

Date/place: January 2010, Ibrahim and Amna's porch, Houston, mid- afternoon, snack time

Cast of characters: Ibrahim, Khadija, Amna, Nani

"Why is my name also Shaban?" asks Ibrahim.

"Well, Muhemmed Ibrahim Shaban," I say looking directly at the five and almost three quarter year old boy staring at me, "it was and is a name that is close to my heart... *Mairae dil kae qareeb hae*," I respond.

"But what does it mean again, Ammi?"

"Ammi, meaning?" repeats Amna, in between bites of banana chips, which my mother is slowly passing out; she is trying to teach Amna how *not* to throw her food.

"You remember *baita*. Shaban is the 8th month of the Islamic calendar, and when many of us try to start preparing for Ramadan. Of course some people prepare all year, but...'[1]

"But Khadija, surely he also knows the other version of the story?" says my mother, smiling.

"Oh yes, I think he pried it out of me last year, didn't you Ibrahim?" I respond, now smiling and blushing a little. "It was in the month of Shaban that I met your father... *Laila-tul Baraa'at*, the Night of Forgiveness."

"Oh, yes, now I'm starting to remember... and he thought you might be a good wife," says Ibrahim very matter-of-factly, with the authority of an adult.

"Yes, something like that, *baita*. I'm definitely still working on that front," I say, perhaps more to myself than anyone else, then, "I think my heart was searching for something and *Allah ta'ala* gave me your father, and then you and Amna. Suffice it to say, it's helped me a lot in my journey."

"Papa and us?" confirms Ibrahim.

"*Jee haan.*"

"Because we've broaden... ed your scope?" says Ibrahim who now sounds as though he may be pushing 40. He also sounds like Abdurrahman who has used that exact phrase in trying to explain our blended families to Ibrahim and Amna.

"*Jee haan*," says my mother, nodding, "broadened and deepened. Do you know that your mother only used to think about water policy before you all came into her life?"[2]

"Well, water is important," responds Ibrahim. Amna who is bilingual with this word, adds, "*pani?*"

"Yes, *pani* is very important, but so is integrating all the different pieces of life, into your life. I thank Abdurrahman, your papa, for helping, your Ammi, and my Khadija, to understand this."

"Ammi," I say, feeling as though the conversation may be getting a little too personal. "*Bohaut shukria*, but how about we head back to our lesson? We have at least another five *surahs* to review, and today we're doing it with Sheikh Husri."[3]

"But Ammi, you aren't done?" says Ibrahim.

"Done with what *baita*?"

"Aren't you going to tell us why your name is Khadija and why Amna's name is Amna, and why Papa's name is Abdurrahman and Nico and why Hafidha Rabia's is what it is? And why you didn't name any one of us *Zalzalah*?"[4]

"How about we park all those good questions except the *Zalzalah* one for another day? Ok," I say, nodding at everyone.

"Ok Ammi, but only if we can call Najma Mumani afterwards. Yaseen told me last week that she was going to have a big day today, maybe an exam or something… and then maybe we can call your other brother to see when Naeem is coming from Qatar," Ibrahim says, looking for my approval. "By the way," he adds, "I think I know why you didn't name either Amna or me *Zalzalah*."

"Why is that?"

"Because it means 'earthquake' and that would be a very strong name."

"Good job," says Amna, clapping. Her sense of timing is, at times, amazing *masha'Allah*.

"But, even though you didn't name me *Zalzalah*, I still think it's a cool *surah*, especially that part at the end where Adam's weight counts. And I also think Captain Kashif would like it."

"*Baita*, not Prophet Adam's, *alayhis salaam*, weight, an atom's weight, but yes, you're on the right track. I think it's cool as well and that Sergeant Faith would also like it. Now, look, we're done with the banana chips. How about we get back to business. *Listos*?" I ask looking at the children.

"*Si, lista*," responds my mother, who may be one step behind Nonna, but is at least one step ahead of us, with her own study (of Spanish). "*Vamanos*," she says beckoning us to head inside.

HIFDH TEACHING NOTE

Zalzalah or 'earthquake' emerged as the focus of the children's discussion, in a broader discussion of the origins of family names. All agreed that '*Zalzalah*' would not be an appropriate name, given the images it conjures up. Using discretion, consider showing some images of earthquakes to your children — somewhat similar to the exercise of (briefly) listening to a loud noise with *Surah Al Qariah*. Another potentially powerful exercise for this *surah* is to show the children a lentil, followed by a grain of rice and finally a grain of sugar or salt. Try to communicate that while each of these items is increasingly small, an atom is much smaller; and yet on the Day of Judgment, attention will be paid to deeds of this (miniscule) size. End your lesson by focusing on increasing the good deeds: what are the good deeds that we may do right now, this day, this hour, this minute?

---

[1] Daylami narrates the following, "Our Holy Prophet [*Salla Allahu 'alayhi wa sallam*] *SAW* has said, Shaban is my month and Ramadan the month of Allah [*ta'ala*]."

[2] As of 2010, approximately 87 percent of the world's population had access to potable water, however, only 61 percent had access to adequate sanitation (which amounts to approximately 2.6 billion people), according to a joint World Health Organization/UNICEF study (*Progress on Sanitation and Drinking-Water –2010 Update Report*).

[3] Sheikh Mahmoud Khalil Husri (also spelled Husary and Husari), b.1917, d.1980, was a world renowned *qari*, and his recordings continue to be in wide circulation, especially amongst aspiring *huffadh*.

[4] *Surah Al Zalzalah* (The Earthquake) is the 99th *surah* in the Holy Qur'aan. As translated by Abdullah Yusuf Ali, "1. When the Earth is shaken to its (utmost) convulsion, 2. And the Earth throws up its burdens (from within), 3. And man cries (distressed); 'What is the matter with it?', 4. On that Day will it declare its tidings, 5. For that thy Lord will have given it inspiration. 6. On that Day will men proceed in companies sorted out, to be shown the Deeds that they (had done). 7. Then shall anyone who has done an atom's weight of good, see it! 8. And anyone who has done an atom's weight of evil, shall see it," (pp.1681-2).

20

CHECKLISTS AND SAINT FRANCIS

Date/place: late January, 2011, around/outside Ibrahim and Amna's apartment, Houston, mid-afternoon

Cast of characters: Amna, Khadija, Ibrahim, Nani

"Mailbox key?" inquires Amna, holding the small silver key.

"Yes, *baita*, the mailbox key. *Chalyae?*"

"*Mein tayyaar hoon*," says Ibrahim, putting on his bicycle helmet.

"Me too, but do we really need both bikes and your briefcase and the soccer ball? We're only going to pick up the mail, and I only have two hands."

"But Ammi, you also have two feet and the top of your head. Remember how we saw women balancing stuff on their heads in Cape Town... and Karachi? But don't worry. I'll put the soccer ball in my brief case, and, of course, the mail, after we collect it, and I'll try to help you carry our bikes downstairs."

"Thank you, *baita*. Ok, checklist: do we have the tissues?"

"Yes," confirms Amna, without necessarily fully understanding the question.

"Do we have the water bottle?"

"Yes," Amna confirms again.

"Ammi, we're only going to pick up the mail," Ibrahim says smiling, "*Chalyae*."

"Ok, ok, let's go. I think I'm ready," then, "*Khuda Hafiz* Ammi," I call out to my mother who has decided not to join us for our little afternoon escapade. She is seated at the kitchen table making notes in her most recent travelogue about the Yucatan, which Nonna sent earlier last week to whet her appetite in a possible trip.

"*Khuda Hafiz, baita*," she says, observing our multi-staged departure. "Have fun," she adds, turning back to her book.

I close the door behind us, take a deep breath and then set out. First I walk the children down the two sets of stairs, before returning for the two bikes. As usual, Bill is on the porch of his garden apartment and immediately engages the children as I take two more trips.

"Well, my angels, good afternoon," he says.

"Good afternoon, Uncle Bill," responds Ibrahim.

"Afta… noon," mimics Amna.

"So where are you off to, now? Any archery today?" Bill inquires.

"Ach… ry," Amna repeats, pulling her right arm back and miming the action, as she has seen her brother do so many times.

"No, Uncle Bill, we're going to get the mail. And maybe we'll play soccer on our way back, or bike. And maybe we'll meet a snake."

"A snake? Don't you think an alligator might be more probable? Or even a leopard?"

"Uncle Bill, there are no leopards here; you should know that," Ibrahim says in his adult voice. "Have you seen any ants today?"

"Hmm, ants? It's colder, and they're a little scarce these days, but look here at my Tiger Beetle. Look how much fun he's having today?" Uncle Bill says, holding up one of his bug cages.

Amna runs right up as if she is ready to hold the insect, while Ibrahim hangs back a bit. I am finally done with bicycle lifting work but not yet ready to get too close to a Tiger Beetle.

"Tiger, tiger," sounds out Amna, "grrr".

"Looks interesting, Uncle Bill. Maybe we can visit more later, after the mail?" Ibrahim says, as if asking permission to leave.

"Ok, catch you later, little angels; and remember, you look after that mother of yours," says Bill waving and smiling at me.

"Bye, bye," I say, then turning to Ibrahim, "*Baita*, do you want to try reviewing *Surah Al Bayyinah* and see if we can get through our own Qur'aan checklist?"

"On my bike?"

"Well maybe on your bike or maybe before you get on your bike; I just thought it might help since we were mixing up some of the *ayaat* inside."

"Not anymore," says Ibrahim confidently, and then, he recites *ayah* seven as though it were his next sentence, "*Bismillah, Innallazeena'amanou wa 'amilus-salihati 'ula-'ika hum khayrul-barriyyah,*" then, "*Illa-llazeena 'amanou wa 'amilus-salihati wa tawasaw bil Haqqi wa tawasaw-bis-Sabr.*"[1]

"*Masha'Allah*, you do have it, and *Surah Al Asr.*"

"Good job," Amna says, sharing her brother's excitement. She hasn't progressed into *Surah Al Bayyinah* yet, but is preserving *Surah Al Ikhlas*, which she learned under her brother's tutelage several weeks back, and will undoubtedly surprise us with a new *surah* soon.

"But Ammi," continues Ibrahim, "I may need another week for *Bayyinah*, to really have it, and not lose my other *surahs*."

"*Baita*, you take as much time as you need. Remember what Papa told you that night when we were working on *Surah Al Fil*: your *hifdh* is not for me, or him, it's for *Allah Subhanahu wa-ta'ala* and also for you; it's like your own treasure map for this world, and *inshaa Allah* you will find lots of treasures as you make your way through it. Do you know that the Qur'aan was revealed to Prophet Muhemmed, *Salla Allahu 'alayhi wa sallam* over 23 years?"

"That's a long time."

"Yes, it is a long time. And we have time, to learn *alhumdulilah*, sort of like our trip to collect the mail."

"What do you mean Ammi?"

"Well, when did we leave the house?"

"I don't know. A while back."

"And if we had just gone to get the mail how long would it have taken us?"

"Maybe three minutes."

"Minutes," repeats Amna, as though she too wants to participate in the conversation.

"Maybe three minutes, if we were running really fast. But at that speed, we probably would not have been able to say goodbye to your grandmother or greet Uncle Bill. And I certainly would not have been able to carry the bicycles downstairs, let alone the soccer ball. We would have missed Tiger Beetle and all the adventures that *inshaa Allah* we are about to have."

"So Ammi, I can have another week on *Surah Al Bayyinah*."

"*Jee haan*. It needs to make sense to you and feel like the blessing that it is."

"Ok, that's good, but what do you think is going to be in the mail box today? Monday, there wasn't too much."

"Well, your Aunt Margaret did say she was going to send you two something special."

"Why didn't she just send an email? Oh, wait I know, I know, because then I wouldn't have seen Uncle Bill's Tiger Beetle and all that other stuff," says Ibrahim, answering his own question. "Ammi, will we see them before next Thanksgiving?"

"*Inshaa Allah*," I respond, as we near the apartment complex mailboxes. "Ibrahim, do you think that we should let Amna open the mailbox again today? It seems she really likes being in charge, of the keys."

"Yup Ammi, let her be in charge, for now."

"Mailbox key," Amna says reaching up to me, to be in charge.

Amna struggles a bit with the key and then finally manages to open our small box. As expected, inside there is a letter from Aunt Margaret. Its contents are, however, a little unexpected.

"What's inside Ammi?" says Ibrahim, grabbing the letter out of his sister's hand, and tearing open the envelope.

"Careful *baita*," I say trying to keep him from tearing the letter as well, and then steadying his hand so I may begin reading.

Dear Ibrahim and Amna: thank you for sharing Thanksgiving with us. It was very special. Thank you also for your recitations. I have never heard anything quite like them before. Immediately below is my favorite prayer. I recite it every day. Love, Aunt Margaret

The prayer of Saint Francis[2]

Lord, make me an instrument of your peace,

Where there is hatred, let me sow love;

where there is injury, pardon;

where there is doubt, faith;

where there is despair, hope;

where there is darkness, light;

where there is sadness, joy;

O Divine Master, grant that I may not so much seek to be consoled as to console;

to be understood as to understand;

to be loved as to love.

For it is in giving that we receive;

it is in pardoning that we are pardoned;

and it is in dying that we are born to eternal life.

"Wow, Ammi, that's really beautiful," says Ibrahim, just as I finish.

"Yes, it sure is. I don't know whether we should write or call or..."

"How about we just think about it for now Ammi and then tomorrow I'm sure one of us will have an idea, maybe even Amna will help us come up with something, or Nani," responds the adult Ibrahim. Then, he adds, "I wonder whether Nani has ever heard it before?"

"I don't know *baita*, but I like your idea of waiting a day and letting the answer come to us. By the way, are you still up for soccer or should we head back."

"Ammi, I'm always up for soccer, *chalyae,*" calls out Ibrahim, who whizzes off on his bike, with Amna following, just steps away.

HIFDH TEACHING NOTE

"It needs to make sense to you and feel like the blessing that it is," explains Khadija, in response to Ibrahim's request for more time on *Surah Al Bayyinah.* Among the most important lessons of this chapter may be, as was introduced in the context of learning *Al Fatihah* (in Chapter 3), that we should not speed through our *hifdh.* Keep a measured pace, do not lose momentum, but do not race. Where more time is requested, allow for it. The associations with *hifdh* should all be positive since the Qur'aan was given as a gift, for us to implement in our lives. What is gained by speeding? And what, perhaps more importantly, might be lost? Linked to issues of pacing, the review that is emphasized in this chapter is critical. Ibrahim is commended for taking his time to sort out the differences between *ayaat* in *Surah Al Asr* and *Surah Al Bayyinah.* Also recognized is Amna's own retention of *Surah Al Ikhlas.* The constant repetition and review serves as glue for her own early *hifdh* work, not to mention the *hifdh* undertaken by Khadija, who also benefits from a slow, measured pace and frequent review, as will be discussed in greater detail.

---

[1] As excerpted from *Surah Al Bayyinah* (98, *ayah* 7), "Those who have faith and do righteous deeds—they are the best of creatures," (Abdullah Yusuf Ali 1989, p.1679). Then, as excerpted from *Surah Al Asr* (103, *ayah* 3), "Except such as have faith, and do righteous deeds, and (join together) in the mutual teaching of Truth, and of Patience and Constancy," (p.1693). Transliteration excerpted from *Tajweed Qur'an* (Abdullah Yusuf Ali & Taha 2007, pp.22, 25). *Ayah* 7 of *Surah Al Bayyinah* and 3 of *Surah Al Asr* resemble one another slightly.

[2] This prayer is accredited to Saint Francis of Assisi, the 12th century monk, responsible for establishing the Franciscan Order. Saint Francis is recognized as the patron saint of the animals and of the environment, and many Catholic and Episcopalian/Anglican churches host ceremonies that involve blessing the animals on October 4th, Saint Francis' feast day.

21

BAGS

Date/place: early February, 2011, outside, Houston (near school/park), mid-day

Cast of characters: Amna, Khadija, Ibrahim, Ms Suzy

The children see me through the window and start running to the door of their one room school house.

"*Salaamu 'kum,*" Amna calls out first, in her slightly abridged form of greeting.

"*Wa alaykum salaam,*" I respond, while simultaneously waving to Ms Suzy who is standing at the door greeting the group of mid-day pick-up parents.

"Ammi, I can read," Ibrahim proclaims, following up immediately on his sister's greeting.

"*Baita,* I know you can; *masha'Allah* you've been reading for months now."

"No, Ammi, I can read in English," Ibrahim asserts. "Listen and look," Ibrahim holds up the small book he has been clutching in his right hand, and, while walking to our car, says the following, slowly: "Once upon a time there was a Little House way out in the country. She was a pretty Little House and she was strong and well built... and that's only the first page. I can read more than that, almost all the way to the second page!"[1]

"That's quite a story, Ibrahim, but you've been reading in English for months as well."

"But, Ammi, I haven't put so many sentences together before. Isn't that great?" I catch Ms Suzy, still at the door, widening her smile, proud of Ibrahim's accomplishment.

"*Masha'Allah,* it *is* great and I am very proud. It looks like Amna is also happy. I think we need to give Ms Suzy a big round of applause." I pause briefly and put my hands together, facing his teacher, in appreciation. Then turning back to the children, I add, "I also think this calls for a double celebration. How about we head to the park?"

"Why double Ammi? What else are we celebrating?"

"What do you think? Don't you remember what happened this morning, before you went to school?"

"Oh yeah, *Bayyinah*."[2]

"What do you mean, 'Oh yeah *Bayyinah*.' That was and is a really big deal. It's your longest *surah* yet *masha'Allah* and it was tough, at first."

"Ammi, it wasn't tough, I just had to work a little harder. Amna helped. And you did too, and so did Papa and Nani. Nonna even listened to me over the telephone and I remember I recited it to Yaseen. I think I'm ready for *Surah Al Qadr*, and the Night of Power."

"*Ahista, ahista baita*, we'll get there, but let's get to the park first for a little picnic."

"Ok, as you wish coach; did you bring ketchup?"

"Kesup?" Amna asks, then making it into almost a song: "Kesup? Kesup?"

"*Baita*, it's a little messy, but yes, we have some ketchup, and some other treats."

I settle Amna in her car seat while Ibrahim buckles himself in. We then head north two streets and then east to the park.

"Ammi, what's in the bag?" Ibrahim asks as we start to disembark. He sees me holding both the lunch basket and something else.

"Well, it's part of our second celebration."

"What do you mean?" Ibrahim inquires.

"Meaning?" Amna, characteristically, repeats.

"Remember, 'oh yeah, *Bayyinah*'? Well, I made something for both of you."

"Why does Amna get something?"

"Hmm, I think I'll let you answer you own question," I say frowning a little bit.

"Ok, ok, you're right she also helped. And she's still doing well."

"Thank you Ibrahim for being so big hearted."

"But Ammi, what is it?"

"How about we find a nice bench and then I'll let you find out."

"Ammi, I can't wait until we find a bench," responds Ibrahim, grabbing at the bag.

"Ibrahim, *baita*, how about our song, *sabr, sabr*, patience, patience, God loves patience." Amna immediately starts smiling, ready for the next line.

"Ok, ok, there's a bench Ammi, come quick, sit," he says, seemingly fearful that he might lose his surprise.

"Close your eyes," I say slowly. Amna immediately squeezes her eyes shut. Ibrahim, however, has another question.

"Why?"

"Because I want to put something in your hand; now, no more questions for a minute; just close your eyes and keep quiet, please." Ibrahim reluctantly obeys. Meanwhile I have opened my bag and taken out two more bags, which I place in the children's laps. Amna opens her eyes, but Ibrahim's are still shut.

"Eyes closed *baita*. Now what do you think it is?"

"It feels soft. And it feels like I could put something inside. Did you make it?"

"Yes, I did, but what do you think you could put inside?"

"Gove," says Amna, putting her hand inside and holding the bag up, almost like a puppet.

"Not a glove," Ibrahim responds, now slowly opening his eyes. "Ammi, did you make me a book bag, with a string?"

"Well yes, sort of; what do you think could fit in there?"

"Not *The Little House*; it's too small, but I think I know where you're heading with this one, Ammi."

"I thought you might. Only if you wish, that is."

"I do wish. And you know, it even looks a little like the black cover for the *Kaaba*. But, Ammi, Amna's too young to have her own Qur'aan bag. So what can she put inside?"

"Well, she has lots of other little treasures so it could simply be her treasure bag for now, until she becomes as big and wise as you *inshaa Allah*. I thought if I only made one there might be some arguments..."

"Ammi, you're a good Ammi," Ibrahim says, "but does this mean I'm not getting my archery stuff?"

"*Baita*, everything is coming, *inshaa Allah*, don't you worry."

"Ok, I just wanted to make sure you didn't forget," Ibrahim looks down as if collecting his thoughts and then addresses me again. "Ammi, do you know I was talking to Najma Mumani once and she told me about the heart and how important it is and how she performs her operations. Then I was just thinking this morning when you got so excited about us passing through *Bayyinah* that it's sort of like heart surgery. All this learning... like I'm learning Qur'aan by heart and I'm almost getting a new heart."

"*Baita*, you have been blessed with a beautiful heart *masha'Allah*, there is no need to get a new heart. Let's just say your heart is becoming stronger and more caring and wise *inshaa Allah*."

"That's cool Ammi, a strong heart, I like it."

"Me too, ok, now how about before we start swinging, a little ketchup, and carrots and hummus? And some pita and, what else?" I say looking deep into my picnic basket for more treats, as the three of us, sit, bundled up, on our park bench, about to start a winter picnic.

HIFDH TEACHING NOTE

Little Ibrahim is triumphant. He can finally read, in English. What is particularly interesting to note about Khadija's remarks is that he already knows how to read, in Arabic: namely that he has been reading his *surahs* in the Qur'aan (albeit after serious preparatory work, as mentioned in the first '*hifdh* teaching note') for several months. The connection between his secular, largely English education, and his Qur'aanic study is important to recognize here. Most children and parents, who adopt an integrated learning approach, will experience a serious learning boon as they become more attuned to detail, develop a greater appreciation for books and reading and finally apply their memory skills, as they are developing through *hidfh*. Finally, as noted at NASA, giving a small treat for accomplishments is key in helping the motivation and momentum of our young learners. Here Khadija has prepared two Qur'aan bags, and although Ibrahim is keen to get his archery set, he does appreciate his mother's loving gesture, together with the special picnic. What treat do you think your special *hifdh* children would enjoy, after completing *Surah Al Bayyinah*?

---

[1] *The Little House* (Burton 1969).

[2] *Al Bayyinah* or *Surah Al Bayyinah* is the 98th *surah* and means 'The Clear Evidence'. It is the longest of the last 16 *surahs*. Although previous *surahs* such as *Aadiyat* and *Zalzalah* have more *ayaat* (lines), the *ayaat* of *Surah Al Bayyinah* are longer.

22

A Carpet

Date/place: early February 2011, Houston, Ibrahim and Amna's living room, en route to the public library

Cast of characters: Khadija, Amna, Ibrahim, Nani

"I want to go flying," I say.

"Me too," seconds Amna.

"Me three," Ibrahim says in agreement.

"I think I'd rather wait for the next plane to come to me," says Nani, who is expecting a visit from her Qatar-based son, my elder brother, Hamza, in about a month, and has been into heavy trip logistics with him.

"Oh Nani, you can't always stay home, *vamanos*," says Ibrahim, urging on his grandmother who had a minor fall last week and has been more reluctant than usual to take part in our excursions.

"Ibrahim, do you know that I'm making up for a lot of lost time?" Nani responds, holding up two of her weekly magazines.

"What do you mean?" inquires Ibrahim.

"Well, when I was about your mother's age, I had four little children running around and I was also trying to cover our community news; I spent about 20 years being very busy. Even though I was writing all that time, I actually don't remember reading much of anything."

"Ammi, that's not entirely true," I say.

"You're right *baita*, I picked up *War and Peace* in 1969 and I finally finished it a decade later, along with Wolpert's *Jinnah of Pakistan*, which I believe I finished in 1985."[1]

"Nani, did it take you 10 years to read a book?"

"It was a very long book *baita*, and remember I had four of you, and a part-time job," responds my mother.

"Well, we just want to go flying Nani, and it's not a long flight. Ammi made up this activity with her magic carpet yesterday, when you were out."

"*Kiya*," Nani says, in a manner that shows Ibrahim might finally have piqued her interest.

"We sit here, at the edge of Ammi's carpet and then we decide a place to go and then we're off. And on our way, first she recites and then me, and of course Amna just keeps reciting *Surah Ikhlas*, over and over. Yesterday, Ammi and I got all the way from *Surah Al Qadr* to *Surah An Nas*, before arriving in New York."

"Did you land in New York?," my mother asks, fascinated by Ibrahim's story.

"Well, we didn't really land, we just stuck our hands out the window, when we passed over Brooklyn and waved at Nonna and then we headed back to Houston for snack and a little *tajweed*."

"You make it sound tasty," says my mother, smiling.

"I don't know, Nani, how Ammi keeps coming up with these things, but she's really working hard to make it interesting," says Ibrahim in his increasingly present adult voice. Meanwhile, I can't help but wonder whether he's after a chocolate for that sort of unexpected praise of what I deem very improvised acrobatics, in an attempt to keep our *hifdh* work fun and fresh.

"Ammi," I say, looking at my mother, "I got the idea from the carpets they work on at their Montessori school. I simply thought it would be good for us all to have a flight or two, and transcend 'the ordinary' during our lessons."

"Hmm, I might just be up for a flight after all," says my mother, putting down her magazines and moving slowly down onto the floor.

"Sit here," orders Amna to my mother who is nearing the small carpet.

"I may need to sit on your lap Nani," offers Ibrahim. "We really don't have much space."

"Ok, I'll take you and your Ammi can take Amna, and then… where are we off to today, Captain Kashif?" says my mother now fully into the game.

"Captain," I repeat, "destination please?"

"We're going to Doha," he says, without a moment's hesitation. "We have some details to discuss with my Uncle Hamza, and then we need to fly over the public library, since our books are almost overdue."[2]

"Books, due," confirms Amna.

"Oh yes, of course, *bohaut shukria baita*, I almost forgot, you know we really do need to go to the library. We've had that book on Harriet Tubman for two weeks now, and all your early reader books…"[3]

"Not so fast, Lieutenant Laila, we're going to Doha first. And it's your turn on *Surah Al Qadr*. And remember it's overnight."

"Those are tall orders, Captain, particularly considering the night flight, how about I start again with the translation?"

"Lation," says Amna, ready for anything.

"Ok, then give me a minute, I need to get off our plane to get my book," I say quickly, taking my translation from the bookshelf. Ibrahim's bookmark with his first Arabic letters marks the *surah* and I start in:

In the name of Allah, Most Gracious, Most Merciful.

1. We have indeed revealed this (Message) in the Night of Power:

2. And what will explain to thee what the Night of Power is?

3. The Night of Power is better than a thousand Months.

4. Therein come down the angels and the Spirit by Allah's permission on every errand:

5. Peace!… This until the rise of Morn.[4]

"Good job Ammi," says Amna, raising her hands up, upon my completion.

"Yes, beautifully read Khadija," then turning to her grandson, she adds, "now how about you, Captain Kashif, will you recite it in Arabic for us?"

"I don't generally recite when I'm holding the steering wheel, let me get my co-pilot, Sergeant Faith," says Ibrahim, who elbows Amna to take his imaginary steering wheel.

"Look at me, good job," says Amna, proud to be playing along.

"Ok, now I think I'm ready, and Ammi, after that you have *Bayyinah*, this time, not me; we're going all the way to *Nas* so keep your seat belts on."

"Ready and waiting, Ibrahim, always, *inshaa Allah*." I say, as he takes off.

HIFDH TEACHING NOTE

Do you have a small carpet? Have you ever considered flying anywhere on it with your children? If you give them the opportunity, they will transport you with their imaginations. All you have to do is be willing to engage. Your next challenge, as a parent-educator, is to help your child understand the connection and channel the imaginative games into a *hifdh* lesson so the verses of *Surah Al Qadr* may come alive. How was the blessed Qur'aan sent down, and why? When do we commemorate *Laila Al Qadr*? Although seat belts may be required for this intense learning experience, their interest is almost guaranteed.

---

[1] The 2006 edition of *War and Peace* by Leo Tolstoy published by Viking spans nearly 1500 pages.

[2] According to a 2008 study by the American Library Association of America, there are approximately 122,000 libraries in the country, of which nearly 100,000 are school libraries.

[3] The month of February is recognized, throughout the United States, as Black History month, which commemorates the struggle and contribution of African Americans. Harriet Tubman is among the most renowned individuals to inspire and lead enslaved African Americans to freedom via the Underground Railroad. The children's book to which Khadija refers in the text is: *'Moses: When Harriet Tubman Led Her People to Freedom'* (2006). "Somewhere between 40,000 and 100,000 slaves escaped to freedom through a loose network of helpers and hideaways known as the Underground Railroad," (Weatherford).

[4] *Surah Al Qadr* (Abdullah Yusuf Ali 1989, p. 1676). As excerpted from the explanatory text, "The subject matter is the mystic Night of Power (or Honour), in which Revelation comes down to a benighted world — it may be to the wonderful Cosmos of an individual — and transforms the conflict of wrongdoing into Peace and Harmony — through the agency of the angelic host, representing the spiritual powers of the Mercy of Allah," (p.1675).

23

THE CASE AND THE CAVE

Date/place: mid-February 2011, Ibrahim and Amna's kitchen, Houston, mid-week, evening

Cast of characters: Khadija, Abdurrahman, Ibrahim, Nani, Amna

"I don't know how to do *Alaq*."

"Sorry, I don't understand," Abdurrahman responds, opening his hands in a manner that reminds me of Nonna.

"I'm trying to start Ibrahim and Amna on *Surah Al Alaq* this week, and I don't know what to do," I say to Abdurrahman who is busy with dinner clean-up as I start on lunch preparation, for tomorrow. "What would *you* do?"

"Come on Khadija, you can crack this case; apply that imagination of yours, and see how many points you can get now; speaking of which, I haven't heard Ibrahim and you talking up the Qur'aan Club for a while now."

"I've tried, but, I really need help with this one; since the flying carpet, I've been a little out of ideas and points, for that matter."

"Well," says Abdurrahman, putting down a plate. "I would make a cave."

"A cave?"

"Yes, you know Ibrahim loves them, provided it's not too scary; he's also always trying to find an excuse to use his series of different flashlights, and well, Amna, seems to enjoy playing along. I remember making cave tents with Geo growing up..."

"I think you just cracked this one, Private Nouman," I say smiling.

"The plate?"

"No the case, silly."

"Who are you calling silly, Ammi?" asks Ibrahim, entering the kitchen, almost on cue.

"No one, no one, but listen your father just came up with a great idea," I say, redirecting the conversation.

"What is it, Papa?"

"I think I'll give your mother credit for this one; I wouldn't have thought of it, unless she had asked me."

"What?" says Ibrahim, looking at both of us, a little bit confused, then adding. "I don't really care who came up with the idea, but I would like to know what it is, especially before Nani and Amna come from the bath because then we won't be able to speak properly."

"Oh, won't we? I don't think you're giving enough credit to your sister, Ibrahim; remember what you said earlier this evening, and I quote, 'Amna is the best sister alive,'" says Abdurrahman, softly chastising his son.

"Papa, she just threw one of her bath toys at my eye; I don't think she's the best sister any more, I've downgraded her. I actually think I hate her."

"Ibrahim, watch your tongue," I shout, then add more calmly, "*Baita,* she's learning, just like all of us; there's no reason to hate her; try to keep showing her the right way."

Abdurrahman adopts a slightly different tactic. "Downgraded her, have you, and who, pray tell, taught you how to downgrade? Or upgrade for that matter," asks Abdurrahman looking more at me than at Ibrahim.

"He picks up everything; they both do," I mouth to Abdurrahman.

"Yes, we're sponges, Papa," says Ibrahim, pointing to his father's hands which are still hard at work with kitchen clean-up. "So please tell this sponge about your and Ammi's idea or the idea Ammi gave to you."

"Ok, but only because you're persistent, not because you downgraded your sister," says Abdurrahman, pausing briefly. "Here's the idea: tonight, right before you go to sleep, rather than reading another chapter in that airplane book, we're going to make a cave and your mother and I are going to recite *Surah Al Alaq* to you. If you or Amna know any of the *ayaat* you can pipe in. And if you're quiet and good, your mother and I will attempt to read the translation together with a little explanation of how Prophet Muhemmed, *Salla Allahu 'alayhi wa sallam,* first received the *surah.*"[1]

"Papa, I already know. He received it in a cave, from *Angel Gibreel…*"

"*…Alayhis salaam,*" continues Nani, now walking in with Amna.

"*Bohaut shukria,* Ammi," I say, turning towards my mother.

"For what?" she responds, looking a bit puzzled.

"The baths."

"Are you kidding? I love this work, and I probably could do a little more of it. Watching you four work, I've actually been thinking, that while all my reading is good, it might be time for me to get back involved, a little."

"Are you going to start that good news newspaper with Nonna?" asks Ibrahim, with excitement in his eyes.

"Well, maybe. I was actually thinking I might start something related to geography. I have always loved the subject and so maybe I could inquire at one of the schools. Maybe in the library or… I need time to mull this one over."

"Geo… graph… y," says Ibrahim slowly, "with Uncle Geo?"

"No *baita*, with maps and movements of people and changes in climates and… it's actually quite a complex subject. I'd like to study it a bit more and then see what I can contribute."

"This all came to you while you were bathing Ibrahim and Amna, and ducking bath toys?"

"No, it's been hatching slowly, over the past week since I explained to the children how busy I used to be, but I need some more time, before it hatches fully. So what about *Angel Gibreel, alayhis salaam*?"

"We're going to do one of Ammi's famous re-enactments again, to help us learn *Surah Al Alaq*, if I can stop hating," volunteers Ibrahim.

"Oh, well that's simple," responds Nani, "just think about all the beautiful verses you're reciting and you won't be able to hate. It's actually what we'd call 'mu… tua… lly exclusive.' You can't hate someone and really live the Qur'aan. And remember that day, we all buried anger."

"I couldn't agree more, Nasheeta, but it sounds more real coming from you, than from either one of us," says Abdurrahman, looking at my mother.

"Easier said than done, Papa," adds Ibrahim.

"Yes, *bambino*, but your Nani is right, and she has some serious experience. I would take her advice."

"And then we can make a cave and use our flashlights?"

"Cave?" inquires Amna, sounding out the word, slowly. And then as though she has fully grasped the sentence, adds, "fast-light, fast-light," and runs full speed ahead back to her bedroom for a flashlight.

"I've also got some reading to do," says my mother, "and some thinking. I wonder whether your children will be able to see any linkages between *Alaq* and geography?"

"Nasheeta, is that a test, and if so, is it for us or for them?" inquires Abdurrahman.

"Hmm, interesting thought," responds my mother. "How about I make it your assignment, Private Nouman? If possible, report back to me, by the weekend."

"Got it," confirms Abdurrahman who is almost always up for a new challenge. "I think the kids will be helping me, though," he adds, smiling at my mother and exiting to join Amna on the next adventure.

HIFDH TEACHING NOTE

Sometimes we run out of ideas, as Khadija admits at the beginning of this scene. She is working overtime to engage her children in a fun and rewarding *hifdh* experience, but with *Surah Al Alaq* she appears to be drawing a blank. In the previous chapter's *hifdh* teaching note, it was mentioned how it is important to be open to the children's imaginations, but here it is Abdurrahman, their father, who ultimately comes up with the idea about what to do. The take-away? As a parent-educator, be open to new ideas, and stay open. Sometimes our children, sometimes our spouses, sometimes our mothers, and mothers-in-law are the ones with the real solutions, given their set of past experiences. No seat belts are required for this *surah* re-enactment of Hira cave; however, flashlights do add to the overall impact. And yes, it is possible to learn and review *tajweed* with a flashlight. You may also listen to your favorite *qari* by flashlight. The fact that the learning is serious does not mean that it needs to be devoid of fun. Rather, with such serious learning, 'fun' becomes critical to keep the attention and excitement of our little learners, as has been emphasized throughout.

---

[1] It is believed that the first five verses of *Surah Al Alaq* also known as *Iqra* (Arabic for 'read') were the first Qur'aanic *ayaat* revealed to Prophet Muhemmed *SAW* by Angel Gibreel AS, in Hira cave in 610 AD. The first five verses are as follows, as translated by Abdullah Yusuf Ali: "1. Proclaim! (or Read!) in the name of thy Lord and Cherisher, Who created—2. Created man, out of a (mere) clot of congealed blood: 3. Proclaim! And thy Lord is most Bountiful—4. He Who taught (the use of) the Pen—5. Taught man that which he knew not," (pp.1672-3).

24

THE STRING AND AT TEEN

Date/place: late February, 2011, Houston, Ibrahim and Amna's living room, Saturday morning

Cast of characters: Yaseen, Abdurrahman, Yasmeen, Abdullah, Khadija, Najma, Nani, Amna, Ibrahim

"What exactly is going on here?" Yaseen inquires, as he walks into our living room, somewhat unannounced. "It looks like you're all stuck in a game of cat's cradle."

"Well, we are, sort of, thanks to your Phuppi jaan and her ingenuity, and by the way, *Assalaamu 'alaykum*," says Abdurrahman. Then diplomatically, he adds, "Isn't it a little unusual that you are so early, especially on a Saturday morning. I thought we were meeting at ten o'clock at Memorial Park?"

Before Yaseen can answer, his sister has also entered our apartment, arm in arm with Najma and my brother. "Phuppi *Jan*, what's happening," exclaims Yasmeen, upon seeing us all, including my mother, seated on the floor with a piece of light, white string around us.

"Khadija, this doesn't look very good," my brother says. "Were you robbed by a very conscientious burglar, who wanted to treat you carefully?"

"No, we weren't *alhumdulilah*. We are learning *Surah At Teen*."

"Sorry, I don't quite get it," Najma says. "What does the five of you sitting cross-legged on the floor, with a white string around you have to do with *Surah At Teen*. I've seen a lot of classrooms, religious and non-religious alike, and I've never seen anything quite like this. I would expect you to be using a bunch of figs to teach the *surah*."[1]

"Your sister in law has a slightly different approach Najma," my mother says. "She wanted to show the children, well, all of us, actually, how what we are learning is actually connected to who we are and what we do."

"Ammi, I'd rather park this for later, when I have less of an audience; I don't think everyone needs to hear my musings about *Surah At Teen*."

"No, no, I'm interested, Khadija. Just because I've never seen anything like this before, doesn't mean it doesn't work."

"Come on Dija," says my brother, sitting down on the couch, together with Yaseem and Najma. "We're listening and you definitely have all of our attention." Meanwhile, Yaseen has sat down next to Amna who is starting to fidget with the string. It almost looks like she is trying to use it as dental floss.

"Amna, no," cautions Yaseen, then, "look, at this," as he starts to demonstrate a little game which involves him looping a piece of loose string around and around his fingers.

"Awe... some," responds Amna. It has become her favorite word as of this week.

"Yes, awesome, now let's listen to your Ammi," Yaseen says pointing towards me.

"Well, this really wasn't meant to be a speech, but I found the children playing with this ball of string earlier this morning. Initially, Ibrahim said he wanted to make a bracelet for our wedding anniversary. And then after about ten minutes of tying toys and trailing them around the apartment (and losing interest in any bracelet making) you two started really fighting," I say pointing now directly at Ibrahim and Amna.

"Ammi, please don't tell them that I bit Amna," says Ibrahim.

"I won't *baita*. What I will tell them, however, is that you and Amna were really fighting, probably the same way that Abdullah and I used to fight when we were young, and of course your Uncle Hamza as well, not to mention your Uncle Geo, and maybe the same way Yaseen and Yasmeen may have fought, once or twice."

"Phuppi jaan, I have neither bit nor hit Yasmeen ever in my life," says Yaseen with a slight tone of self-righteousness.

"Oh, yes you have; you're actually lying," shouts Yasmeen, as though something has been brewing.

"Do not shout at me, Yasmeen, I am your bhai jaan," responds Yaseen, getting up and walking over to his sister as if to threaten her.

My mother intervenes before any of us. "Ok, ok, boxer one, in your corner," she says, indicating that Yaseen should move over towards her. "Boxer two, you just wait it out over there. We're going to resume this fight in just a minute, once the referee is done, Khadija, please continue."

"Ammi, that was good," I say. I also catch Abdullah nodding at my mother.

"*Bohaut shukria*, remember I trained for this job. Now please *do* carry on."

"Ah, yes, the fight. Well, Ibrahim and Amna started fighting, or continued rather, and I asked them to stop, which they did eventually, after quite a lot of tears had been shed."

"And a book had been torn and a salt shaker had been broken," adds Abdurrahman.

"Papa, I did not break the salt."

"No, the salt broke itself, and it was an accident; you just happened to get in the way. Let's listen to your mother though; remember we also want to go to see the turtles this morning, in the park."

"The turtles? I thought we were going for a walk," says my brother.

"That too, I wanted to point out the turtles to the kids, briefly; we've been reading the *Tortoise and the Hare* and I think it would be nice to see one of our creatures in action," I say.[2]

"Phuppi jaan tortoises and turtles are not the same," pipes in Yaseen, applying what sounds like some of his new science trivia.

"Yes, yes, but they are cousins of sorts, and they are also the closest things I can find at Memorial Park to help illustrate this story and what I think is a very important lesson, especially when it comes to learning *surahs*."

"Khadija do you ever stop?" asks Najma, somewhat rhetorically.

"Well, there's always something to teach and learn, so I guess, no, not really, but yes, Abdurrahman is right let's finish this one up. Anyway, I took the same ball of string which initially was to be used for a wedding anniversary bracelet and then was the object of the fight. First I asked both children to hold on to it to show them how they are connected to each other."

"Because when you're connected to someone you really shouldn't hurt them," says Ibrahim, paraphrasing the earlier lesson.

"And then, just as you all walked in," I continue. "I was trying to show something more. Our recitation is not simply words. For all this *hifdh* work to make sense and make a difference, our actions should be connected, like this string, to our recitation. When we fight, and hurt each other we fall down and become 'low' like in *ayah* five.[3] On the other hand, when we don't fight and we make our love manifest, by helping and being kind, then we do as *Allah Subhanahu wa-ta'ala* has intended for us and what He actually moulded us for."

"You got this from a piece of string Khadija?" says Najma, a little bit in disbelief. "What was your real source?"

"*Bhabi*, do you ever stop?" I say, also with a slightly rhetorical tone. "You know very well, the source was and is life; I'm simply trying to help connect it to the Qur'aan, for our children."

"I know, I know, don't take me wrong, I'm actually impressed. I think I might be able to use some of this material with my two little boxers," says Najma looking at Yaseen who is still standing near my mother. "Now, how about a quick cup of tea, right Amna?" says Najma, standing up and them walking over to give Amna an affectionate squeeze.

"Ok, a *quick* cup of tea," cautions Abdurrahman, who knows how long his in-laws can spend drinking tea. "And then we're off, to catch a turtle-tortoise or two."

"Catch them? No Papa, we're just watching them, we want to see how slowly they go."

"Something like that," I say, smiling. "Maybe we can let the turtles explain when we get there, *inshaa Allah*."

HIFDH TEACHING NOTE

"I was trying to show something more," says Khadija. "Our recitation is not simply words. For all this *hifdh* work to make sense and make a difference, our actions should be connected, like this string, to our recitation. When we fight, and hurt each other we fall down and become 'low' like in *ayah* five [of *Surah* At Teen]. 'Then do We abase him (to be) the lowest of the low.' On the other hand, when we don't fight and we make our love manifest, by helping and being kind, then we do as *Allah Subhanahu wa-ta'ala* has intended for us and what He actually moulded us for." Enough said, with regard to 'teaching notes'. It's time to implement it; use a string, or a fig, or simply engage your children with their *mushafs*, but let the real lessons of the *surah* shine through.

---

[1] *At Teen* (as in *Surah At Teen*) may be translated as 'The Fig', in reference to the first *ayah*.

[2] Refers to the *Tortoise and the Hare*, among Aesop's fables.

[3] *Surah At Teen* (95), "1. By the Fig and the Olive, 2. And the Mount of Sinai, 3. And this City of security—4. We have indeed created man in the best of moulds, 5. Then do We abase him (to be) the lowest of the low—6. Except such as believe and do righteous deeds: for they shall have a reward unfailing. 7. Then what can, after this, contract thee, as to the Judgment (to come)? 8. Is not Allah the wisest of Judges?" (Abdullah Yusuf Ali 1989, pp. 1669-70).

25

TRAINS

Date/place: early March, 2011, Houston highways, mid-week, mid-afternoon

Cast of characters: Ibrahim, Amna, Khadija

"Why not a train?"

"A what?" Amna inquires.

"A train, *un tren*, choochoo, choochoo," says Ibrahim, using both arms to mime the wheels of a train.

"Why do you say that?" I ask, then add "By the way, nice use of your Spanish, I didn't think you had caught that word, yesterday."

"Ammi, do you honestly think I would forget the word for train? Anyway, to answer your question, all these cars, around us, seem to be going in the same direction. I think most of them might be going to the rodeo, or nearby.[1] So why don't we attach one car to the next and then put the cars on a railroad and then we could all get there faster, right? Do you remember in Cape Town how we had those special trains at the World Cup and those m... uttle buses?"

"Yes, *baita*, the shuttle buses and the trains, and yes they did help move people more efficiently, but they do involve a cost and not everyone always wants to go exactly to the same place. After all, some people are not going to the rodeo right now. Some are simply driving home, or going out to get some milk, or butter, or... perhaps going to a..."

"Park," calls out Amna, who recognizes our exit and the park nearby.

"Yes, the park, *inshaa Allah* we are going there too," I affirm.

"But you could have different stops on the train, one for the rodeo, and one for the milk store and one for the park," proposes Ibrahim.

"*Baita*, I fully agree, but even then some people would still choose to have their own private space. Different cultures have different norms. And the culture we're in right now is primarily a driving culture. People really like their cars and the freedom to move freely as well as live more spread out, which pretty much necessitates a car."[2]

"Necess... i... tastes, like makes a taste?" asks Ibrahim.

"No, it means, makes it necessary," I say, trying to clarify.

"I wish I was in a train culture, with a house near the track," Ibrahim says, frowning and sighing a bit in his dramatic way.

"Well, you know, your Papa takes a bus to work every morning, so maybe one of the days when you don't go to school in the morning, we could go with him. And then we could ride the bus back and stop for some milk on the way?"

"Good job," says Amna. It's not clear if she likes the milk idea or the bus idea.

"Yes, maybe a good idea, speaking of which, do you want to try reciting *Surah Al Inshirah*, since we still have a couple more minutes of waiting out this traffic jam? We could use the recording of Sheikh Husri and you could try to recite the *ayaat* before him."

"Ammi, I already have *Al Inshirah*," says Ibrahim with confidence.[3]

"*Kiya*?" I say, somewhat in disbelief, considering we only started reviewing the *surah* two days ago.

"I got it, or maybe it's better to say, Allah gave it to me. And then, I've got a real surprise for you. I also got *Surah Ad Duha*!"

"What?" My hands turn slightly on the wheel as Ibrahim's news really is a surprise for me. "*Baita*, what are you talking about? We haven't even started *Surah Ad Duha*, how can you have it already?"

"Nani and I practiced it when you were bathing Amna last night and we even finished the drawing of it. I drew a big sun for the morning light.[4] I also heard you working on it and that helped. As for *Al Inshirah*, it's one of Papa's favorites and so I hear him recite it a lot in his prayers, especially those two *ayaat* that he loves: "*Fa-'inna ma'al usri yusra. Inna ma 'al'usri yusra.*"[5]

"You're like a TGV today," I say, still quite stunned by Ibrahim's surprise.

"TV?" queries Amna.

"Not quite, TGV, it's French, *Train à Grande Vitesse*, and means a very fast train. I once took a TGV from Paris to Lyon and back when I was visiting one of your uncles."

"I want one," says Ibrahim.

"Me too," is Amna's customary response.

"A TGV?" I say to both children who I can see nodding in the rear view mirror. "Well, they're not like cars, I don't think people own them, but *inshaa Allah* one day we'll ride one. And in the meantime, how about we find a quiet piece of shade at the park to hear your beautiful *surahs masha'Allah*, but first we check out that train activity. If I remember correctly, you really liked that model train, and so did most of the other kids, the last time we were there."

"Ammi, it's not a TGV."

"No it's not, but it's what we have, for now *alhumdulilah*, so let's enjoy it. If we wanted a fast train right now we would have to drive all the way to Nonna's house which would mean more traffic. Or wait for a little while in California where I think they might be building something."

"Ok, Ammi, but I still want a ticket, someday."

"Inshaa Allah," I say, pulling into the parking lot of one of our two neighbourhood parks.

"Ammi, look here," shouts Amna, catching me off guard. I look back at her, expecting to see a big spill or something caught in her car seat, but instead she is pointing out the window, at the sky. "Look, here," she repeats.

Ibrahim bends his neck to try to peer out her window. "Ammi, I think Amna likes the clouds; you know they look like cotton marshmallows today."

"Cotton marshmallows? That doesn't sound very tasty," I respond. "Do you know what I see though?" I say, getting out of the car and starting to unlatch Amna.

"No wait, me first, do you know what I see?"

"Ibrahim, you interrupted me."

"Sorry, it's just I don't want the clouds to disappear. Just one minute, Ammi, look, now, it looks like a TGV, look, it really does, a long, fast train, that could take us all the way to Nonna's house and maybe even back to that place where your brother lived, or maybe back to Allah?"

"Maybe," I say, swallowing hard, not quite knowing what else to say, about this momentary miracle of time and space.

HIFDH TEACHING NOTE

Why not, in addition to reciting in a mosque and at home, recite in our cars? En route to school, en route to errands? Let the car ride which occupies, for many of us, so much of our time, become part of our *hifdh* journey as well? Here, Ibrahim is challenged to recite *Surah Al Inshirah*. Rather than simply have him recite alone, however, Khadija has given Ibrahim the opportunity of reciting each *ayah* before Sheikh Husri (almost in a competition of sorts); that is, before she learns, much to her surprise, that he has already moved on to *Surah Ad Duha*. Work with your children (not against them), give them lots of nurturing educational experiences and prepare to be surprised, by *Dhuha* (the glorious morning light) and much more *inshaa Allah*. Both of these *surahs* also make great candidates for calligraphy. Consider excerpting *ayaat* five and six of *Surah Al Inshirah* or *ayah* 11 of *Surah Ad Duha* and have the children copy out the Arabic text. Use a nice piece of paper, add some colors or shapes and make either a small poster or a bookmark, which could be given as a gift. Little by little, as we start incorporating Qur'aan into the many facets of our life, *hifdh* becomes a way of life.

---

[1] The Houston Livestock Show and Rodeo has been operating since 1932; in 2011, the 3-week event attracted nearly 2.3 million visitors (and their vehicles).

[2] According to the November 2010 Navdeq report, the US cities with the worst rush hour traffic are as follows: New York, Washington D.C., San Francisco, Seattle, Los Angeles, Philadelphia, Chicago, Dallas-Ft.Worth, Atlanta, Houston (available via http://corporate.navteq.com).

[3] *Surah Al Inshirah* is the 94th *surah* in the Qur'aan and may be translated as 'The Expansion of the Breast', which is symbolic of the heart, among other things (Abdullah Yusuf Ali 1989, p.1666).

[4] *Surah Ad Duha*, the 93rd chapter of the Qur'aan is also known as 'The Glorious Morning Light.'

[5] Transliteration excerpted from *Tajweed Qur'an* (Abdullah Yusuf Ali & Taha 2007, p.20). Abdullah Yusuf Ali translates the verses as follows: "5. So, verily, with every difficulty, there is relief; 6. Verily, with every difficulty, there is relief," (p.1666).

26

STAGES

Date/place: early March, Houston, Ibrahim and Amna's living room, Wednesday evening

Cast of characters: Amna, Ibrahim, Khadija, Abdurrahman

"*Kufuwan alaq!*"

"Amna, it's '*kufuwan ahad*', not '*alaq*',"[1] corrects Ibrahim, elbowing his sister out of his way. "And anyway I'm right in the middle of my performance, so now you're the one who's interrupting."

"My turn," is Amna's rebuttal.

"Ammi," says an exasperated Ibrahim, who was, indeed, right in the middle of presenting his *surah*, which is neither Amna's version of *Ikhlas* nor *Alaq*, but rather a first attempt at *Surah Al Layl*.

"I know *baita*, she did interrupt, but she is trying to copy you, which you should take as a compliment."

"Ammi, this is *not* a compliment, this is an interruption. Now I can't find my place and I'm lost." In frustration, Ibrahim jumps on the kitchen chair on which he is standing (and onto which Amna has climbed up) and the chair starts to sway.

"Whoa," says Abdurrahman, sensing that his son is starting to get worked up and we might have a major accident on our hands. "How about Ammi and Amna head into our bedroom and Ibrahim and I carry on with the performance, and see how many points we can get?"

"Good idea, *bohaut shukria*," I say, picking up Amna and exiting before she can resist. "Please carry on Mr. Ibrahim, or was it Kashif?"

"Thank you, yes, it is Kashif, Captain Kashif," responds Ibrahim, immediately changing his tone and his mood. "This is my night job, reciting *surahs* on kitchen chair stages; so sorry you won't be able to stay."

"*Inshaa Allah* we'll be back," I call out.

"Papa, are you ready for me now?" queries Ibrahim, who seems to have switched out of his Kashif role and tone momentarily.

"Yes, *bambino, pronto,*" says Abdurrahman.

"Well, could you give me the first *ayah*? Amna did distract me and I can't see the *surah* clearly in my mind anymore."

"Sure, 'By the Night as it conceals the light'," Abdurrahman reads out.[2]

"Papa, that's the English. I need the Arabic."

"Oh, hmm, I thought you could translate."

"Papa, I'm still only five."

"Really, last I heard you were turning six in two months and you were already planning for your 7th birthday?"

"Papa, I'm still very small when it comes to my *surahs*; remember when you told us about feeling spiritually small before you started your own *hifdh*?"

"Ibrahim, I can't believe you remember that."

"I do, and I also remember 22 *surahs*, can you believe that? It's just this one, my 23rd, that's really tough."

"*Masha'Allah, bambino* 22 *surahs*… but wasn't *Surah Al Bayyinah* more difficult? Didn't you spend two weeks working on that one with Ammi and Nani and Hafidha Rabia?"

"You're right, *Bayyinah* was challenging, but we got it and then last week, remember, I got two for one; I still can't believe that. Maybe that's why I was expecting this to be easier."

"Ok, how about we treat this like one of your missions. Do you remember when you helped save the whooping cranes?"

"Yes, I used *Surah Al Quraysh* in Aransas," says Ibrahim with a new sense of confidence.

"Well, how about we say that you're about to embark on an even bigger mission."

"The whales?" asks Ibrahim.

"If you wish," responds Abdurrahman. "Or perhaps you could be trying to save someone who was unjustly imprisoned and this *surah* will help."

"Papa, it sounds like a real adventure."

"It is Ibrahim. It really is. The *surah* itself is an amazing adventure as well, but you're right, there are some difficult parts. Take for instance this *ayah*," says Abdurrahman, picking up Ibrahim from his kitchen chair and carrying him over to the couch. He settles Ibrahim in his lap, which makes Ibrahim look very small, and then picks up his *mushaf*. "Look, here, *ayah* seven. Then, look again, *ayah* ten."

"I know Papa," says Ibrahim. "Ammi showed them to me. There's only one letter different in them. One letter makes all the difference in the world."[3]

"I think that's amazing *subhanAllah*. Only one letter, between 'bliss' and 'misery'."

"There must be something like that in Italian, too?" suggests Ibrahim.

"Perhaps there is. You'd have to ask your Nonna since I'm not much of an expert. But let's stick with *Surah Al Layl* for just a minute longer and not get distracted. You know, taken from a different angle, you actually get an *ayah* for free. All you have to do is remember one new letter, not the whole *ayah*."

"Yup, I was also thinking that. It makes it easier. Then there are only 20 *ayaat* plus one different letter. It's not quite so long. And we also hear the word 'Husna' twice."

"You see. It's as though *Allah Subhanahu wa-ta'ala* is helping you out, giving you clues and shortcuts…"

"To help get to the end and save the prisoner."

"Sure, right, our adventure."

"Do you think we wrongfully prison-ed Amna just now in the bedroom with Ammi?"

"Well, I'm sure she would like to recite and to hear you. It's just she has a hard time sharing the stage sometimes. Remember she's still just two."

"I know Papa. Ammi is always reminding me of the same thing. Maybe I should go get her, and Ammi, and let her present whatever she wants and then maybe she'll give me a little space."

"It's worth a try, Captain."

"Ok, clear the deck, Sergeant Faith is due back any moment," says Ibrahim, jumping out of his father's lap and racing to our bedroom to invite Amna back on stage.

"But Papa," Ibrahim calls out, just before opening the bedroom door, "please don't tell them I couldn't remember the first *ayah*."

"Don't worry," responds Abdurrahman. "You've got it all."

HIFDH TEACHING NOTE

Siblings have the potential to be wonderful companions, most of the time. Sometimes, however, right at the critical moment, they steal the stage. For the first (or second or third) child, his/her sibling(s) may actually seem to sabotage the performance. How as parents do we react, so as to bring peace and order? Do we lash out and mimic our children (who may be angry and jealous), or do we respond in a calm and collected manner, and find a way out? It is all easier said than done, but the consequences of reacting and not checking our own angry streak are grave. Living our *hifdh* means trying to be cognizant of the Qur'aan at all times, and maintaining a spiritual and real connection to *AllahSWT*. In this scene, Khadija and Amna retreat to the bedroom to avoid conflict and Abdurrahman carries on with the lesson. After they exit, Ibrahim is able to continue, without interruption and actually make real progress, although he does need a pep talk during this episode. Along with Amna's absence and Abdurrahman's overall encouragement, the idea of a 'free' *ayah* helps Ibrahim advance through his 23rd *surah*, *alhumdulilah*. Have you incorporated the idea of 'free' *ayaat* into your lessons to help lighten the load? What are other strategies that could help our little *hifdh* stars advance, with ease?

---

[1] Excerpted from the last *ayah* of *Surah Al Ikhlas* (112), meaning 'unto Him'; transliteration excerpted from *Tajweed Qur'an* (Abdullah Yusuf Ali & Taha 2007, p.28).

[2] First *ayah* as excerpted from *Surah Al Layl* (92), (Abdullah Yusuf Ali 1989, p.1658).

[3] Ibn Mas'oad *RA* narrates that Rasulullah *SAW* said, "Whoever reads one letter of the Book of Allah is credited with one blessing and one blessing is equal to tenfold the like thereof in its reward. I do not say that Alif Lam Meem is one letter, but Alif is one letter, Lam is one letter and Meem is one letter," (Shama-il Tirmidhi Hadith Collection).

27

Reunions and Understanding

Date/place: mid-March 2011, mid-week, en route to IAH, Houston, post-*magreb*

Cast of characters: Ibrahim, Amna, Nani/Nasheeta, Abdurrahman, Khadija

"*Baita*, they're arriving in an hour, don't you think we should get on the road?"

"Ammi, I'm still working. Can you give me five more minutes, please?" I say.

"Four minutes and then Abdurrahman and I are on our way," my mother responds.

"With me," adds Ibrahim.

"And me," says Amna.

"I get the picture. So please now, just give me four minutes without any interruption," I say, gently closing our bedroom door and trying to resume the 21st *ayah* of *Surah Al Mutaffifin*, which I have been struggling with, together with the 20 preceding *ayaat*, for the past two weeks.[1]

"Time's up," an ever eager Ibrahim says, knocking on the door.

"*Baita*, that wasn't even two and a half minutes," I respond. "Please, we agreed to four."

"Ammi, do you want to be late for your brother who has just been flying for 24 hours to come and see you."

"*Baita*, he is also coming to see you, and attend a conference. I am not the sole purpose of his journey."

"Ammi, quit stalling, we're leaving, now," says Ibrahim stridently.

"Ok," I finally say, relenting. I put my *mushaf* down, together with the translation that I have been carrying. Then, reconsidering, I slip both into my purse, take up Ibrahim's hand and make my way to the front door where everyone else is waiting, making a mental note about the *hadith* regarding one who struggles in learning.[2]

"Abdullah and company are meeting us at the airport," Abdurrahman volunteers.

"Really? Did you coordinate that one?"

"Yes, when you were behind that closed door of yours, your mother and I worked out the final logistics including the fact that Hamza will ride in Abdullah's car, together with Mary, and you and I will take Naeem."

"Provided Mary allows us," I say.

"Mary should allow us; wasn't the plan that Naeem will stay with us for the first couple of days?"

"No, no, that they *all* will stay with us," I respond.

Abdurrahman looks at me as though something has been lost in translation. "And your mother?"

"Oh, don't you worry, *bambino*," says my mother, responding directly to the query about her whereabouts, and taking up his term of endearment for Ibrahim and Amna. "I am also swapping beds for a couple of days to make a little more room on this side of the city."

"Nasheeta, I didn't mean it like that. I simply misunderstood. I thought that we were all meeting at the airport, as you and I and Abdullah just discussed, and then that Naeem was going to be with us, and that he and Ibrahim were going to do a *hifdh* camp with Khadija."

"And Mary was going to hang out in the Woodlands, alone, while Hamza pontificates downtown about oil in the Gulf...?"

"I didn't think about that," says Abdurrahman with a tinge of awkwardness.

"Ok, so are you sure we are all going to the right airport," I ask, trying to bring a little more clarity to our plan, as we shut the door and begin making our way to the parking garage.

"Yes, Ammi, we are, we are going to go north, right now."

"And is that right?"

"Yes, it is," asserts Ibrahim.

"It is not," Amna then contradicts.

"Khadija, I think we're headed to IAH and so is Abdullah and any other logistics will work themselves out along the way, *inshaa Allah*," offers Abdurrahman.

"Ok, so who votes for news and who votes for review?" I ask, settling the children into their car seats.

"I could do with a little of both," my mother responds.

"I need help with *Surah As Shams*,"[3] says Ibrahim, lacking his usual confidence, "Ammi, you're not the only one who's struggling with your *ayaat*."

"Is that a consolation?"

"I don't know what a cons... lation is but if it's anything like a translation, then no, I get the translation, it's the Arabic *ayaat* that I'm struggling with," Ibrahim says, bringing a smile to everyone's face, including Amna's.

"You'll get plenty of help, *bambino*," responds Abdurrahman, "but I think your Nani is right, let's also do a little news, first. A lot is happening right now, and we might be able to catch the tail end of BBC at this hour." [4]

"And then, you'll give me *Surah As Shams*," Ibrahim persists.

"Give it to you, no," I respond. "I don't have that sort of power. I will, however, do everything within my power to help you learn, including go letter by letter with you through the whole *surah* and perhaps I'll get a point for that."

"And then will I have it?"

" *Inshaa Allah*, but just think about each of the *surahs* that you've learned so far. Each time the process is a little bit different. Sometimes it's the…"

"Drawing," Ibrahim continues, "and sometimes it's Hafidha Rabia and Sheikh Husri and even Private Nouman, and Your 'Qur'aan Club'… and sometimes it's the writing, and sometimes it's…"

"Me," says Amna, understanding more than we could possibly imagine.

"Yes," I say, nodding. "Sometimes, it is you, Sergeant Faith… Ammi, are you buckled in?"

"I'm in, I'm learning and I have buckled my seatbelt, yes," responds my mother.

"Are you going to give us a geography lesson then?" inquires Ibrahim, who has been following his grandmother's new pursuits.

"No, no geography now, *baita*; first BBC, then *Surah As Shams* for you and then maybe we can turn to your mother's *surah* as well, since she's sharing your sense of struggle."

"Ok, that works, but just one more thing, there's a she-camel in my *surah* and I think Naeem has seen one before. Isn't that cool?" [5]

"Yes, it is," responds my mother. "Perhaps, once he's rested just a little bit, you can ask him all about the she-camels in Qatar. You might even be able to find a link with the rodeo." [6]

"*Kiya*?" Ibrahim says looking at his grandmother.

"Camel racing… cowboys… I think there must be a link, but yes, let's listen in and see what is happening," says my mother, hushing Ibrahim, as she starts to adjust the radio dial.

"I'm listening, but I just want to add one last thing," says Abdurrahman, turning to my mother who is sitting next to him in the front seat. "You know, you are part of our family, and you are welcome wherever we are."

"I know *baita*, I know," says my mother, patting him softly on the shoulder. "*Bohaut shukria*, but no need to explain or justify… come on, now, we've got places to go and many people to see and the BBC is waiting for me, whether they know it or not. I need to hear about what's happening," says my mother who turns up the volume, as we pull out, into the well lit night, including strings of green Christmas lights, commemorating the just passed Saint Patrick's Day, which adorn many shops and houses as we drive on.

HIFDH TEACHING NOTE

The plot thickens. Here we have two *surahs*: *Surah* Al *Mutaffifin* and *Surah* As Shams — with Khadija learning the former, and Ibrahim the latter. We also learn of three new family members arriving from Doha. There are the added logistics of Nani leaving, and a meeting to coordinate with Abdullah, Najma, Yaseen and Yasmeen at the airport. How, amidst all this divergent activity, does the aspiring *hafidh* keep the focus, especially with the request to listen to the BBC? Quite simply, *hifdh* is part and parcel of life, particularly home-based *hifdh*, and so constant adjustment and a significant degree of flexibility is required. We stay the course by keeping the *mushaf* close at hand, having recourse to audio recordings, and trying to inculcate a culture of *hifdh* at home, but be prepared for interruptions and resistance and, to the extent possible, learn to take your *hifdh* on the road so that it becomes a real journey, and the learning is ultimately transformative. It should be noted, as with earlier *surahs*, *Surah As Shams* lends itself to drawing, which often helps reinforce the learning for young *hifdh* students, given the beautiful imagery, particularly in *ayaat* one-ten.

---

[1] *Surah Al Mutaffifin* is the 83rd chapter in the Holy Qur'aan and translated as 'The Dealers in Fraud'. The *surah* is 36 ayaat, and working backwards, starting from *Surah An Nas*, *Surah Al Mutaffifin* is the longest in terms of both number and length of ayaat encountered by the characters to date.

[2] Aisha *RA* narrates that Rasulullah *SAW* once said, "One who is well versed in the Qur'an will be in the company of those angels who are scribes, noble and righteous; and one who falters in reading the Qur'an, and has to exert hard for learning, gets double the reward," (Sahih Muslim Hadith Collection).

[3] *Surah As Shams* is the 91st chapter in the Qur'aan and translated as 'The Sun'. Immediately below is the translation provided by Abdullah Yusuf Ali (pp.1654-1656). "1. By the Sun and its (glorious) splendour; 2. By the Moon as it (the Sun); 3. By the Day as it shows up (the Sun's) glory; 4. By the Night as it conceals it; 5. By the Firmament and its (wonderful) structure; 6. By the Earth and its (wide) expanse: 7. By the Soul, and the proportion and order given to it; 8. And its enlightenment as to its wrong and its right;- 9. Truly he succeeds that purifies it, 10. And he fails that corrupts it! 11. The Thamud (people) rejected (their prophet) through their inordinate wrong-doing, 12. Behold, the most wicked man among them was deputed (for impiety). 13. But the Messenger of Allah said to them: "It is a She-camel of Allah. And (bar her not from) having her drink!" 14. Then they rejected him (as a false prophet), and they hamstrung her. So their Lord, on account of their crime, obliterated their traces and made them equal (in destruction, high and low)! 15. And for Him is no fear of its consequences."

[4] On December 17, 2010, Mohammed Bouazizi, a 24-year-old fruit and vegetable street cart vendor in Sidi Bouzid set himself on fire to protest persistent injustice and humiliation. This act subsequently caused a series of protests across Tunisia, and has been linked to many uprisings throughout the Arab world, including in Algeria, Bahrain, Egypt, Jordan, Oman, Syria, and Yemen, with the overwhelming demand being for recognition of civil rights and economic justice, as well as a larger call for democracy.

[5] See *ayah* 13 of *Surah As Shams*.

[6] In 2002, the United Arab Emirates banned the use of child jockeys (under the age of 15) in camel racing due to repeated cases of abuse. Increasingly popular, in both the UAE and Qatar, are robot jockeys, which have, however, come with a set of their own controversies as well, including the use of (illegal) electric shocks (Solon, 2011).

28

BAMBOO FOR DINNER
AND OTHER STORIES

Date/place: late March, 2011 Houston Zoo, mid-afternoon[1]

Cast of characters: Ibrahim, Amna, Khadija, Mary (Ibrahim and Amna's aunt, wife of Khadija's brother, Hamza), Naeem (Mary and Hamza's son), who are visiting from Doha

"Do you miss Amna?"

"What?" I say, reaching out to help Amna climb a step.

"Do you miss her?" Mary repeats.

"Sorry, I don't understand. She's right here, just look at her," I say, pointing to Amna who has unlatched her hand from mine and has cupped both hands together and extended them to form a baby elephant trunk.

"Roar," says Amna.

"*Baita*, that's a lion sound, not an elephant one," I respond, "elephants make more... actually, I can't seem to think of an elephant's call, Mary?" I say turning back to my sister-in-law.

"Well, why don't we listen," Mary says very matter-of-factly.

"Good idea. By the way, I don't miss Amna, but I do miss the boys. Do you know where they are?" I ask.

"The boys, look, just over there, behind the bamboo shoots. I think they may be trying to climb the fence, but don't worry, it's kid friendly and they can't really climb all the way over; and no, I wasn't talking about this little Amna, I was speaking of your sister," says Mary.

I don't quite know how to respond. Mary sees the bewilderment on my face.

"I've never heard you speak about her Khadija, and yet you named your daughter after her," says Mary.

"Yes, with Ammi's blessings, but ultimately Amna's namesake is Prophet Muhemmed's, *Salla Allahu 'alayhi wa sallam*, mother."

"Khadija, why don't you talk about her?" Mary persists. Meanwhile my little Amna looks like she is ready to climb in the cage with the elephants as well. I take her hand again and try to distract her.

100

"We miss her a lot," I say. "And I think my mother still feels responsible."

"For what? Hamza has told me your mother had nothing to do with her death. It was the other driver, and even he may not have been ultimately responsible," counters Mary.[2]

"If Ammi had kept her home on that day..." I say, reminiscing.

"Something else could have happened. Khadija, it was an accident," Mary's tone is strong, almost apologetic. She looks directly into my eyes, which I then turn to look at the boys, who are climbing back down.

"Ammi simply feels as though she didn't do enough to..."

"Ammi," calls out Ibrahim, as he runs up to me. "Look there!"

"*Kahan, baita?*"

"There, there, it's that bird walking in the elephant's tracks."

"Yup," says Mary. "He's having a meal, just like the elephant, but he's eating insects."[3]

"Really, that's so cool, mom," says Naeem, as, if not more, fascinated than Ibrahim.

"Just a quick question, what have you two been up to? It looked like you were going to catapult over the fence and I was going to have to call in the guards."

"Oh that was just one of our games. We were tracking the elephants, but don't worry, no ivory. We just had to give some healthy shots," responds Ibrahim, "but Ammi, listen to this, Naeem has been showing me all these cool mines."

"What?" I say.

"Mines, panda..mines," says Ibrahim, spreading open the palms of his hands.

"Pantomimes?" I ask, trying to decode.

"Yes, panto... mimes. He gave me a ppp... mime for all of *Surah Al Balad*."

"What?" says Mary.

"He learned them at school Aunt Mary," says Ibrahim turning to his aunt, then continuing. "They're really cool, especially all the hand motions for the *ayaat* that I was confusing, Ammi. Do you remember the one about the orphan that I kept confusing with the day when there is not a lot of food?"[4]

"Naeem, when did you learn this at school? I never remember you talking about it," says Mary, still trying to understand her son.

"Oh, maybe I showed *Abbu*," says Naeem. "I don't remember. Anyway, it was in Qur'aan class. We had this guest who showed us all these drama activities, which were really fun."

"Oh," says Mary, slightly detached.

"Ammi," this time it is Amna calling out. "Meow," she then says. She is beginning to show real signs of boredom.

"Amna, do you want to see the lions?" asks Naeem.

"Yes, me, big cat," responds Amna, in her increasingly adult tone, which she is learning from Ibrahim.

"Are you ready for the lions, Mary?" I say turning back to her.

"Just give me one more minute here, I actually want to take a second look at the bamboo," says Mary.

"What?" Ibrahim and I both say, forgetting that Mary is a botanist, and unlike the average person takes a serious interest in plants.

"Aunt Mary, what's ban… doo?"

"Bamboo, Ibrahim, bamboo. Elephants love to eat it, for breakfast, lunch and dinner. Recently our zoo in Doha called me to look into some different varieties. So I'm keen to see what exactly these guys are eating."

"Which guys?" queries Ibrahim.

"Sorry, the elephants."

"Oh," says Ibrahim, taking in all this new information. I sometimes wonder how he processes it all, but it seems to get digested each day, like another meal. "Ammi," he then says, "what were you talking about when we were catching elephants?"

"Amna," I say, not thinking.

"I thought you didn't talk about her," says Mary looking at me intently.

"Oh, we talk about her all the time," responds Ibrahim. "Actually she talks about herself all the time: I walk, I eat, I need, I spill, I hurt," he says, mocking his sister.

"I wish I had a little sister," says Naeem, looking up at his mother.

"No you don't. You wouldn't be able to get anything done or keep anything for yourself. And somebody, who everybody else thinks is cuter than you, would always be taking up your space and time," says Ibrahim.

"*Baita*, those are pretty harsh words," I say.

"Ammi," responds Ibrahim, changing his tone, "I do love Amna, it's just I would never want Naeem to have to deal with all the issues I do."

"It's ok. I like issues. And there's extra space on my four wheeler," offers Naeem.

"Naeem you are not going to put a baby on the four wheeler," Mary says vehemently.

"Mary, are you expecting a baby," I ask quietly turning to her.

"No, we're considering adopting. We'll see. There's a lot to work out, but I am keen to talk to your mother about her children and how she handled them all.

But, don't worry, I'll tread lightly. I'm starting to understand the sensitivities. Suffice it to say, she has a lot of insights," says Mary.

"*Sahih*," I say more to myself than anyone else.

"And so do you," continues Mary. "Although I don't quite understand what you're up to with all this Qur'aan work lately with the children. Hamza and I have also spoken about it; he's equally confused why you've parked your career."

"We're on an adventure," I say, not ready to recount the whole story.

"We sure are," seconds Ibrahim, "now, *vamanos a ver los leones*," he calls out, grabbing his cousin's hand and running ahead, toward the lions.

HIFDH TEACHING NOTE

Camaraderie is essential, and yet, for the home-based learner, it is sometimes a missing ingredient (or at least, a little harder to come by). In this scene, Ibrahim learns that his cousin Naeem is also doing *hifdh* (in Doha); and several of Naeem's 'mimes' for *Surah Al Balad* help to make the *surah* literally easier to grasp. Although Khadija is actively involved in her children's *hifdh* journey, and they all have the support and guidance of Hafidha Rabia, having a *hifdh* companion or buddy of a similar age proves fun and very helpful for motivating the learning process. The 'buddy' need not live on the same block nor necessarily in the same town. In this age of electronic media, there are many possibilities; however, frequent (real and/or virtual) interaction helps. Ultimately, we want to encourage, healthy (not hurtful) competition, in which all companions strive to please *AllahSWT*.

---

[1] The Houston Zoo was established shortly after the discovery of oil (in Humble, Texas) in 1905. As of 2011, the Houston Zoo is among the leading zoos in the United States--with over a million and a half (human) visitors each year, and home to more than 6,000 animals from 900 different species.

[2] "Road traffic injuries are a leading cause of death, killing nearly 1.3 million people annually. Approximately 90 percent of these deaths occur in low- and middle-income countries... In March 2010 the United Nations General Assembly adopted resolution 64/2552 which proclaimed the period 2011–2020 as the Decade of Action for Road Safety. The goal of the Decade is to stabilize and then reduce the forecast level of road traffic fatalities around the world by increasing activities conducted at national, regional and global levels," (World Health Organization, 2010).

[3] The cattle egret often travels with the elephant and other large herbivores and feeds off the insects that are kicked up as the larger animals walk. It represents one of the many 'symbiotic relationships' that abound in the animal kingdom.

[4] As excerpted from *Surah Al Balad* (90), *ayaat* 12-18 (Abdullah Yusuf Ali 1989, pp.1651-2): "12. And what will explain to thee the path that is steep?- 13. (It is:) freeing the bondman; 14. Or the giving of food in a day of privation 15. To the orphan with claims of relationship, 16. Or to the indigent (down) in the dust. 17. Then will he be of those who believe, and enjoin patience, (constancy, and self-restraint), and enjoin deeds of kindness and compassion. 18. Such are the Companions of the Right Hand."

29

ALWAYS READY

Date/place: late March 2011, mid-week, early morning, before work/school, Ibrahim and Amna's home

Cast of characters: Abdurrahman, Ibrahim, Amna and Khadija

"Can I have that pin?"

"Which one?"

Ibrahim reaches into his father's bureau drawer and pulls out a small pin, which he then cusps in his hand in front of Abdurrahman.

"It's burning," Ibrahim says.

"Yes, I know," responds Abdurrahman.

"Why?"

"It was a symbol for Vladimir Lenin, and socialism."

"What do all those letters mean underneath? They are not Arabic and they don't really look English. I don't think they are Spanish or Urdu..."

"*Masha'Allah* Ibrahim, for an almost six year old you've got quite a grasp of languages, but you forgot to mention that they are also not Italian," says Abdurrahman, smiling at his son.

"Papa, you have never read me a story book in Italian so that's why I don't know what the letters look like. Are you sure they are not Italian?"

"Yes, I'm sure, but are you sure Nonna has never read you a bedtime story in Italian? I'd be surprised. To answer your earlier question, though, you're forcing my memory into a space it hasn't been in years, but I think it's Russian, pronounced, *Vsegda gotov*, meaning 'always ready," says Abdurrahman.

"Vessa gov?" attempts Ibrahim.

"What?" says Amna, hearing all the early morning chatter, from the children's room. Wanting to take part, she rounds the corner and sees Ibrahim's hand extended, and then says "Wassa glove?" holding out her hand.

"*Vsegda gotov,*" repeats Abdurrahman, "but I'm going to let your mother explain the balance. I'm going to be very late for our morning teleconference with

Dubai."

"It's ok, you can run off to Dubai now, and I can explain everything to Amna," reassures Ibrahim. Ibrahim then looks down at his sister and says, "It belonged to Lenin, and it is burning and it means 'I'm ready'."

"I'm ready?" queries Amna.

"Yes, I'm ready," repeats Ibrahim.

"You are, are you?" I say, coming from the kitchen, passing Abdurrahman in the hall, and handing him his lunchbox as he races out the door. "It doesn't really look like you're ready. You're still in your pyjamas and I don't think you've had anything to eat."

"No, Ammi, I'm not ready. Lenin is ready and so is Papa. But Papa said you'd explain more. I think I need to know more."

"About what, exactly? The Bolsheviks?" The front door has already closed behind Abdurrahman. I wish I had been fully debriefed before he left.

"This pin," says Ibrahim, opening up his hand to show me his latest treasure.

"Oh, that," I respond. "I think that when your Nonna used to travel with *The Times* she would pick up pins and other trinkets for your Papa and Uncle Geo. I think that came from when she visited the Former Soviet Union, just after the end of the Cold War."

"The cold war?"

"Yes," I say, slowly, anticipating a long series of questions to follow.

"Why was the war cold?" says Ibrahim, as is to be expected.

"Very good question, but is there any way we may answer it later? Then, I can dust off my history books to give you a well informed answer and we can quickly get ready for school. Papa's not the only one who might be late for this morning's meetings."

"Are you late, Ammi?"

"Well, I might be, and you might be too if we keep talking about this pin with fire and the Cold War."

"Ammi, do I have to recite even if we're late?"

"Well, we can recite on the way to school, in the car, like we normally do. You can bring along your *mushaf* just for reinforcement. And then we can do a little more this afternoon *inshaa Allah*."

"But Ammi, I don't want to; since Naeem left, it's just not as fun anymore."

"Oh *baita*, come on. You're exaggerating. You did a beautiful drawing last night of *Surah Al Fajr* and I shouldn't have to remind you that you enjoyed it. And remember, we have that weekend project to take a picture of a sunrise? How about this afternoon, we try going on our flying carpet again?"

"Can we fly to where the pin came from?"

"Fly?" says Amna, increasingly interested.

"Yes," responds Ibrahim, "Ammi says this afternoon we're going on a trip to a cold place, and she's going to tell us a lot of interesting stories about history." Pausing, Ibrahim then turns back to me. "Ammi, was Lenin like the people who we were learning about yesterday… the 'Ad people… or was he like Prophet Muhemmed, *Salla Allahu 'alayhi wa sallam?*" [1]

"*Baita*, that's another big question. Ok, Lenin was not a Prophet, but, from what little I know, he was committed to bringing about social change and equality, unlike the 'Ad people."

"What?" says Amna, after my brief explanation.

"Lenin was not like Pharaoh," responds Ibrahim to his sister.

"Not like Fara?"

"No," I say, trying to accelerate the tempo. We have the potential to spend the whole morning in a pseudo history lesson with what feels like Doctor Seuss mediating. "Come on, breakfast, teeth brushing, quick recitation and then, one, two, three…"

"…up we go," Ibrahim finishes my sentence.

"Ibrahim, we're flying this afternoon *inshaa Allah*. We've got a little work cut out for us this morning."

"Ammi, why do we always need to practice reciting?"

"Ibrahim, is there any way we can answer that later?" I say, on the verge of exasperation.

"No, Ammi, this is really important. It's not history. It's not flying lessons. I actually really need to know why we recite every day."

"Didn't you explain this to Yaseen once?" I say, thankful for the sign we still have in our home about the importance of reviewing. [2]

"Yes, but I need another answer Ammi; that's not working for me this morning," responds Ibrahim, not budging.

"Ok, where's that pin of your father?" I ask.

"Here," says Ibrahim, opening up his hand.

"Fire," says Amna.

"Yes, fire. Now, you didn't give me a chance to look back at my history books, yet, but if I remember correctly, and if I overheard properly, just ten minutes ago, your father said that that little slogan under Lenin's name means 'always ready' in Russian. *Sahih?*"

"Yes," says Ibrahim, nodding.

"Well, one way of looking at your revision is…"

"…being like Lenin."

"No, not necessarily, but it may be being 'always ready.'"

"Ready for what?" asks Ibrahim.

"Well, ready to use each of your different *surahs* in your prayers and actually communicate with Allah *Subhanahu wa-ta'ala* in special ways… ready to help teach and explain them… ready to learn."

"Ammi, those are big tasks."

"Yes, but you've started *masha'Allah*. And you're making really wonderful progress. And each day that you remember and live your *surahs*, you grow *inshaa Allah*."

"Ammi, I don't want to recite in the car; I just want to hear about the Cold War."

"How about we do half and half, and try to earn some points too?"

"Well… that sounds ok. I think I could do that, and it also sounds like what we did when we went to pick Naeem at the airport…" says Ibrahim.

"…and what we do, every day," I conclude.

"Ammi, we've never spoken about the Cold War before."

"Yes, but we have talked about trains, and *Hajj* and birds and I think many, many other subjects under the sun, either before or after our recitation."

"You may be right," responds Ibrahim.

"Right," seconds Amna.

"Do you think we should simply do school at home today?" offers Ibrahim.

"I think Ms Suzy is waiting for you this morning, Ibrahim," I say. "How about we put the pause button on for four hours and then we conclude all this really important discussion after lunch?" I suggest.

"It's a deal, but remember don't forget to look at history when I'm gone. I want to know it all. Or maybe you could ask Lieutenant Laila to look into it for you since you're pretty busy," he says, with a big grin.

"It's a deal," I say.

"Deal," agrees Amna.

Ibrahim looks at us, smiles again, and then, starts walking toward the kitchen. *Inshaa Allah* we are on our way.

HIFDH TEACHING NOTE

Almost every day, we wake up and prepare for school and work, but do we prepare for our *salah* and our communion with *Allah*SWT? If we were to prepare for the latter, how exactly would we go about it? Surely learning His*SWT* Book is a major part of this, together with learning and applying the *sunnah*. In terms of learning the Holy Qur'aan, in *hifdh* one does not simply read or learn by heart once; to actually preserve the Qur'aan in the heart, one must review, constantly. Ibrahim remarks, "I don't want to; since Naeem left, it's just not as fun anymore." How then as parents, do we keep the *hifdh* spark, day after day? How do we convey the importance, the love and the excitement of living the Qur'aan? In this episode, Khadija mentions some photography (they plan to take a picture of a sunrise to aid in the learning of *Surah Al Fajr*). In addition, Khadija offers the flying carpet activity again, which Ibrahim immediately seizes. He wants to explore the world — a pursuit embraced by children of all ages. Where does the Qur'aan feature in your exploration? Have you ever tried to make it the journey map, and let it be part of the adventure? Why not try it?

---

[1] References verse 6 from *Surah Al Fajr*: "6. Seest thou not how thy Lord dealt with the 'Ad (people) — 7. Of the (city of) Iram, with lofty pillars," (Abdullah Yusuf Ali 1989, p.1645)

[2] See Sabr & Cacti (Chapter 14).

30

WATER PROJECTS AND
THE DAY AFTER

Date/place: early April, 2011, Houston, in front of Ibrahim and Amna's Montessori school, mid-day

Cast of characters: Nani, Khadija, Ibrahim and Amna

"*Baita*, he's not a water project."

"*Kiya*," I say.

"Ibrahim is not a water project," my mother starts to clarify.

"And neither is Amna, for that matter," I respond, still not knowing where she is heading.

"I think you should ease up," she says.

"In what regard?" I ask.

"I think you know," says my mother.

"Are you referring to what happened last night?" I query.

"Well, yes, and no. Khadija, I am also referring to other instances over the past six months. I've seen you with your two beautiful children. *Masha'Allah* you're doing a wonderful job, including all that 'Club' stuff, but sometimes I feel as though you are doing too much, and they are part of one of your massive South Asian water supply programs."

"Ammi, I thought we agreed to disagree with regard to our different approaches to Qur'aanic education. You engaged a *maulvi sahib* to teach the four of us, and Abdurrahman and I have opted largely to rely on each other, with some expert advice on *tajweed* and *hifdh* from Hafidha Rabia, and have a more integrated approach."

"But, *baita*, Ibrahim needs to play more, without a *hifdh* lesson, however fun and engaging it may be, hanging over him; he says it, he shows it, and last night he really showed it with that temper tantrum," my mother responds.

"How will we get to *Surah Al Baqarah* then?" I say, starting to get defensive.

"I thought that getting to the end wasn't your point. I thought it was all about the journey and the learning along the way," my mother says. "That's what you've been explaining to the children and even to Yaseen and Yasmeen over many months."

"Yes, of course, but there is also an end goal."

"And I thought that end goal was to reflect the character and teachings of Prophet Muhemmed, *Salla Allahu 'alayhi wa sallam*?"

"Which we will only fully know by understanding the Qur'aan and the *sunnah* and our teachers," I say.

"Khadija he is not yet six. Amna is still two."

"Ammi, I realize this. I appreciate your concern. And I also understand that I bring to my own teaching a few years of field experience in the water sector, but I am trying my best."

"Khadija, I know that *baita*. And I know that you only want the best for these two little angels. But Ibrahim was very upset last night. God forbid he associates his lessons with fear or anxiety. We all know what can happen when the Qur'aan or any other holy scripture is taught under real pressure."

"Ammi, please don't say that. I've been trying so hard to make this fun. I got a little upset last night, and he reacted, strongly. I probably shouldn't have pushed him to continue, but he was right on the cusp of actually finishing *Surah Al Ghasiyah*.[1] Some people say it's precisely at the point where a child is resisting that you should push him, and others…"

"Others, your husband, and I believe your Hafidha included, would say that there is always time, and room for a more gentle approach, particularly when it comes to Qur'aan. Khadija, this is not a Math class; this not a Science exam; this is Qur'aan. It is revelation, and if you really want to understand it and help to teach it, you have to do it with love and tenderness, being ever mindful of the stage of your student," concludes my mother.

"Ammi, I am sorry," I say, looking down. "I may have lapsed into my seriously adult field manager mode last night. I just got so frustrated with him not wanting to finish," I say.

"Khadija, you have amazing talent *masha'Allah* and you have done a lot of good in this world, and *inshaa Allah* you will continue to do good both with the Qur'aan and back in the field, but go easy on your children. They are children. I know some schools of thought say it must be 24-7, but let life breathe, deeply, in and between your lessons. And give yourself a break, too."

"Ammi, I know," I say, tearing up a little. My back also sags and I feel as though I am wilting in my seat. "Do you think I should simply shelve this project?"

"What project?" says my mother, now seeking clarification.

"This work, this *hifdh*. Shouldn't I call a *maulvi sahib* to take over?"

"Absolutely not. You've started something really wonderful and *masha'Allah* you are all nearing the end of *Juz Amma*. But just remember always learn and teach with and in the spirit of love, even if it takes a little longer, to get to the end. Do you know that today, at the ripe age of 71, I have just sat in my first

110

geography class."

"Yes, Ammi, I just picked you up from the University."

"I know you know where I was, but can you appreciate how long it has taken me to get here?"

"Ammi, you've been to a university before."

"Many, yes, but not to this particular geography class," says my mother, continuing. "It has taken me, meeting Nonna and Abdurrahman, and appreciating their stories. It has also, and I thought I would never say this, taken losing my Amna and your father and trying to recreate meaning and purpose in my own life. Naeem and Ibrahim and Yaseen and their incessant questions have pushed me in this direction, not to mention Yasmeen's own geography class. If I had tried to accelerate or bypass any of these experiences or the lessons from them I would never be who I am: an old woman who is still traveling through this world, hopefully on toward the next, with increasing peace in her heart."

"Thank you, Ammi."

"For what?"

"For traveling, for learning and for teaching us all."

"You are always welcome, *baita*. Remember we are all always learning here," says my mother getting out of the car. The door to the children's school has just opened, and we line up with the other parents near the door, as is customary.

"Look there they are. I wonder what kind of questions we are going to have today," says my mother somewhat rhetorically.

"Nani, why are you here?" says Ibrahim to his grandmother as he approaches us.

"*Assalaamu 'alaykum* to you too," says my mother. "Your dear mother picked me up early from class."

"Oh, yeah, how did it go?" asks Ibrahim.

"I felt young again," says my mother.

"In a good way?" asks Ibrahim.

"Yes, in a good way. The course has already started so I'm simply sitting in at this point, until the end of the semester, but I also feel like I've 70 solid years behind me, supporting my learning, just like you; you have five years backing up yours," responds my mother.

"I'm two," says Amna, as though she'd like a little more attention.

"No, you are almost three," says Ibrahim.

"No, I'm two," repeats Amna, not quite grasping the concept of advancing to another year.

"Well, you're going to be three soon, whether you like it or not," says Ibrahim.

Then, "Ammi, do you know what Lent is?"

"Lent or Lenin? I thought we already finished off with Lenin last week?"

"Yes, we did; no I said, L… e… n… t," Ibrahim repeats very slowly.

"Ok. Are we starting with that question now or did you want to pick up some of the questions from earlier this morning? I thought you wanted to know more about the Yucatan from Nani."

"No, she filled me in on the Yucatan. I was just sort of testing her before her class to see if she knew the subject. You know Nani's class was studying the Yucatan today; isn't that cool. It's like that book that Nonna sent her a long time ago."

"It wasn't so long ago Ibrahim," I say. "Ok, so, we're on to Lent, are we?"

"Yes," responds Amna.

"My friend, John Henry, mentioned it during show-and-tell this morning," says Ibrahim.

I pause and look at my mother, who I don't remember ever talking about Lent with us when we were growing up. "*Baita*, what little I do know is that Lent is sort of like Ramadan. It's a period of sacrifice and introspection before Easter. I think it is 40 days and is connected to Christ's, *alayhis salaam*, own trials in the desert."

"Ammi, it sounds like you know a lot."

"Well, whatever I know is thanks to your Aunt Margaret," I respond. "When we all called her to thank her for the Saint Francis Assisi prayer, she and I eventually came to the subject of Ramadan and then Lent," I respond.

"Life is sort of like that," says Ibrahim.

"Like what?" I respond.

"Like what you describe, coming back to things. By the way, Ammi, you promised me we were going to bury anger after school today, after what happened last night."

"Did I?"

"Yes, or at least that's what Papa and Nani suggested when you slammed the door and I shouted," says Ibrahim.

"Where do you think we should go to bury it this time?" I ask, blushing a little at Ibrahim's depiction of last night.

"Well, Memorial Park of course. That's where we always go," Ibrahim responds.

"*Baita*, I hope you don't associate Memorial Park only with burying anger."

"No, of course not. When I think of the Park, I think of bikes and squirrels and Nonna being with us, and our last visit with Naeem and Yaseen. I also think of Robin Hood and archery."

112

"Well, that's heartening," I say.

"Ok, so we're off to Memorial Park," affirms Nani.

"Yes," responds Amna.

"And then we can recite again," offers Ibrahim.

"Only if you're ready *baita*," I respond.

"Oh, Ammi, I'm ready; in fact, this morning at school, I was actually going back over those lines in my head, *Fazakkir, innama 'anta muzakkir, Lasta 'alayhim bi-musaytir,*[2] and I think I may finally have them. Not because of last night, but simply because, well, like you always say, everything comes as a gift from Allah *Subhanahu wa-ta'ala.*"

"*Masha'Allah,*" I say. "Does that mean you want to recite it all here, now?"

"No, I want to wait for the Park, and then, maybe if you're all good," says Ibrahim, slowly smiling at all of us, "I'll give you a *surah* gift."

"*Accha hae,*" both my mother and I respond.

"Let's go," beckons Amna, and we are all off again.

HIFDH TEACHING NOTE

"This is Qur'aan," Nani instructs. "It is revelation, and if you really want to understand it and help to teach it, you have to do it with love and tenderness, being ever mindful of the stage of your student," she concludes. According to her, there is no room for coercion. When the child resists, then do not push further. A temper tantrum should not be part of a lesson, no matter how important. Khadija admits that this is one school of thought, which, it should be added, she has largely demonstrated up until this point, especially during the learning of *Surah Al Bayyinah*; however, another school of thought pushes back, at the moment of resistance, to challenge the aspiring *hafidh*. In somewhat of an about-face, Khadija seems to be adopting this more rigid approach, which her mother likens to her former project management style. She cautions, and Khadija ultimately listens. It is a fine line of sorts, to have *hifdh* be part of life and yet also to have specific lessons. Take your temperature and your children's to make sure your combination is working, well, and sustainably. While serious, the learning should stay fun; and both the players and the coach must take breaks. "Breathe, deeply, in and between [...] lessons," Nani advises. What do you gain after all by (swiftly) completing *Surah Al Ghasiyah*, but simultaneously losing the love for Qur'aan?

---

[1] *Surah Al Ghashiyah*, translated as 'The Overwhelming Event' is the 88th *surah* in the Qur'aan, consisting of 26 *ayaat* (Abdullah Yusuf Ali 1989, p.1640). Abdullah Yusuf Ali summarizes the *surah* as follows: "Its subject matter is the contrast between the destinies of the Good and the Evil in the Hereafter—on the Day when the true balance will be restored: the Signs of Allah even in this life should remind us of the Day of Account, for Allah is good and just, and His creation is for a just Purpose," (p.1639).

[2] *Ayaat* 21 and 22, as excerpted from the transliteration of *Surah Al Ghashiya* (Taha, p.16), meaning, "21. Therefore do thou give admonition, for thou art one to admonish. 22. Thou art not one to manage (men's) affairs," (Abdullah Yusuf Ali 1989, p.1642).

31

SEAGULLS

Date/place: mid-April, Houston, Ibrahim and Amna's apartment, early evening, Friday

Cast of characters: Abdurrahman, Ibrahim, Amna, Khadija, Nani

"So what's on for tonight?" asks Abdurrahman after dinner.

"You get to choose. Ammi and I found two movies at the public library, *'The Gull'* and *'The Prince'*," responds Ibrahim.

"*'The Gull'*?" questions Amna.

"No *baita*, not *'The Gull'*, *Jonathan Livingston Seagull*," I say.

"Oh, right, right," says Ibrahim nodding. "You know, Uncle Bill gave us the idea," he then adds.

"And *'The Prince'*?" Abdurrahman queries, seeking clarification.

"Yes, *The Little Prince*," I respond, "but it's in French with English subtitles."

"Khadija, that might be a little difficult for the kids," says my mother.

"No, I like French," Ibrahim affirms. "I heard it in *Babar* and also in *Madeleine*."

"Well, well," says my mother. "Then, don't let me get in your way. *On y va.*"

"What does that mean?" asks Ibrahim.

"If I remember correctly, it means 'let's go' or 'let's go there'."

"Nani, did you also learn French watching *Madeleine*?"

"No, not exactly. I think I picked up one or two phrases on the job, many, many years ago. French used to be more prevalent, as it was considered the international language of diplomacy."

"I don't know what that means," responds Ibrahim.

"It's ok. Let's park the subject for tonight, and we'll get back to diplomacy when you're seven *inshaa Allah*. Now, enough about my little history and the history of French, what movie are we going to see?"

"I vote for *'The Gull'*," says Abdurrahman.

"Really Papa, are you sure you don't want to see '*The Prince*'?"

"Well, there's always tomorrow," responds Abdurahman. "I remember reading the book, *Jonathan Livingston Seagull*, a very long time ago, when I was just a little older than you."

"You mean when you were six?" asks Ibrahim.

"Hmm, let's just say six plus seven," Abdurahman responds.

"You mean when you were fourteen," Ibrahim answers.

"Try again," says Abdurrahman.

Ibrahim spreads his fingers out wide and starts counting. "I meant, when you were thirteen," he says, correcting himself.

"Yes, maybe around then."

"Did Nonna give it to you?" asks Ibrahim.

"Nonna give it to you," mimics Amna, making it a statement rather than a question.

"No, like you, I got it from the public library. You know we also had those growing up."

"Really," says Ibrahim, sounding astounded. "You had libraries?"

"Yes, and cars too," says Abdurrahman, smiling. "Ok, so why don't Amna and I start working on the popcorn, and Ibrahim you can take the lead clearing the dishes, deal?" suggests Abdurrahman.

"Papa, do I have to? Ammi was going to review with me before we started the movie."

"Oh so you want a dish exemption to do your Qur'aan work, do you?" says Abdurrahman raising an eyebrow and looking at both Ibrahim and me.

"Yes," Ibrahim and I respond in unison.

"Well, I think it sounds… reasonable, for tonight. But tomorrow morning, Amna and I are going to ask you to help with the pancake clean-up. And we might just go off and recite Amna's favorite, *Surah Al Alaq*, together. You got that," says Abdurrahman.

Ibrahim nods his head, and I pat Abdurrahman on the shoulder, then add, "Thanks, I owe you a lot. Ok, Ibrahim, let's go get *Surah Al Al'aa*."

"I'm going to help Abdurrahman if that's ok," offers my mother. "Why don't the two of you work in my room so that it's more quiet."

"Thanks Nani," says Ibrahim. "Don't worry I won't play with all your newspapers and books and letters, this time."

"Thank *you*," says my mother, "but be quick, we've got a film and popcorn and, who knows, your father might even treat us to a game of charades afterwards."

"Ok, we're coming," calls out Ibrahim, who is two paces ahead of me, and already entering in Nani's room, which is close to the kitchen.

I have his *mushaf* as well as my own, together with two Qur'aan stands and my translation, which I balance as we sit down, on the floor.

"Ammi, that was nice of Papa and Nani, don't you think," says Ibrahim.

"Yes, very nice, and Amna too. Now, let's try to focus and not take too much time out from helping them. Do you remember what we were discussing earlier today?"

"*Al Al'aa* is high," says Ibrahim.

"Almost," I respond.

"Higher," offers Ibrahim.

"Highest," I say. "*Al Al'aa* means 'highest', and describes Allah *Subhanahu wa-ta'ala.*"

"And Jonathan?" asks Ibrahim.

"What?"

"The gull," says Ibrahim.

"Not quite. As we read, *Jonathan Livingston Seagull* strives to get high, very high and he manages to transcend his pack, but he doesn't reach Allah, because Allah…"

"… is the highest," says Ibrahim, finishing my phrase.

"You got it," I say. "Do you remember what comes after that first *ayah*?"

"Something about creation," says Ibrahim.

"Yup, and…?" I ask.

"Ordering," Ibrahim says.

"Almost, Allah creates and gives order and proportion."

"Oh yeah, oh yeah, like this," and Ibrahim mimes two boxes with his fingers, "now I'm starting to remember it."

"Ammi," cries Amna from outside the door, interrupting my train of thought.

"Oh no, is she coming in now?" says Ibrahim with frustration in his voice. "Then we'll never finish."

"Wait just a minute, *baita*, let me see what is wrong. Meanwhile, please look into your *mushaf*, I want to see if you can get the first three *ayaat* clearly." Then, opening the door, and seeing Amna, I say. "What's the matter?"

"Papa popcorn," says Amna, with tears in her eyes.

"*Kiya*?" I ask.

"Papa popcorn eat," repeats Amna.

116

"Ammi, she's distracting me," calls out Ibrahim from behind me.

"Ok, *baita*, just give me one more minute; meanwhile please keep reading, I'm coming."

Amna is looking at me, but pointing at her father who is standing nearby with a full bowl of popcorn.

"That was fast," I say. "You know we're just nearing the third *ayah*."

"So we'll wait for you, on the porch," suggests Abdurrahman, "and Amna can start eating."

"What about me?" Ibrahim calls out, seemingly excluded.

"Oh don't you worry *bambino*, you've got your own bowl and it's actually bigger than Amna's. We're not going to touch it until you get through the eighth *ayah*," says Abdurrahman.

"Ok, Ammi, that's just almost to the end of the page. Let's finish, quickly," says Ibrahim as though there's a fire under him.

"*Baita*, don't worry, they won't eat your popcorn. And they won't start the movie. And they definitely can't play charades without you. As your uncle often says, 'you *are* the party' so don't worry about being left behind."

"Which uncle?" asks Ibrahim.

"Many of them, it's not important now. Ok, let's start from the top again. I am going to re-read the translation, up until *ayah* eight and then we'll recite down together slowly *inshaa Allah*.

1. Glorify the name of thy Guardian-Lord Most High,

2. Who hath created and further, given order and proportion;

3. Who hath ordained laws. And granted guidance.

4. And Who bringeth out the (green and luscious) pasture,

5. And then doth make it (but) swarthy stubble.

6. By degrees shall We teach thee to declare (The Message) so thou shalt not forget,

7. Except as Allah wills: for He knoweth what is manifest and what is hidden.

8. And We will make it easy for thee (to follow) the simple (Path)." [1]

"I like the part about it being easy to follow the simple path," says Ibrahim as I conclude.

"Me too," I say. "Ok, so are you ready for the Arabic?"

Ibrahim nods. "But Ammi, let me be ahead this time."

"Absolutely, this is your lesson, go right ahead."

"Ok, so, *Authu Billahi Minishaytonir Rajeem, Bismillahir Rahmanir Raheem*," then stopping, Ibrahim looks at me, "but Ammi, do you think Jonathan could have burned his wing?"

"I don't know *baita*; you give me food for thought, meanwhile let's finish this *surah* and then see what the film shows us."

"Food for thought?"

"Yes," I say, dodging the question for now, "ok, *Authu Billahi Minishaytonir Rajeem, Bismillahir Rahmanir Raheem,*" I start back in, but Ibrahim takes over, asserting himself. And as I ease my voice out, he is already almost to the end of the 'simple Path'.[2]

HIFDH TEACHING NOTE

Flight has been a recurring theme in this *hifdh* journey — from the Whooping Cranes to the flying carpets. Here, it is *Jonathan Livingston Seagull* coupled with *Surah Al Al'aa* that raises the aspiring *hafidh*. Popcorn is promised as is a potentially fun, family movie, afterwards. What is also important to note is that the lesson is brief. It is a quick review, with the undivided attention of Khadija focusing exclusively on one *surah*. *C'est tout, tout court.* There is no need to overburden, especially when such enthusiasm is shown. Remember, stay the course, but no temper tantrums, please.

---

[1] *Surah Al Al'aa*, verses 1-8 (Abdullah Yusuf Ali 1989, pp.1636-37).

[2] Books referred to in this Chapter are as follows: *Jonathan Livingston Seagull* (Bach 1970); *The Story of Babar* (Brunhoff 1933); and *Madeleine* (Bemelmans 1939).

32

TARIQ

Date/place: early April, 2011, Houston, the roof of the parking garage attached to the apartment building, evening

Cast of characters: Abdurrahman, Ibrahim, Amna, Khadija

"I think this may be my favorite moment today."

"Why? Because you're with us?"

"Well, yes, that too," responds Abdurrahman, looking down and putting his arm around Ibrahim. "But I also just love being up on this roof, especially after sunset."

"I love roof," says Amna, on cue.

"Me, too," I add.

"Did you ever go up on a roof when you were a kid, Papa?" inquires Ibrahim.

"The roof? Of course, Geo and I lived up on our roof, almost. We probably spent more time on the roof than inside the house, much to my mother's chagrin."

"What does that mean?" Ibrahim asks.

"Nonna would have liked us to spend less time with our sling shots on the roof and more time inside, probably, helping or reading or…"

"Or boxing?" says Ibrahim.

"Oh, so you remember?"

"Papa, how could I forget? It was cold and Amna took over but I still thought that punching bag was super cool. I wish we had one."

"*Inshaa Allah*, as soon as we get settled, your Ammi and I will make a plan."

"We will, will we?" I say, more to Abdurrahman than to either child.

"Come on Khadija, it's harmless," says Abdurrahman.

"Fine, but let's first find a house. I don't think we have room just yet in our apartment."

"Once we get settled, Papa said," repeats Ibrahim, looking at me and taking my hand.

"Settled, Ammi," mimics Amna.

"Yes, settled, *inshaa Allah*," affirms Abdurrahman. "By the way, do you know what I did this evening coming back from work?"

"You read the newspaper," says Ibrahim.

"You're partly right, I did glance at the headlines, and then…"

"And Qur'aan," exclaims Amna.

"Also correct," responds Abdurrahman, "but there was something more as well, what do you think Khadija?"

"You finished a poem?" I say.

"How did you know?"

"I didn't. I guessed. You always tell me it's what you would do if you had just one more minute in the day. I think the last time you wrote was around *Ashura*."

"How many extra minutes did you have today, Papa? But before you answer, do you know that there are 60 minutes in an hour? And there are 60 seconds in a minute. Ammi taught me that today. And she also showed me how it can't be eight 60 one, on her watch."

"So you were late, again?" asks Abdurrahman.

"No, not really, just on time," says Ibrahim, smiling.

"Your mother is a serious teacher."

"Very serious, but she is also seriously fun," responds Ibrahim. "We mostly learn at the park and *inshaa Allah* we're getting lots of points for all our work."

"Well that's nice to hear," I respond, "by the way, I am still waiting for the poem."

"Me too," says Amna.

"I can give you a poem Ammi," says Ibrahim, seemingly upstaged.

"*Baita*, I am sure you can. You are writing beautifully these days, but let's hear what your father has to say. It's been a long time since we've heard his verses."

Abdurrahman takes a small piece of paper out of his pocket and unfolds it slowly.

"A tissue?" asks Amna.

"Not quite," says Abdurrahman. "Will you listen?"

"Not mine?" says Amna, seeking clarification.

"Well, yes, it is yours, but first you must listen. Will you sit and listen?" says Abdurrahman again, sitting down himself and beckoning to the children to do the same.

"Why did you write it?" asks Ibrahim.

"How about we listen first and then we answer that. You might even know the answer by the time we get to the end."

"I listen," says Amna, asserting herself.

"Great, *on y va*," responds Abdurrahman.

"Hey, wait, that's what Nani said last week when we were talking about *Madeleine*."

"Yes, I remembered," says Abdurrahman. "Now, let's respect your mother's wishes and listen. And by the way, the title is 'To Count the Blessings'," Abdurrahman takes a deep breath and begins.

As this sun sets

The question persists

Did we see the blessings of the day

Each moment as the myriad rays

In a rainbow

That fit like a halo

'Round our head

Enlightening

Brightening

Yes, did we see the blessings of the day

Or did we dismiss

As trite and replayed

All that passed our way

Letting the little things

Fray our patience

And plunge our spirit into dismay

Yes, did we see the blessings of the day

The stars that shine throughout

Night and day

And the angels that pass

Guiding us on our way to

That light that beckons us

Ever-onward, ever-upward

The choice is ours to make.

As Abdurrahman concludes, no one says anything for at least 30 seconds. The children simply stare at their father; meanwhile, I try to replay some of the lines in my head again. Finally, Ibrahim breaks the silence.

"Did you write that poem to help me learn *Surah At Tariq*?" asks Ibrahim.

"Why do you say that?" responds Abdurrahman.

"There was a star inside," says Ibrahim.

"Inside what?" I inquire.

"Inside the poem," Ibrahim says.

"Right," says Abdurrahman. "There was a star, but there were also angels."

"In the poem, yes," confirms Ibrahim. "But there are no angels in *Tariq*. And there was no '*hafidh*' in your poem."[1]

"What?" Abdurrahman says.

"No '*hafidh*'. Remember '*In-kullu nafsil lamma 'alayha hafi[dh]*'," says Ibrahim.[2]

"You're strong," says Abdurrahman to his son.

"No, I'm still learning," responds Ibrahim, fully grasping his father's comment.

"Well, then maybe you will be open to another interpretation. I actually think there may have been a reference to a *hafidh*, in my poem as well."

"What do you mean?" asks Ibrahim

"Meaning?" repeats Amna.

"You're almost to *Surah Al Infitar*, which I recited last night during my *Isha* prayers. And in that *surah*, there is a reference to angels appointed over us, protecting us."[3]

"And so in your poem there were angels, protecting?" queries Ibrahim.

"Yes, right at the end, I mentioned them briefly," says Abdurrahman.

"That's very cool," says Ibrahim. "And I also liked your rainbow."

"Rainbow?" asks Amna, not quite grasping the reference. "Don't see rainbow."

"No, neither do I, not now, at least," responds Abdurrahman. "Maybe tomorrow *inshaa Allah*."

"No Papa, she can understand," says Ibrahim. Then looking at his sister, he takes her hand and says very slowly. "No rainbow in the sky. Rainbow in Papa's poem. Understand?"

"Listen tissue?" is Amna's less coherent response.

"Listen poem, and *Tariq*. Look see the *Tariq*," says Ibrahim now pointing above us to a star.

"I think they both get it," I say to Abdurrahman. "And I also think they will be our teachers soon."

"Khadija, they already are," responds Abdurrahman. "And don't worry, I won't go off and buy a boxing bag, but to tell you the truth, I think we are settled, even now."

HIFDH TEACHING NOTE

Keep reading: poems, stories, history, biography. Keep reading, keep listening, keep watching, and keep exploring with your children. They will absorb, and their *hifdh* journey will become all the more animated. Here, Abdurrahman has opted to share a poem, to which Ibrahim immediately latches on, thinking that his father has recited the poem to help him learn *Surah At Tariq*, 'The Night Star'. A dialogue ensues that involves Abdurrahman testing his son's knowledge of the *surah*. Rather than simply asking him to recite the *surah*, Abdurrahman questions Ibrahim about specific words and concepts, challenging him to literally think outside of the *surah*, similar to what Khadija did in Chapters 14 and 15 when she asked the children to look for '*sabr*' and then '*haq*'. This type of review is a great way to keep the children involved and motivated, while keeping any tedium at bay. If it's time to learn *Surah At Tariq*, perhaps it's also time to go star gazing, with your *mushaf*.

---

[1] '*Hafidh*' is based on the Arabic root, meaning to to preserve, protect. A *hafidh* of the Qur'aan, as featured throughout *A Qur'aanic Odyessy*, is one who preserves or protects the Qur'aan. In addition, the Qur'aan has countless references to '*hafidh*' (and other forms of the word), namely protectors/preservers.

[2] Transliteration of the fourth *ayah* of *Surah At Tariq* as featured in *Tajweed Qur'an* (2007, p.15); and is translated as follows: "There is no soul but has a protector over it," (Abdullah Yusuf Ali 1989, p. 1632). *Surah At Tariq* is translated as 'The Night Star' and is the 86th *surah* in the Qur'aan.

[3] *Surah Al Infitar* (82) *ayah* 10: "But verily over you (are appointed angels) to protect you," (Abdullah Yusuf Ali 1989, p.1613).

33

THE FASTS AND HOLY FRIDAY

Date/place: end April, 2011, Houston, Ibrahim and Amna's living room, mid-afternoon, Thursday

Cast of characters: Ibrahim, Nani, Khadija, Amna

"Nani, are you fasting?"

"Why?"

"Because I don't see you drinking *chai*, and normally you always have a cup of *chai* at this time, and then you sit down on the couch and read the paper. And I was talking to Uncle Bill last night, when we went up on the roof, and he said that he was going to fast on Friday," Ibrahim says.

"You're very observant *masha'Allah*. But remember, now I have my geography class so I don't always sit down with the paper; sometimes I have homework," responds my mother, smiling. Then continuing, she adds. "Yes, I guess Bill and I are both fasting, but on different days, me today, him tomorrow."

"But are you celebrating Easter?" queries Ibrahim.

"No, not exactly. I am fasting because I need to make up one last fast before *Ramadan* starts. I was traveling back from your Uncle Hamza's home in Doha last year and then I was sick, and so I missed six days of my fast…"

"And Easter?" Ibrahim repeats.

"Easter is a slightly different topic, which your Nonna and your Aunt Margaret will hopefully be able to explain to you in better terms, and of course your Papa. For me, Easter, like Christmas, is always a good reminder of Christ, *alayhis salaam*. I am grateful for the example."

"Of who?"

"Of Christ, *alayhis salaam*."[1]

"But then why is Uncle Bill fasting tomorrow?" Ibrahim asks.

"Bill fast," repeats Amna, then adds. "I fast. You fast. Bhai jaan fast." She picks up one of her legos from the living room floor and makes the sound of a car engine.

"Not yet, you're too young," responds Ibrahim. "And so am I, for a whole day…

124

so why is…"

"It's Good Friday," I respond, putting down my book, and giving my mother a brief break with Ibrahim's questions.

"And so?"

"And so, one of the ways in which the day is commemorated is for Christians to fast and pray and reflect on what happened to Christ, *alayhis salaam*," I respond, sitting down on the couch, next to my mother.[2]

"How do you know Ammi?" asks Ibrahim.

"Like Nani said, it was your Nonna and Aunt Margaret. They've taught us all," I say.

"But what is good about Good Friday?"

"I think there are different right answers to that question but one of them is that the actual meaning of the word 'good' has changed over time and that it might be called more aptly 'Holy Friday'."

"Why?"

"Because according to Christian belief, Christ, *alayhis salaam,* was crucified on that day, which was followed by his resurrection and ascension to Heaven," I respond, raising my hands skyward for emphasis, but with some tentativeness in my voice, not knowing if the theology will make sense to Ibrahim. I look at my mother for affirmation.

"We could wait for Abdurrahman and Nonna to finish," suggests my mother, who understands that I am treading lightly.

"But why is that good? I don't really want to wait for Papa for the answer," Ibrahim responds.

"*Baita*, I'm not a theologian, but as I understand it the reason why it is good is because Christ, *alayhis salaam,* is considered by Christians as the means to salvation, and Good or Holy Friday leads to Christ's resurrection and ascension to Heaven which in turn leads to the understanding that he was and is the son of God."

"And why is that good?"

"It is good because it brings people, Christians, closer to God," I respond. "But yes, I would like to have your father and Nonna and Aunt Margaret confirm all this. I think what's important for you to grasp, especially in the context of your *hifdh*, is that we revere Christ, *alayhis salaam,* and can learn much from his teachings, but don't consider him to be the son of God," I add.

"Because of *Surah Ikhlas*?"[3]

"Yes, *Surah Al Ikhlas* and other *surahs* as well. *Inshaa Allah, ahista ahista* we'll get there," I respond.[4]

"Papa told me last night, after we saw Uncle Bill, that Christ, *alayhis salaam,* was hurt," says Ibrahim.

"Yes, he was hurt; he was persecuted, as were many of the Prophets and believers," my mother says.

"And then he tried to help me learn an *ayah*," Ibrahim continues.

"Which one?" I say, curious to know whether Ibrahim has retained the teaching.

"*Ayah* eight," says Ibrahim.

"Do you remember how it goes?" I inquire.

"No, only that people were hurt, simply for believing," Ibrahim responds.

"I'm hurt," interjects Amna, pointing to a scab on her right arm.

"No, you're not, silly," says Ibrahim. "That's a baby hurt. We are talking about serious hurts."

"Well, where is your *mushaf*?" I ask, trying to close the loop on *ayah* eight.

"Here, here," says Amna, getting up and running over to the dining room table. My mother is, even while fasting, quicker in her response than any of us, and she gently plies the Qur'aan out of Amna's hands, before Amna can do her now customary ripping, otherwise known as her experimentation with books.

"*Bohaut shukria, baita*," says my mother to Amna.

"Thanks Amna," adds Ibrahim. "Ok, do you want me to read it to you?" asks Ibrahim, looking at me.

"If you wish," I respond. "Read or recite. I was actually thinking that we might also try to finish up *ayah* nine now and then do our review game so we have a little more time."

"For what?" asks Ibrahim.

"To prepare Nani's *iftari*," I respond.

"*Baita*, look, you have the children, please don't worry about me. I can easily fend for myself," says my mother.

"Ammi, give us the opportunity, please; they'll also enjoy it."

"Will we make fruit chaat and samosas, like we do in Ramadan?"

"I eat samosas," says Amna.

"Me, too, I eat a lot of samosas," says Ibrahim to his sister, pretending to chew a samosa in his mouth. "But first I finish *ayah* eight and nine, ok?" he adds, looking for his sister's approval.

"*Ayah* eight?" questions Amna.

"Yes, *ayah* eight," responds Ibrahim, opening up his *mushaf* and starting to read out loud. "*Wa ma naqamou minhum 'illa 'any-yu'minou bi-LLahil-'Azaazil-Hameed.*"[5] Pausing, Ibrahim then says, "Ammi, do you know, Uncle Bill also said he could take us to see the butterflies at the Museum."[6]

"Before or after Holy Friday?" I ask.

"He said we could go next week, after school."

"Great," says Nani. "I also want to see them."

"What?" asks Ibrahim.

"The butterflies. I love them. I love the idea and the reality of metamorphosis."

"Meta source?" repeats Amna.

"No, meta morse," says Ibrahim.

"Almost, it's meta... mor... pho... sis," my mother says slowly.

"I can spell that," offers Ibrahim.

"I'm sure you can, especially the 'ph' part. I'm also sure that your cousin Yasmeen would want to come along."

"Ok, we can call her, but why do you love meta... mor... pho... sis?" says Ibrahim very slowly, counting out the syllables on his fingers.

"It's an amazing miracle *baita*, and it is happening all around us, all the time. A creature transforms, completely, from egg to caterpillar to brilliant butterfly," says my mother.

"I'm butterfly," pronounces Amna, flapping her arms in front of her grandmother.

"Yes, you are, you are a beautiful Amna-butterfly. And I love you lots," says my mother taking her into her arms and kissing her.

"Ammi, why can't the butterfly simply be born as a butterfly?" says Ibrahim turning to me.

"Because life is about change and transformation and growth," I say. "The butterfly may actually be one of our most vivid examples of that."

"I have to turn six, soon and grow up."

"Yes, quite soon in fact, and Amna, too."

"Not two, Ammi, three," says Ibrahim.

"Yes, three, also," I say. "We'll come to that in English soon *inshaa Allah*. Now, where were we? I thought we were going to tackle *ayah* nine and then play review. For some reason I feel we've already traveled to the butterfly exhibit."

"No, we're just daydreaming Khadija. Don't worry you're getting us back on track," responds my mother with a smile.

"Ok, Ammi, I'm ready," says Ibrahim, "especially since I need to finish up so I can start preparing Nani's samosas. You know, I think Uncle Bill might like one too, to break his fast, tomorrow," says Ibrahim.

"Beautiful idea, *baita*," I say. "*Chalyae*?"

"Chalyae," affirms Ibrahim and once again picks up his *mushaf.*

HIFDH TEACHING NOTE

In addition to explaining public holidays, such as Martin Luther King Day, are you also able to integrate some knowledge of other religions? Helping our little learners to understand and navigate the culture in which they live is essential for them to appreciate our interconnectedness. What is good about Good Friday? How can you explain this fact, and link it to the Qur'aan? Furthermore, can you make a connection, as Khadija tries, with Christ's (peace be upon him) persecution and the events that unfold in *Surah Al Buruj,* as described in *ayah* eight. If we start to see the continuum of history and *deen,* these sorts of linkages start to emerge, together with real meaning. Try not to shy away from this significant opportunity to learn and teach.

---

[1] Maryam (Mary) is also revered by Muslims for her piety. "O Mary! Allah hath chosen thee and purified thee—chosen thee above the women of all nations," (Abdullah Yusuf Ali 1989, 3:42, p.138). See also: *The Miraculous Baby* (Khan 2004, pp.2-14).

[2] The Jewish holiday of Passover, commemorating the Israelites freedom from slavery, started on the 19th of April 2011, just one week before the celebration of Easter, and includes rituals of fasting as well, namely abstaining from eating any products with leaven (due to the fact that the Israelites fled in such haste that there was no time to let the bread rise). Passover spans approximately one week.

[3] *Surah Al Ikhlas* (112), (Abdullah Yusuf Ali 1989, p.1714), as first discussed in Chapter 6. "In the name of God, Most Gracious, Most Merciful 1. Say: He is God, the One and Only; 2. God, the Eternal, Absolute; 3. He begetteth not, Nor is He begotten; 4. And there is none comparable to Him."

[4] See for instance, *Surah Al Baqarah* (2:116), (Abdullah Yusuf Ali 1989, p.49); *Surah An'am* (6:101), (p.324); *Surah Al Tawbah* (9:30), (p.446).

[5] Excerpted from *Surah Al Burouj* (85th *surah*), translated as, "And they ill-treated them for no other reason than that they believed in Allah, exalted in Power, Worthy of all Praise," (Abdullah Yusuf Ali 1989, p. 1628).

[6] The Houston Museum of Natural Science was founded in 1909 and is considered among the top museums of natural science in the United States. In 1994, the Museum added the Cockrell Butterfly Center. Apart from their important piece in the plant and animal kingdom (as noted in detail at the Museum's exhibit), butterflies have been depicted in Egyptian hieroglyphs, dating 3500 years, and play an important symbolic role in art worldwide.

34

THE MOTHS

Date/place: late April, Museum of Natural Science, Houston, late-afternoon, mid-week

Cast of Characters: Uncle Bill, Yasmeen, Yaseen, Ibrahim, Khadija, Amna, Nani/ Nasheeta, Beatrice

"Look at that beauty," says Uncle Bill pointing up, at a small wall hanging.

"I don't see anything beautiful; in fact, I think it's quite the opposite," says Yasmeen, recoiling.

"That's because you're a girl," teases Yaseen, "and you get scared easily."

"I'm not scared; I simply said that a plain, brown moth, behind a piece of glass, is not a 'beauty', with all due respect to Uncle Bill. I don't think there is anything wrong with that. Anyway, we came here to see the butterflies, not the moths," says Yasmeen, in a slightly defensive tone.

"Yasmeen," says Uncle Bill, slowly, turning to my niece. "Why do you think butterflies are beautiful?"

"Well, I love their colors. I've actually never seen such brilliant colors before, not on any fashion model, not even on any bird."

"We had designs like that at the World of Birds," says Ibrahim, as though he used to work there.[1]

"What?" says Yasmeen.

"Remember, the World of Birds. We took you there when you visited us. I went with you then, and I probably went fifty times before and afterwards as well."

"*Baita*, maybe not 100," I say.

"Ammi, we went a lot. And I know that I saw beautiful colors, like on those butterfly wings."

"Ok, ok," says Uncle Bill, trying to mediate. "Let's not get into an argument here. And this isn't a competition. Yasmeen, you are absolutely right. The butterflies are beautiful. And Ibrahim, you are also right. Although I've never been to your 'World of Birds', there are many exotic birds with extraordinarily beautiful and diverse patterns. Now, let Yasmeen finish what she was trying to say, and then give me a minute to explain."

"Explain what?" questions Ibrahim.

"Yasmeen, first," responds Uncle Bill, "then, me."

"Ammi, Yasmeen not sharing," says Amna, who up until now has been engrossed at looking at a beetle.

"Yasmeen is sharing her thoughts and her knowledge," I say, "I think it's us who are being a little impatient and not sharing our time. *Sabr, baita, sabr*. Now listen to Yasmeen, please."

"I also think that they are beautiful because they transform. They evolve from almost nothing, and well, that's it," says Yasmeen, folding one arm into another and leaning against one of the exhibits; seeing cockroaches on the other side, she cries out "Ahhh" and jumps away.

"See, I said you get scared easily," responds Yaseen.

"Yaseen, those are cockroaches. They are not moths. And there was no warning sign," says Yasmeen, still shaken by how close she got to the bugs, even with a plastic separation between her and them.

"It's ok," says my mother, who was previously occupied in talking to Beatrice, Uncle Bill's wife, who has also joined us for our afternoon outing, and played a pivotal role by driving half of our brood (as Uncle Bill no longer drives and my mother has yet to learn). My mother reaches out for Yasmeen's hand, and gives her a hug.

"Bug," says Amna. "Big bugs," she then repeats.

"Yes, a lot of them. Ok, now it's my turn, provided Yasmeen is alright, and Yaseen can demonstrate a little compassion," says Uncle Bill smiling at Yaseen. "Not everyone is as brave as you, and has ants for pets," he adds.

"They're not my pets, Uncle Bill; they are simply a hobby.[2] I would have a wolf if my father allowed," responds Yaseen.

"You would have a wolf?" says Ibrahim, wide-eyed.

"Yes, I would," says Yaseen in a very matter-a-fact tone. "Wouldn't you?"

"I don't really know how I would feed it," responds Ibrahim. "And I don't know if it could fit in our apartment. But maybe I could take yours for a walk? I have my Russian pin as protection."

"*Baita*, please, let's listen to Uncle Bill. He was going to explain something to us, important. Remember he's the expert here," I say, trying to steer away from Ibrahim's new found interest in a pet wolf.

"Well, the boys certainly have a lot of adventures and a lot to say. And I personally have very fond memories of *Peter and the Wolf*, which Yaseen is bringing back, but in the last 60 plus years or so, I've learned a little bit about insects. And the reason why I like moths is because they undergo an extraordinary metamorphosis, like butterflies, but then they are mostly

130

nocturnal and they are also camouflaged."

"Cama what?" says Ibrahim.

"Cama flat," says Amna as though the question were posed at her.

"Yes, thank you Amna, good effort. Ibrahim, they are camouflaged, meaning they may hide themselves, for example on the bark of a tree. Just look at this one here; my now, famous 'beauty', thanks to Yasmeen," says Uncle Bill. "You wouldn't be able to see this one if you were walking in the forest; you could easily mistake it for part of the tree."

"That's cool, Uncle Bill. I want to dress up like a moth," says Yaseen.

"And go for a walk with your wolf?" says Beatrice, showing a sense of humor that I had not fully appreciated until now.

"No, I own ants," responds Yaseen as though Beatrice has misunderstood.

"Yes, I realize," says Beatrice, letting the subject go, with grace, and a smile.

"I also want to dress up like a moth," says Ibrahim. "Ammi?"

I also smile, then beckon Ibrahim to come towards me. Meanwhile, our motley crew continues to make its way through the exhibit with Uncle Bill in the lead, gently instructing.

"What, Ammi, can't I dress up like a moth and walk Yaseen's wolf one day?"

"*Bilcul baita*, the world is your oyster, but since we're not having our normal lesson this afternoon, I just wanted to run through one line with Captain Kashif before we embark on our next adventure."

"Here?" Ibrahim asks, looking at me, with surprise, and then around at the exhibit.

"Yup, it will be quick. Do you remember what we read this morning?"

"Really?" Ibrahim says, reluctantly.

"Yes," I nod. "Let's do some review quickly, on this bench cum spaceship, and then get back to Uncle Bill and the gang."

"In *Inshiqaq*?"[3]

"Yes," I say.

"There were a lot of *mudood*, and full-mouth letters and some *qalqalahs*."[4]

"Ok, and…" I say, looking for something more.

"No butterflies," responds Ibrahim, being evasive.

"Correct, no butterflies," I respond. "But there was that amazing verse about 'going from stage to stage'; do you remember that one?"

"Full-mouth letters and some *qalqalahs*."

"Yes, you already said that. Come let Lieutenant Laila give you the first word:

La-tarka…"

"La-tarkabunna tabaqan 'an-tabaq," says Ibrahim, with confidence, finishing the *ayah.*[5]

"That's enough, great," I respond.

"But Ammi, it's only one *ayah*, don't we need to do more?"

"No. I said it was only going to be one line this afternoon. I just wanted to remind you of it quickly, here, with all these amazing butterflies and moths, in our midst," I say.

"Going through meta… mor… pho… sis," says Ibrahim, smiling, as though he's really grasped the lesson.

"Jee haan," I say. "Now how about we get back to the group and the butterflies?"

"And the moths, Ammi," says Ibrahim pulling me up from our bench. "And you know what I might even have a game for you before we rejoin the pack. Name the *ayah* that reminds you of that," he opens the doors to the butterfly sanctuary and spins around finally pointing at the waterfall.

I am speechless, for a moment. I didn't expect the sanctuary to be so beautiful, and I didn't expect Ibrahim to ask me this sort of question. *"Baita*, I don't know what exactly you're looking for," I say.

"An *ayah* about water, flowing, under gardens," says Ibrahim, in his teaching mode.

"I can think of a couple," I say, "that is, from the *surahs* we learned together so far."

"So give me a brother-sister pair, or a mother-son pair, like Hafidha Rabia always says," says Ibrahim.

"Well, that's a nice clue. *Surah Al Buruj* and *Surah Al Bayyinah*, the *ayaat* about there being rivers under which water will flow," I respond.

"Good, but, how about the actual *ayaat*, and the difference between the two of them, and *inshaa Allah* you'll get a point for that one." There is a bench by the entrance to the sanctuary and Ibrahim sits down on it, taking the lead in our unexpectedly extended lesson. Meanwhile, I catch a glimpse of my mother and Beatrice, Amna, Yaseen, Yasmeen and Uncle Bill up ahead. My mother waves to us.

"Just a minute," I call out to my mother, "we're coming."

"After I hear those *ayaat*," says Ibrahim, swinging his legs on the bench and looking down at his watch.

"Ok, I need to think, give me a minute. I'm not sure I want to recite the whole *surah* out loud here, at the exhibit, so yes, just give me a minute to sort through the verses, in my head," I say, working my way down in *Surah Al Bayyinah* first.

"Two minutes," says Ibrahim.

"Are you timing me?" I say, somewhat astounded by Ibrahim's assertion.

"Come on, you know this, Ammi. You could do it, in 30 seconds, if you weren't distracted by all these colorful designs."

"Ok, *Bismillahir Rahmanir Raheem, Jaza'uhum 'inda Rabbinhim Jannatu,*" I say starting in with *ayah* eight of *Surah Al Bayyinah.* Ibrahim starts to nod his head, in encouragement.[6]

HIFDH TEACHING NOTE

A moth's camouflage is powerful, as is the transformative and beautiful nature of a butterfly. In this scene, we accompany the children to the Museum of Natural Science, along with Uncle Bill and Aunt Beatrice. To the extent possible, let science be a playground for your children. Teach them the scientific method, and let them engage in (supervised) experiments. Most importantly, try to instill in them the importance of observation. Are they able to spot a butterfly? A moth? What shades of colors do they see? How many different shades? The Qur'aan testifies to the extraordinary bounty of creation, and to the infinitely diverse patterns that exist. Observation helps to make manifest our faith as we stand in awe and wonderment at HisSWT creation, including as mentioned in *Surah Al Inshiqaq,* the 'ruddy glow of Sunset' (*ayah* 16). What have you observed today with your children? And what have you observed in your *surahs* that testifies to the majesty of creation? Make it fun (and interesting), and use binoculars.

---

[1] The World of Birds, in Houtbay, South Africa, is among the largest bird parks in Africa and among the few large bird parks worldwide, with approximately 3,000 birds, as of 2011.

[2] See *Amr and the Ants* (El-Magazy 2000) for insights into keeping ants as pets. See *Surah Al Naml* (27th *surah*) for an account of "men pitted against a humble ant," (Abdullah Yusuf Ali 1989, p.937). See *The Ants* (Holldobler 1990) for an extensive treatment of these extraordinary creatures.

[3] *Surah Inshiqaq* is the 84th *surah* in the Qur'aan and translated as 'The Rendering Asunder' (Abdullah Yusuf Ali 1989, p.1622).

[4] *Mudood* mentioned previously in Chapter 16, and as defined in the glossary are as follows: Arabic grammar terminology referring to the elongation of a letter. There are seven full mouth letters: خ، ص، ض، ط، ظ، غ، ق، which are always pronounced with a full mouth. *Qalqalah* refers to an echoing sound made on any of the five letters (د، ج، ب، ط، ق) when there is a *sakiin* (stop). See Tasheelut Tajweed for a more complete discussion of *tajweed* (Curriculum Development Board/Kwa-Zulu Natal Taalimi Board 2006).

[5] Excerpted from Abdullah Yusuf Ali (1989, p.1624), 19th *ayah* of *Surah Al Inshiqaq,* translated as: "Ye shall surely travel from stage to stage."

[6] The two *ayaat* (from *surahs* up to *Inshiqaq*) that both mention water flowing in gardens, are *Surah Al Bayyinah* (98:8): "Their reward is with Allah; Gardens of Eternity, beneath which rivers flow; they will dwell therein for ever; Allah well pleased with them, and they with Him… " and *Surah Al Buruj* (85:11): "For those who believe and do righteous deeds, will be Gardens beneath which Rivers flow: that is the great Salvation, (the fulfilment of all desires)," (Abdullah Yusuf Ali 1989, pp.1679 and 1628). The transliteration included above is excerpted from *Tajweed Qur'an* (2007, p. 22).

35

WATER, AGAIN

Date/place: early May, 2011, Houston, Ibrahim and Amna's kitchen, mid-afternoon, mid-week

Cast of characters: Amna, Khadija, Ibrahim

"I'm thirsty."

"Yes, *baita*, just a minute. I want to put this away," I say, pointing at my world map.

"Ammi, I'm thirsty," repeats Amna, sounding increasingly desperate.

"*Baita*, I'm coming, now, now."

"Like in South Africa," says Ibrahim, to both Amna and me. "Do you remember?"

"I'll remember as soon as I get Amna a glass of…"

"*Thunda pani*," shouts Amna.

"It's coming, *baita*," I shout back, abandoning my clean-up efforts and racing to the kitchen sink before Amna moves into temper tantrum mode.

"Wow, that was fast, Ammi, not like the 'now-now' that I remember," says Ibrahim, seemingly impressed.

"*Bohaut shukria baita*," I say, handing Amna her glass of water. "I do, however, wish that I had more of a Montessori set-up here, and the two of you could simply pour yourselves a glass of water when you desire, but I am always bracing for the next spill and so…"

"I help myself," says Ibrahim.

"Yes, and you're also well versed in opening and closing the refrigerator door, but I don't feel ready for Amna," I say.

"Ammi, she's a lot more grown up than you think. I've always thought that," Ibrahim says.

"Always?" says Amna.

"Always?" I repeat.

"Almost always," says Ibrahim, "but Ammi, I think you should stop running around and serving water and get back to work. You are presenting on Friday."

"On Friday?" questions Amna.

"Yes, Friday, before *Jumu'ah*," says Ibrahim.

"*Baita*, we still have time, but thanks for the encouragement. I'm actually mostly done. I just want to cut out some labels for you all to stick on the map," I say.

"What kind of labels?"

"Water war labels," I respond.

"What?" says Ibrahim.

"Matter wars," says Amna, making her hand into a gun and pretending to shoot it. "Pow, pow," she says, for the full effect.

"Amna, stop it," says Ibrahim, brushing Amna's hand away from his face. "Ammi, what did you say?"

"Not 'matter', Amna, water war labels," I repeat.

"What are those?" Ibrahim asks. Meanwhile, Amna keeps up her game, although now she's calling out 'Spiderman' beyond Ibrahim's reach so he can't swat her.

"I want to put labels on this map to demonstrate the different areas around the world where there has been conflict due to water," I say.

"Well, we've never had one," asserts Ibrahim.

"*Baita*, we have. Just look here; for almost a decade, between the 1870s and 1881 there were disputes about water rights in New Mexico, which borders Texas. And there was violence. Then look here, in South Africa, just seven years ago, there were violent uprisings due to lack of clean water and sanitation. Again, there was violence, and considerable damage. Across India and Pakistan, which you know well, there have been many conflicts, including one in 2001 in Karachi," I say, pointing intermittently to my map.[1]

"But why did people fight?"

"Because we need water to survive. It's essential. Without clean water, we will die," I respond.

"Is that why you work on water?" asks Ibrahim.

"What do you mean?" I say.

"I mean, why, before you started doing this *hifdh* work, you worked on water, because it's so important," says Ibrahim.

"Well, there are many very important things in this world, *baita*, but, yes, water is essential, and I was motivated by the fact that with some knowledge and strong policies and resources, people can live peaceful, productive lives, and water issues may be resolved."

"Did Ms Suzy ask you to teach us that on Friday?"

"In part. I think she mainly wanted me to come in for Earth Day and give you some conservation tips," I say.[2]

"Earth Day," Amna repeats with a big voice, opening her mouth wide, finally off her Spiderman tangent.

"Yes, Earth Day," I say.

"Ammi, wasn't that two weeks ago?" asks Ibrahim.

"Officially, yes, it was, but there has also been considerable focus throughout the month of April and even into May."

"And every day is Earth Day, right? Just like you taught us, every day is Mother's Day," says Ibrahim.[3]

"Oh I see, are you listening now?"

"Trying," says Ibrahim, then continuing he adds, "Ammi, do you really think that's right, to talk about war?"

"Yes, I do, because I think that you and John Henry and your other friends at school understand right and wrong and fighting and peace as well, if not better, than the rest of us."

"You may be right," says Ibrahim.

"Now, since I'm finishing up my work, how about we try out *Surah Al*…"

"Ammi, I told you earlier, I got it. You don't need to quiz me on it. I actually got the first packet," says Ibrahim.

"All the way up to *ayah* six? How did that happen?" I ask.

"I think the packets are helping: that, and actually having the *ayaat* on your note cards; somehow the *surahs* don't seem so long anymore when I dissect them and make them into smaller bundles," Ibrahim says.

"Bunnies," says Amna, nodding as though she's ready to lead the conversation. "I like bunnies a lot, ribbit."

"Amna, that's a frog noise."

"No, Ibrahim, I actually think she was trying to say 'rabbit', we just didn't understand her," I say. "And, now, I want to hear your *ayaat*, because if you have them, then I'm going to be really, really impressed."

"I do have them, Ammi, just listen," and Ibrahim starts in with the first *ayah*, followed by the second and third. On the third *ayah*, he stops.[4]

"Ammi is it a *geem* or a *kha*?" he then asks.[5]

"Baita, I need to check," I say, turning to the bookshelf in the living room, taking up a *mushaf* and leafing through to the line in question. "It's a *kha*."

"Rabbit," he then responds, with a twinkle in his eye.

"Well, yes," I say, smiling. "Ok, you said you could get all the way to *ayah* six *inshaa Allah*."

"Ammi, I can get there and then I can even go beyond," Ibrahim says with confidence, as though he is about to compete in a running race.

"*Masha'Allah*. You know, I just thought up something else we could do once you're finished with your recitation," I say.

"What?" says Ibrahim.

"We could identify all the water *ayaat* to help us in our review today," I respond.

"You mean in all the *ayaat* up until *Surah Al Mutaffifin*?" says Ibrahim, sounding exhausted, and abandoning his earlier enthusiasm.

"I thought it would be easy and fun; after all, you already quizzed me on those two in *Surah Al Buruj* and *Surah Al Bayyinah* from last week."

"Do those count?" Ibrahim asks.

"Sure, why not. How about we finish up the beginning of *Mutaffifin* and then see what we can find, looking back into our *mushafs* and our translations?"

"Before our swim?"

"Yes, *baita*, for just 30 minutes, before our swim, nothing less, nothing more," I respond.

"Ready," he then says.

"Me too," says Amna, then, "ribbit, ribbit. I'm a frog," and she jumps in front of me, as though she's one step ahead, and already ready for splashing in the pool.

HIFDH TEACHING NOTE

What do we do when the *surahs* get longer? First the *surahs* did not get longer over night. This little team has been building its stamina for the past many months, and slowly working up to longer *surahs*. By making the lessons fun, Khadija is also helping to keep the sheer length from seeming overwhelming. Abdurrahman's pep talks help, as does the companionship of cousin Naeem, among others. In this scene, Ibrahim also makes mention of the 'packets' and 'bundles' which are helping him to digest *Surah Al Mutaffifin*, with which Khadija was grappling, as we heard previously (in Chapter 27). Although there are some 'free *ayah*', *Mutaffifin* poses a challenge for many learners due to the similarity in *ayaat*, coupled with the length. Breaking it up into discrete sections (or as Ibrahim has termed it 'packets') has the potential to make it more palatable. He also makes mention of keeping the different packets on different note cards and carrying them with him, another potential method for overcoming the length. Consider listening to and reading the *surah* with your children (including the translation). Ask them where they see/hear the different sections and where it would be most intuitive to demarcate parts. You may have suggestions, but it is important for it to make sense to the children. Try to maintain the same sections throughout your lesson and encourage them, to the extent possible, to incorporate the *surah* in their *salah* using this packet/section approach. First, for instance, encourage them to use just one section of the *surah* in the first *rak'ah*, then the second in the second *rak'ah* and so on, until through their *fard, sunnah* and *nafl* prayers they have actually completed the *surah*. As endurance and memory build, they will be able to tackle two sections in the first *rak'ah* and *inshaa Allah* eventually the whole *surah*. Practice, practice, practice, and take baby steps.

---

[1] See Pacific Institute (2010), Water Conflict Chronology Map.

[2] "Each North American uses two and a half times more renewable fresh water than the world average—and could unleash a proportionately prodigious new supply to productive uses simply by adopting readily available, high efficiency practices and technologies," (Solomon 2010, p.448). The Zaky series provides an instructive list of (general environmental conservation) tips in 'The Earth Has a Fever,' especially geared toward Muslim children (One 4 Kids Productions 2010).

[3] The South African musician Zain Bhikha has helped to spread the *sunnah* of respecting one's parents, especially one's mother, in the children's *nasheed* (religious song): 'Your Mother,' (from the album, 'I Look I See', Yusuf Islam, 2006).

[4] *Surah Al Mutaffifin*, translated as the 'Dealers in Fraud', is the 83rd *surah* in the Qur'aan. The *surah* "condemns all fraud—in daily dealings, as well as and especially in matters of Religion and higher spiritual Life." (Abdullah Yusuf Ali 1989, p.1615).

[5] See *The Talking Book* (published by Bayyinah Institute) for the pronunciation of all Arabic letters, http://bayyinah.com/tajweed_book/main.html; http://understandquran.com also provides basic as well as sophisticated grammar and recitation instruction.

36

Super Men and Women

Date/place: mid-May, 2011, Houston, Ibrahim and Amna's school, morning

Cast of characters: Ms Suzy, Khadija, Ibrahim, Amna, John Henry and other students

"The Earth Goes Around The Sun

The Earth Goes Around The Sun

12 months, 52 weeks, 365 days in a year

And Ibrahim turns one…"

The chorus goes on.[1] I sit next to Ibrahim and John Henry, on the floor, while Amna is on my lap and a little boy named Salvador is seated on my other side.[2] Ibrahim rises and sits, circumambulating the candle, holding a small globe. The scene is reminiscent of Cape Town, where Ibrahim also attended a half-day Montessori program, and the associated birthday celebrations. I am amazed how certain lessons and rituals transcend such broad borders.

"And how did you feel?" asks Ms Suzy, who is seated on the other side of Salvador.

"What?" I say, lost in thought.

"What did you feel, when he turned three?"

"Three? Oh yes, well, it's always been a lot of work, but also a lot of fun. When Ibrahim was three, he learned how to ride a bike, and shortly thereafter Amna arrived and then, towards the end of the year, he started learning the alphabet."

"In Arabic, not English," says Ibrahim, who is familiar with his own history. "I started the English one a little before that," he adds.

"Yes, of course," says Ms Suzy, who has grown increasingly accustomed to our multi-lingual-cultural household, since the first day we met her, seven months ago.

After another 10 minutes of sharing photos and circumambulating, we have finally arrived at six.

"Khadija, you've done well," says Ms Suzy.

"Thank you," I say, not knowing whether she is referring to the synopsis of our lives, or as a parent in general, or in simply bearing with the outbursts of laughter and chatter with the class.

"But, it's not over, right, boys and girls? Now, Ms Khadija is going to talk to us about water," says Ms Suzy, looking at the children and nodding her head. "And we're going to show Ms Khadija that we are excellent listeners, now, one, two, three, let's begin."

"Thank you, again," I respond. I spoke to Ibrahim's class in Cape Town, but never on the subject of water. Looking out at the children, I realize that I am relatively prepared to speak about water, but not to three, four, five and now six year olds. Amna, I might add, is in the two year old, half-day, Montessori class, but has a 'pass' to sit in with the elders today, and yet, I also don't think I'm prepared to speak to her on the subject.

"Ok, let's begin," I say. There is an awkward pause, for a minute. I see John Henry looking at Ibrahim, perhaps wondering why I haven't said anything yet.

"Right, now, who drank water this morning?" I ask. One child raises her hand.

"Anyone else?"

"Not me, I had orange juice," says a little boy, whose name I do not know.

"Ok, well, do you know if it was from concentrate?" I ask.

"What?" the boy responds.

"Did your parents add water to the juice?"

"I don't know. Aren't you supposed to talk about water, not orange juice?" says the boy. Another awkward pause follows.

Ms Suzy turns to me, addressing me in an interview style, "Khadija, tell me, you know a lot about water, and, from what I've heard, you've worked on water projects all around the world. Now, do you want to show us the map you prepared?"

"Yes, sure, I made a map," I say.

"Matter wars," volunteers Amna. I feel as though I am losing more ground and may soon be dismissed for poor performance.

"No, not 'matter wars' Amna," says Ibrahim, then continuing, "water wars. Remember Ammi explained it to us earlier. People fight over water."

"Wow, that's cool," says the boy who drank orange juice earlier this morning.

"Not so cool," responds Ibrahim. "Some people died."

"I'd like to have a water war. I would bring all my water guns," says John Henry.

"Boys and girls, please, Ms Khadija is here to talk to us and not vice versa. We are here to listen and learn, and at the end, we can each ask a question, but please let's turn our attention to Ms Khadija," says Ms Suzy, who is still trying to facilitate my teaching.

"Thank you. You're right John Henry, a water war with a plastic water gun, in your backyard or at the park down the street would be fun, in the summer, when you're hot and playing with your friends. However, it would not be much fun if there were real guns and the consequences were life and death," I say. The children, including those who were chatting, all fall silent.

"Imagine if you turned on the tap, and there was no water to drink. Imagine if you tried to take a shower, and you didn't have enough water to clean yourself. Or imagine if you didn't have any water pipe running to your house and you had to walk to a village center and wait in line, for the water," I say.

"What?" says a little girl, wearing a pink sundress seated across from me in the circle.

"This is the reality of many people. Do you know that approximately 900 million people living in the world today do not have access to clean, drinking water; that's almost 15 percent. And almost 40 percent don't have access to adequate sanitation," I say, holding up a pie chart that Ibrahim, Amna and I decorated on the back of one of our old cereal boxes.[3]

"Then how do they live?" says the girl with the pink sundress. I see Ms Suzy initially shushing the girl but then deciding to let the conversation flow.

"They live on the edge. It is precarious," I say.

"What does that mean?" says the boy who drank orange juice.

"Their life is difficult, extremely difficult," I respond.

"I'm getting scared," says the girl with the pink sundress.

"I'm scared," mimics Amna.

"Ms Khadija, why don't we talk a little about some of those water conservation tips you mentioned to me earlier, like turning off the tap when you're brushing your teeth?" says Ms Suzy, assessing that this may be too much for her students. "Maybe we can return to your map, later," she then adds.

I look down at my map, which I spent more than a day preparing, and can't help feeling a bit defeated. I haven't been able to communicate what I thought was truly important about water, and now I'm being asked to change the subject, prematurely. I am somewhat consoled by Ibrahim and Amna, who seem unphased by the course of the conversation. In the back of my head, I also cannot help but hear Ibrahim's voice, from earlier this morning, reciting *Surah Al Infitar*: "*Wa 'inna 'alaykum laha-fizeen,*"[4] as well as recall his glee in finding another word stemming from the root ha-fa-dha.[5] Taking a deep breath, I look at the girl seated across from me.

"Sorry, what is your name?" I ask the girl with the pink sundress.

"Hannah," she replies.

"Ok, Hannah, is Superman scary?" I ask her.

"No, he's not scary, but the people he fights against are very scary," Hannah clarifies.

"Very, very scary," repeats Amna, again.

"Well, I agree with you, and not having sufficient water can be extremely scary; and these issues are actually part of our world, not Superman's world."

"What?" says Salvador.

"Superman is make-believe, right? It's a character we read in a book or see on a television, but people having insufficient water is actually a fact of life that is happening here and now, in our world," I respond, trying to help the children understand the urgency of the situation.

"Really?" says Hannah.

"You may not see it, but it is happening. And it is linked to you turning off the tap when you brush your teeth," I say.

"How?" asks John Henry.

I stop for a moment, hearing the silence in the room. "You have to go home and think about it, and then, next week, if Ms Suzy agrees, I will come back and hear you tell me how and why, and hopefully pave the way for you becoming super men and women?" I say more to Ms Suzy than any of the children.

"Well, that's quite a tall order, but we'll do our best," says Ms Suzy, then she adds, "Khadija, I really want to thank you for coming in this morning. It's not always easy to speak to young children, so many of them, in the language that they understand, but you've done well. So we'll see you again, next week?"

"Yes," I say, nodding and getting up.

"And if possible, we'd like to hold on to the map until then," says Ms Suzy.

"It is yours," I respond, before hugging my two little superheroes.

HIFDH TEACHING NOTE

Khadija has gone off on a limb, of sorts. She's taken her development economics to the children's school and is trying to engage the class (of 3 to 5-year-olds) in thinking about water wars and conservation. The *surah* on which the family is working, namely *Infitar*, does not feature prominently in this episode, but it is still present, in the background. The memory of Ibrahim's voice from the morning lesson steadies Khadija and the beauty of the *ayah* "But verily over you (are appointed angels) to protect you," (82:10). However 'background' this may seem, this is actually *hifdh* in action, namely *ayah* coming to our aid and helping us to make meaning and peace of our lives. Sometimes the miracles are audible and visible and sometimes they are simply for the sight and sound of one aspiring *hafidha*. May you be blessed with many such miracles *inshaa Allah*.

---

[1] These verses and/or a slight variation are used in the celebration of life activity, typical in many Montessori classrooms worldwide, to recognize a child's birthday. A candle is lit to signify the sun, and then the child holds a small globe and moves around the candle, representing the completion of one year. At the end of each rotation, the parent/guardian is invited to recount an anecdote from that year, including how s/he felt.

[2] Salvador means 'savior' in Spanish and is a common boy's name. 'San Salvador', the capital, of El Salvador (the Savior), may be translated as the 'Holy Savior'. Approximately 1.5 million El Salvadorians presently live in the United States, with the migration prompted largely by the civil war spanning 1979 to 1992 (however migration has continued in recent years due to persistent poverty in the country as well as crime).

[3] See Chapter 15, footnote 2.

[4] *Ayah* 10, excerpted from *Surah Al Infiitar* (82nd *surah* in the Qur'aan), translated as "The Cleaving Asunder." The *ayah* is translated as "But verily over you (are appointed angels) to protect you," (Abdullah Yusuf Ali 1989, p.1613).

[5] Most Arabic words are derived from three letter roots; the root 'ha-fa-dha' (ح ف ظ) means to protect/preserve; as previously mentioned (see Chapter 32, footnote 1), a '*hafidh al Qur'aan*' is one who protects/preserves the words and message of the Qur'aan by learning it by heart.

37

A LITTLE ORANGE SURPRISE

Cast of characters: Amna, Nonna, Ibrahim, Khadija

Date/place: Late May, Houston, Ibrahim and Amna's living room, mid-afternoon

"One more."

"One more what?" asks Nonna, who is seated between the two children.

"One more, tiny," responds Amna.

"One more, tiny what?" Nonna repeats.

"Book," says Amna, picking up *The Perfect Orange*.[1]

"Amna, I think you might be scared of the hyena in that one," cautions Ibrahim.

"Not scared," asserts Amna, flipping through the book to her favorite page, where the little girl presents her orange to the king. "I eat orange," she then adds, jumping down from the couch and running over to the fruit bowl in the kitchen, where I am working and quietly enjoying watching the children with Abdurrahman's mother. She then picks up a clementine and returns to Nonna. "For you," she says smiling, and extending her hand with the small citrus, as though she rehearsed the scene.[2]

"*Grazie, grazie*," says Nonna, and gives Amna a big kiss.

"What about me?" asks Ibrahim.

"Oh, *bambino*, you know how much I love you, but your sister just did a very special act of kindness," responds Nonna.

"And me?" says Ibrahim, seemingly jealous of Amna's attention.

"And you also do such acts all through the day, but you're a big boy now. Can you believe you're six now?" Ibrahim nods his head at his grandmother. "And so," she says continuing, "I don't always reward you immediately like I do with Amna."

"You make me wait for a hug and a kiss?" Ibrahim inquires.

"No, those are always in abundance; in fact here's one right now," says Nonna, taking him up in her arms.

"That's too tight," says Ibrahim.

"My turn," says Amna, pushing against her brother, to get inside Nonna's embrace.

"Don't worry there's enough for everyone," replies Nonna, putting her arms around both children.

After a minute, Ibrahim touches his grandmother's cheek gently and asks, "Nonna, when are you going to give me my present?"

"Well, that's rather forward," says Nonna, "but since you asked, I was thinking, that we might read one more story and then…"

"Then, I can open it?" says Ibrahim eagerly.

"Slowly, yes," says Nonna, "but you're not allowed to tear the wrapping paper; I want to reuse it for Amna," she says smiling.

"What?" says Ibrahim.

"I'm just joking. It's your gift and you can open it any way you wish, but yes, let's finish one more story, first, and then I'll enjoy my clementine and you can enjoy your gift."

"And me?" says Amna, a bit left out.

"Well, you'll help me eat my little orange and then, we might just have to find another treat, ok?" Amna nods her head in agreement. Meanwhile, I wonder what my mother-in-law has planned, but continue to observe from the sidelines.

"Nonna, may I choose the next one?" asks Ibrahim.

"Absolutely," she replies.

"You know Ammi and Papa gave me this one last night; they said I could read it, all by myself, and that it might help me with *ayah* five."

"What's *ayah* five?" asks Nonna.

"There are wild animals in *ayah* five," responds Ibrahim.

"What?" repeats Nonna, not yet following.

"Sorry, it's been a while since I recited to you. I actually think I haven't recited since…" Ibrahim pauses and closes his eyes as though he is trying to read something in his memory. "…since, February, and *Surah Al Bayyinah*," he says slowly. "We're up to *Surah At Takweer*, now, and this week we've been working through the beginning."[3]

"And so your devoted parents bought you a book to help you with another book?" says Nonna, starting to put the pieces together.

"Well, it's Qur'aan Nonna, it's not just a book. It's a very big, holy book, and we read it all the time," responds Ibrahim.

"Yes, *bambino*, I'm starting to understand that, but what I don't understand is how *Where the Wild Things Are* fits in exactly," says my mother-in-law, looking

145

more at me than at either child.[4]

"Nonna, let's just start reading and then I'm sure we'll figure it out," says Ibrahim with enthusiasm. He turns the first page and starts to read, slowly.

"I'm scared," says Amna, looking in at the pictures.

"It's ok, *baita*," I say, beckoning for her to join me in the kitchen and give her grandmother and brother a little time together.

"A roy..al… rumpus," says Ibrahim nearing the middle of the book. "What's that?"

"Why don't you look at the pictures," suggests Nonna.

"Oh, yeah, not such a tongue twister then," says Ibrahim, in a more reflective mode. Then he adds, "So where's *ayah* five, Ammi? I don't get it. Do I have to finish the whole book?"

"Not exactly. It was actually your father's idea, the book, that is. He remembers it from when he was a kid. I never read it before last week. He said that it might help you with *ayah* five, seeing all the wild animals," I say.

"You're right Khadija. Geo and Nico loved this growing up. Our copy was tattered. I wonder if I still have it?" says my mother-in-law.

"You mean Papa read this?" says Ibrahim, increasingly interested.

"Yes, he did, many, many times."

"Many times," repeats Amna. "Orange?" she then asks.

"Almost," responds Nonna. "The investigative journalist in your grandmother would like to get to the bottom of this *ayah* five story first."

"Carmen, I think we should bring Abdurrahman into the discussion. Again, it was his idea, not mine. He simply thought that it would help Ibrahim visualize the wild beasts referenced in the *surah*," I say.

"But Ammi, in *ayah* five the beasts come to human houses," says Ibrahim, recalling our lesson from last night.

"Well in *Where the Wild Things Are* the wild beasts play with Max and they make him king," says Nonna, perhaps clarifying more than we could have on our own. "I think I know where my son might be going with this one," she then concludes.

"Maybe Papa could finish the story tonight," offers Ibrahim.

"I think that's a very good idea," I say.

"So, is it time for my gift, Nonna?" Ibrahim then asks, taking up her hand in his.

"Well, you've been a patient *bambino*, so yes, it's time."

Ibrahim disappears for a minute into the guest room where my mother-in-law has been staying as of two days. As is customary, she has come to visit us to celebrate Ibrahim's birthday. She and I agreed to spread out her gifts over a couple of days. This is the last one and allegedly the most important.

"Nonna, did you really?" says Ibrahim, still from inside her room. He knew exactly where the last gift was and had agreed to our plan of pacing them over two days.

My mother-in-law simply nods her head, again, looking more at me.

"Ammi, you're not going to believe this? Nonna gave me a…" and Ibrahim walks out of Nonna's room, holding an archery set above his head. "Look at this," he says and puts it on my lap.

"Wow, awe… some," responds Amna, starting to pick up the bow.

"Whoa, Amna," I respond, not quite knowing what to do with either the bow or arrow, but eager to keep it from her grasp. I was actually planning to wait a little longer to give Ibrahim any real archery gear, considering he had been playing make-believe Robin Hood so well for the past many months, but my mother-in-law obviously thought otherwise.

"*Grazie*," I say slowly and somewhat formally, turning to Nonna, then add, "Ibrahim, please go thank your grandmother for her very generous gift."

"Thank you, thank you, thank you, thank you," says Ibrahim, running to Nonna and giving her a bear hug. "You made my day; you made my year; you made my life!" His excitement is boundless.

Nonna takes him up in her arms and simultaneously smiles at me. "It's ok Khadija; we'll all be careful. And Ibrahim is only going to use it in the park, right Ibrahim?"

"I… I guess so, unless of course, there are any wild animals in the house, Ammi," he says, looking at me and smiling. "Do you remember Halloween here in Texas?"

"Yes, *baita*, I do; you, in the form of Salahuddin dress-up, defended me from wild beasts for over a month," I say. "I am very grateful to you for this, and I am also grateful to your grandmother for her generosity and her stories and… her imagination. She's very good at playing along," I say, starting to appreciate Ibrahim's joy and Nonna's intuition.

"Can we go to the park tonight?" asks Ibrahim.

"We might just have to make a plan," I say.

"I could call Papa now and tell him to meet us there. We could have a picnic and archery and then finish *Where the Wild Things Are* and the other one we got from the library," says Ibrahim.

"Oh, I want to finish *The Three Questions* now," says Nonna, picking up the library book.

"My orange," says Amna, remembering a forgotten promise.

"Oh Amna dear, I'm so sorry," responds Nonna. "You're right; it is your turn now, so why don't you come here and help me peel this orange, and I will read you one last book."

"I like this one a lot," says Amna, picking up *The Three Questions* and turning to the second to last page with the red kite, which has caught her attention since we found the book at the library last week.

"Well, since it's also your day, I'll read that to you," and Nonna starts in: "…there is only one important time, and that time is now. The most important one is always the one you are with. And the most important thing is to do good for the one who is standing at your side," Nonna stops to embrace both children, as though on cue.[5]

HIFDH TEACHING NOTE

Nonna connects the dots. She is neither *maulvi sahib*, nor even Muslim, but she is a grandmother, the mother of Abdurrahman and she knows, among many things, *Where the Wild Things Are*. In her own, respectful way, she communicates what the absent Abdurrahman could not, namely how *ayah* five of *Surah At Takweer* may be connected to this short book by Maurice Sendak. These insights are helpful as they make the message of the Qur'aan more tangible for her ever-exploratory and questioning grandson and they also help connect that message to Nonna's own experience. On many levels, *dawah* is at work, through lived experience, abundant hugs and the openness to hear and appreciate different stories. How are you demonstrating *dawah* with your little ones? What form does it take? What are the many stories you are telling and hearing to give them an all embracing world view, and one rooted in Qur'aan and compassion?

---

[1] *The Perfect Orange: A Tale from Ethiopia* (Araujo 1994).

[2] Londt in *How to Memorize the Holy Qur'an* makes explicit mention of citrus (p.49) in aiding memorization. The author also recommends a host of different foods, however, proper hydration is critical as well.

[3] *Surah Al Takweer*, the 81st *surah* in the Qur'aan, is translated as 'The Folding Up.' *Ayah* five as referenced above is translated as follows: "When the wild beasts are herded together (in human habitations)," (Abdullah Yusuf Ali 1989, p.1606). As mentioned in Chapters 20 and 21, *Surah Al Bayyinah* is the 98th *surah* in the Qur'aan. Ibrahim has largely followed the pattern of completing one *surah* per week, together with daily review of back *surahs*; there is, however, a slight change as the *surahs* lengthen towards the end of *Juz Amma*, however, the pace is maintained more or less as his character's own skills develop.

[4] *Where the Wild Things Are* (Sendak 1963).

[5] *The Three Questions*: Based on a story by Leo Tolstoy (Muth 2002).

38

PIECES

Date/place: early June, Houston, Ibrahim and Amna's living room, Friday evening, dinner time, just after *magreb*

Cast of characters: Nani/Nasheeta, Nonna, Amna, Ibrahim, Khadija, Abdurrahman

"Wonderful news."

"What?" says Nonna, looking over at my mother, who has, after greeting us, just sat down on the couch to take off her shoes.

"Naeem is going to have a baby sister," says my mother responding, but directing her words more to Ibrahim and Amna.

"What?" says Amna. "A big brother?"

"No," says Ibrahim. "She said, 'a baby sister'." Then turning to his Nani, he continues, "Is it true? Will Naeem really get an Amna? And may we play with her?"

"Ibrahim, Naeem lives in Doha," says Nonna, reminding her grandson of the geography.

"Yes, that's true," says my mother, "but of course when you go to visit him or when he comes to see you or when you meet in the middle, then…"

"I play with baby brother," says Amna, finishing off her sentence.

"Baby sister," corrects Ibrahim again.

"Well, logistically challenging play-dates aside, that is truly wonderful news," says Nonna.

"Absolutely," both Abdurrahman and I second, looking at each other and then the children.

"Yes, yes, *alhumdulilah*," says my mother. Approaching Nonna, she adds, "Hamza and Mary called me just before Abdullah dropped me this evening; you know they have been considering adoption for so long, but Mary couldn't see how to make all the pieces work."

"I can't either," says Ibrahim.

"I can't neither," mimics Amna.

"Oh, of course you can, *baita*," I say, approaching both children, and sitting down next to them. "Just look here, you've already completed almost the whole frame."

"What frame?" asks Ibrahim.

"She means all the outside pieces," offers Abdurrahman, who has also joined me on the floor.

"Papa, that's easy for you to say; you're 35 years older than me," responds Ibrahim, "and you don't have an Amna playing alongside you."

"Come on, *bambino*, you're almost done; now, here's what Geo and I would do," he says, patting Ibrahim affectionately on the back and picking up the puzzle top cover, which reveals a striking picture of the solar system, and which I took out to help us review *Surah At Takweer*, during our afternoon lesson.[1]

"I know, I know," says Ibrahim. "All I have to do is look at the box top, and pretend I really am an astronaut, and then I have the key."

"You got it," says Abdurrahman.

"I got it," says Amna, snatching the box top and racing off toward our bedroom.

"Amna, please," I call out.

"It's mine," she retorts, not turning around.

"Amna, that's not fair; I'm going to give you to Naeem too, if you don't give it back," says Ibrahim, in a way that shows this is not the first time today that Amna has done something to provoke him.

"Amna, please now," says Abdurrahman. "Come help us finish; we know you can do it."

"No," says Amna, defiantly, from the end of the hall.

"Well, then your Nonna, might just have to find something for you in her room," says Nonna, just at the right time.

"For me?" says Amna, sensing she might get something better than the puzzle box top.

"Yes, you, now, come, listen to your father, and your mother and your brother and come into my room and let's first find *Brava Strega Nona* and then that old dinosaur you were playing with earlier tonight."[2]

"Dinosaur?" says Amna, wide eyed.

"Yes, dinosaur; I think I have Daisy the dinosaur packed in somewhere here."

"In the bottom drawer," says Amna, as if solving her own puzzle. She drops the box top at the end of the hall and races into Nonna's room.

"I got it," says Ibrahim, running over to the discarded box top, as though it really holds the answer to his puzzle.

150

"Teamwork," says my mother, "well done, parents and grandmother number one."

"I think we share that spot, Nani," says Nonna, calling out from her bedroom, where Amna is finally distracted.

Settling down next to Ibrahim, my mother then asks. "Naeem has big news, but so do you, don't you?"

Abdurrahman shoots me a gaze, wondering where my mother might be going with her question.

"I don't know. What were you thinking of?" asks Ibrahim.

"Something about school," she responds.

"Oh yeah, I had a good day at school," he says, so focused on his puzzle that he doesn't even raise his head.

"Well, I think it's something more, isn't it?" says my mother, fishing.

"Ammi, it's still in the works," I say. "We're actually all discussing it. Ibrahim saw the new school last week, and he really liked it. Nonna also came, together with Abdurrahman. We have another couple of days to make a decision."

"Well, from what I've heard, including from your brother, it sounds like an excellent option: a small Islamic school, with a fully integrated academic curriculum, and a good, shaded playground; who could ask for anything more?" says my mother.

"I think our major question at this stage is whether Ibrahim wants to take on the *hifdh* work full time or integrate it as we have been doing, and have Khadija continue to take the lead in teaching the children," says Abdurrahman.

"But, she's doing well, and so is he," says my mother, smiling at Ibrahim and me.

"Yes, but Khadija's also decided to take on some water work," Abdurrahman responds.

"More at the Montessori school?" asks my mother.

"Perhaps, but something else too; last week one of my former colleagues sent me a very interesting project," I say.

"And how would that work?"

"She'll work from home, part-time," responds Ibrahim, still focused on his puzzle, but obviously following the conversation closely now. "So when we're at school; Ammi will do a little work, but when we're home she'll be our mother-teacher, again."

"And the *hifdh*?" asks my mother.

"*Inshaa Allah* that will continue for me too; we're going to try to make it all work," I respond.

"We're going to juggle," says Ibrahim, looking up and smiling, as though he's just learned a new metaphor.

"Juggle, eh?" says Nani. I can't help but expect Nonna to arrive on the scene and start to juggle in front of all of us, given her flare for playing along, but she has closed her door momentarily, and is out of ear shot, with Amna.

"Well, it sounds very exciting. Knowing all of you, you will make it work, even Amna, *inshaa Allah*. Now, weren't we supposed to have dinner tonight?" asks my mother. "I thought you were cooking Khadija?"

"Ammi, I made something, but you have your son-in-law to thank for the rice. I just can't seem to get the timing right."

"Oh, *baita*, how about you focus on the *hifdh*, and the children and water, and you leave the rice to me and Abdurrahman?" says my mother, patting me gently.

"I have no complaints," I say.

"But you know what, Nani, she bought us olives and dates," says Ibrahim.

"Well, that sounds good. I don't see why we can't eat them in the place of rice?" says my mother, smiling.

"And do you know why?" he asks.

"They are delicious, nutritious and look good on the table," my mother responds.

"Something else," says Ibrahim.

"Well, knowing your mother, at this stage in her life, it must have something to do with a... *surah*," says my mother.

"You've got it Nani; but now guess which, and which *ayah*," says Ibrahim.

"Ibrahim, this is too big a test for me; remember I'm a retired community journalist who's dabbling in geography these days," says my mother.

"You are too modest, Nasheeta," says Abdurrahman. "You are also raising grandchildren, not to mention giving us cooking lessons, and teaching us Urdu."

"Yes, yes, and that's all very hard work; ok, which *surah*?" says my mother, dismissing Abdurrahman's comment and starting to play along.

"I'll give you one clue; it begins with an 'ein', and remember we're still in *Juz Amma*," Ibrahim says.[3]

"Well, I would hope so," says my mother. "You're not allowed to finish *Juz Amma* without some fanfare. Ok, an 'ein' eh?"

"Yes, an 'ein'," responds Ibrahim.

"I am going to take the liberty of looking in my *mushaf*," says my mother, pulling a small Qur'aan out of her purse.

"Nani, that's sort of cheating, you were supposed to just recall the *surahs* from memory," says Ibrahim.

"Ibrahim, you did not stipulate that from the beginning, and furthermore, I am not doing *hifdh*, it's you and your mother, and your father and Amna, and Naeem; you might have even piqued Yasmeen's interest, last I heard," says my mother, smiling quite broadly now. "But because I am not a *hifdh* student, and I am your elder, you have to give me a little more allowance."

"Ok, let's just say, you may look at the table of contents, very briefly," Ibrahim says.

My mother flips to the back of her *mushaf*. "I don't think it's *Surah Al Alaq*," says my mother, "although that does start with an 'ein'," she adds.

"Ammi, I think Ibrahim wants you to find a *surah* that starts with an *ayah* that starts with an ein," I say, trying to clarify.

"Oh goodness, well then looking at the table of contents is not really going to help," says my mother, with a slight sign of concern on her face. "Ibrahim you may have trumped me here. And you know your Nani is really quite hungry. Why not bring me one of those olives and then you can explain it all to me," says my mother.

"Nani, we're on *Surah Al Abasa* right now," Ibrahim responds, dutifully bringing the tray of olives and dates to my mother and presenting it to her.[4]

"*Bohaut shukria baita*, and so, now help me to connect the pieces," she responds.

"Ammi, brought the olives and dates to help us think about *ayah*....Ammi, which one is it again?" says Ibrahim turning to me.

"Oh Ibrahim, you know this; now, how about I give you one chance to look in your *mushaf*."

"I got it," says Amna, opening Nonna's door and bursting out with her normal excitement and intensity. She is clutching Daisy the dinosaur and the new *Strega Nona* book that apparently Nonna brought to help introduce more Italian into the children's lives.

"Amna, just hold on for a minute; you're not allowed to interrupt this time. Ammi just asked me a very important question," says Ibrahim in his serious voice.

Amna senses her brother's seriousness and does not advance. Meanwhile, Ibrahim goes to the bookshelf and takes down his *mushaf*, flipping to *Surah Al Abasa*.

"I've got it now," he says.

"And what exactly would that be?" asks Nonna.

"It's sort of a long story, Nonna, but it helps explain why we're eating olives and dates with the biryani tonight."

"Oh, I thought the olives were just a Sicilian touch and the dates, well, they seem to always be part and parcel of your meals," says Nonna.

"There's something more tonight, Mama," Abdurrahman says to his mother.

"*Ayah* 29, Ammi," says Ibrahim, looking at me, for approval.[5]

"*Ayah* 29?" says Amna quizzically.

"Yes, you got it," I say. "Now, how about we serve your father's rice and my vegetables together with some more olives and dates?" I ask before any of us start off in a new direction.

"Good idea," affirms my mother, and she pulls out a chair and beckons for Nonna to sit down, next to her.

"And then, after dinner, we can all call Mary and Hamza to congratulate them," says Nonna.

"And Naeem," says Ibrahim. "It's going to be a lot of work for him, and I might need to give him some advice," he adds.

"I advise," says Amna.

"Ok, ok, advisors, please be seated, now; dinner is being served," Abdurrahman says as he carries the steaming pot of biryani to the table, and I follow suit with my date and olive platter.

HIFDH TEACHING NOTE

What treat will you prepare to accompany your lesson today? If there is a reference to food in a *surah*, it is highly recommended to try to incorporate a little snack or even a meal, featuring such food, to help make the *surah* come alive. In this episode, Khadija serves dates and olives to highlight *ayah* 29 of *Surah Al Abasa*. You could also incorporate a review game to see how many other *surahs* include the same (food) reference. Take the lesson into the kitchen, put on your aprons and *bon appétit*.

---

[1] As translated by Abdullah Yusuf Ali, *ayah* 15 of *Surah At Takweer*, "So verily I call to witness the Planets that recede," (p.1608), which he explains as follows: "The appeal here is made to three things [verses 15-18], the Planets, the Night, and the Dawn. (1) The Planets have a retrograde and a forward motion, and during occultation, hide or disappear behind the sun or moon, or are otherwise invisible or appear stationary. They behave differently from the millions of stars around them. Yet they are not mere erratic bodies, but obey definite laws, and evidence the power and wisdom of Allah."

[2] *Brava Strega Nona* (DePaola 2008).

[3] The Arabic letter referenced in this passage is: ع pronounced 'ein'.

[4] *Surah Al Abasa* is the 80th chapter in the Qur'aan, the 3rd last in *Juz Amma* (the 30th section of the Qur'aan), and is translated as 'He Frowned' (Abdullah Yusuf Ali 1989, p.1600).

[5] *Ayah* 29 is translated as follows: "And Olives and Dates." *Ayah* 29 follows from *ayah* 24 in the same *surah*: "24. Then let man look at his Food, (and how we provide it): 25. For that We pour forth water in abundance, 26. And We split the Earth in fragments, 27. And produce therein Corn, 28. And grapes and nutritious plants, 29. And Olives and Dates," (Abdullah Yusuf Ali 1989, p.1602).

39

PHARAOHS

Date/place: mid-June, mid-week, Houston, neighborhood park, mid-afternoon

Cast of Characters: Ibrahim, Khadija, Amna

"I don't know about Pharaoh."

"What exactly does that mean?" I ask.

"I don't understand why he did what he did," responds Ibrahim.

"What made you think of that?" I inquire.

"Last night," Ibrahim says.

"Last night, Friday," says Amna, who is trying to contribute her bit to the conversation.

"No, last night was Wednesday," corrects Ibrahim, then continuing, "and anyway, you're not allowed to interrupt me," he says pointing his bow and arrow at her.

"Ibrahim," I say sternly, "do not point that at your sister's face."

"Not, me," says Amna, waving her index finger back and forth in front of her brother, as if to correct him, this time.

"But Ammi, she's always interrupting me. I can never finish a sentence," says Ibrahim with a sigh of exasperation.

"I'm sorry Ibrahim, but that is no reason to threaten her with your bow. Remember, the ground rules are…"

"Only use the bow and arrow in the park, and don't kill anyone or anything," says Ibrahim, finishing off my sentence.

"Ibrahim," I say, quite strongly, looking down at him.

"I mean, don't hurt anyone or anything," he says, back-stepping a bit.

"Don't hurt me," mimics Amna, again waving her finger.

"Ok, so, if you would just put your bow and arrow down for a minute, and promise never to threaten us with it again, then we can all discuss Pharaoh; and, please, let's be a little more tolerant and let Amna also have her say," I say, looking at both children.

"I'm listening, Ammi, and I promise," says Ibrahim, laying his weapon down on the ground.

"I'm too listening," adds Amna, following her brother's cue and putting her small(er) bow and arrow down as well, which Nonna and I were prompted to buy after she coveted her brother's one.

"Ammi, could we sit under a tree instead; it's sort of hot right here," says Ibrahim.

"Sure, wherever you like," I say, picking up both bows and arrows and following Ibrahim's lead. He finally settles on a big tree, which also has a series of good tree climbing branches.

"Ammi, is it ok if we climb as we discuss?" he asks.

"Yes, *baita*," I say, smiling, now understanding his reason for wanting to get out of the sun, "but first tell me again why you thought of Pharaoh."

"That film Papa put on for us, about Egypt," responds Ibrahim.[1]

"What about it?" I say.

"Well, I don't understand why the Pharaohs thought they were God," says Ibrahim.

"Ibrahim, do you know what?"

"What?" he says.

"You ask good questions *masha'Allah*," I say.

"Thank you, Ammi, you do too," Ibrahim responds.

"Now, just let me open my *mushaf* for a minute," I say, taking a small Qur'aan out of my knapsack, which I carry for instances like this.

"Here?" Ibrahim asks.

"*Baita*, I need to find something quickly. Ok, listen to this," I say reading out of the *mushaf*, "Fa –qala 'ana Rabbukumul-'a-la."[2]

"Ammi, I know, that's why Papa showed us the film; he wanted us to see Pharaoh and help us imagine that part of *Surah An Naziat*," says Ibrahim, not missing a beat. Then he adds, "but what I don't understand is why Pharaoh acted that way in the first place."

"I'm thirsty," says Amna, letting go of her branch and coming over to me. She unzips the knapsack and takes out our thermos, unaided.

"Well done, Amna," I say, applauding her for her independence.

"I did it by myself," she says.

"I see *baita*, and that's very good work," I respond.

"Ammi, please. Remember Pharaoh," says Ibrahim, still holding his branch and doing what looks like a possum trick.

"*Baita*, I will, but you please be careful. Ok, Pharaoh. Wait, just a minute. Do you see what Amna just did?" I ask.

"By myself," she repeats.

"Yes, but ultimately, there is something greater right?" I ask, looking more at Ibrahim.

"You mean we're puppets?" asks Ibrahim.

"No, not puppets," I say. "We are all working, struggling and trying by ourselves, but ultimately Allah *Subhanahu wa-ta'ala* is behind us, as the Creator and the Sustainer."

"So Pharaoh thought he was Allah?" says Ibrahim.

"Yes," I respond.

"But why?" Ibrahim persists.

"Well, it's all in your Qur'aan *baita*, and we've already read a lot about it.[3] It seems it's almost ingrained in humankind to constantly think of oneself as God and forget the real God," I say.

"But why would the real God do that, if He is really in control?" asks Ibrahim.

"Well, it's sort of like a test for us," I say.

"I don't like tests," says Ibrahim, still hanging upside down.

"Think of this one as a test for which you receive lots of rewards," I respond.

"Ok, I like this test then," Ibrahim says.

"Me too," says Amna, slowly making her way up her brother's branch. I think twice about removing her, in anticipation of a quarrel, but let it go for the time being.

"So what's the biggest reward?" asks Ibrahim.

"Heaven," I say, "and peace within."

"What?" says Amna.

I wonder how to explain the next piece. I have both children's full attention. "You know Hafidha Rabia may be able to do this better than me," I say.

"Ammi, don't leave us hanging," says Ibrahim, obviously borrowing an expression from his father. "I get the Heaven part, but what do you mean, 'peace within'?"

"Ok, let me try. My sense is that someone who thinks they are God has a misunderstanding of the order of the universe, including his or her own place in the universe. Do you remember *Surah At Takweer* and the puzzle you did? And then do you remember how we spoke about how small our earth is within the solar system, and how our solar system is part of a galaxy, and that galaxy is part of a greater universe? Just think how small we, you and me and Amna, really are, in the universe? We should always strive to do good in the world, but none of us could create or regulate such a universe. And so it is incorrect ever to claim that we are God. No matter how tall we build our pyramids, ultimately, if we seek to glorify only ourselves, our efforts will end in naught, nothing, zero," I say, first tracing an imaginary pyramid in the air and then making a circle with my index finger and thumb. I then add, "As a person's quest to be God continues, as we saw with Pharaoh, so too does his anxiety or discomfort, since this role is God's alone, and generally this is part of his own destruction or demise," which I illustrate first by raising my index finger up towards the sky and then changing direction quickly to let my whole hand fall close to the ground.

"Ammi, Amna thinks she's in control, and maybe that's why she cries, because she's not at peace inside," says Ibrahim. "I, however, know that you are in charge and then Papa, and then of course Allah," he adds.

"*Baita*, Amna is learning, and doesn't really cry that much; bottom line, I think she accepts that she shares power with you and many others," I say, smiling, relieved that some of my soliloquy made sense.

"Ammi, I think the world would be a more peaceful place if there were fewer Pharaohs in the world," says Ibrahim.

"*Baita*, I agree, a lot more peaceful. But just think you have that wisdom as well as the hands and heart and mind to act upon it."

"Does this mean we are going to do our review now, all the way down to *Surah An Nas*?" asks Ibrahim.

"In 10 more minutes *inshaa Allah*. I think you have a tree to climb first, and then some snack to eat," I say.

"I snack," offers Amna.

"Yes, *baita*, I know, but first climb tree," I say holding her hand to assist her as she makes her way up the branch, towards her brother.

"Ammi, also remember, you have another *Strega Nona* book to read us," calls out Ibrahim, moving swiftly up the branch, as Amna pursues him.[4] "Nonna gave you an assignment last week, remember, before she left?"

"Yes, *baita*, I do. I'll try to make good on my commitment too; and of course, we also have Nani's book about the sheep in Spanish, to read, after that," I add.[5]

"After," says Amna, nodding her head. Then she asserts, "First, tree climb, and no Pharaohs," once again waving her index finger to make sure we both understand.

HIFDH TEACHING NOTE

The Pharaohs of Ancient Egypt are no longer with us, but power hungry men and women, seeking to glorify themselves alone, still abound. Their hubris almost always brings their nemesis, and it is this lesson that we should try to communicate as we discuss the Pharaohs of history and today. One way to teach this important aspect is show the rise and fall of many such rulers. They are evident in *Surah An Nazi'at* as well as being mentioned extensively throughout the Qur'aan. You could start by discussing this theme in *Nazi'at* and then do word searches on 'Pharaoh' to show how/where it appears in other *surahs*. It could be an opportunity for a review as well as a preview of (sections of) *surahs* to come. In addition, *Nazi'at* also lends itself to drawing, particularly *ayaat* 27-33. Consider for example, "On high hath He raised its canopy, and He hath given it order and perfection." (79:28). Let your young learners meditate on these *ayaat* and see how they express the words in pictures, even as they may potentially be racing to the finish line (with the near-completion of *Juz Amma*, now only 1 *surah* away).

---

[1] The author suggests the following, albeit with parental guidance, for younger children: *Instant Expert*: A Quick Guide to Egypt, History Channel (2010).

[2] Pharaoh's assertion after Prophet Moses, *Alayhis salaam*, tried to lead him back to God, translated as, "Saying, 'I [Pharaoh] am your Lord, Most High;' *ayah* 24, excerpted from the 79th *surah*, *Surah An Naziat* ('Those Who Tear Out') (Abdullah Yusuf Ali 1989, p.1595).

[3] The 30th *Juz* is full of references to humankind's idea that s/he is fully autonomous and all powerful. See *ayah* 7 in *Surah Al Alaq*: "In that he looketh upon himself as self-sufficient," (Abdullah Yusuf Ali 1989, p. 1673). See *ayah* 5 in *Surah Al Balad*, "Thinketh he, that none hath power over him?" (p.1650). There are also countless references to Pharaoh, and the punishment he received, throughout the 30th *Juz* to reinforce this message, including in *Surah An Naziat*, "But Allah did punish him [Pharaoh], (and made an) example of him –in the Hereafter, as in this life (*ayah* 25, p. 1595).

[4] See 38th Chapter.

[5] *Donde esta la oveja verde?* (*Where is the green sheep?*) is a wonderful bilingual children's book that teaches basic Spanish/English phrases (Fox 2004).

40

THANK YOU NOTES

Date/place: late June, Houston, Ibrahim and Amna's living room/kitchen, evening, after *magreb*

Cast of characters: Abdullah, Ibrahim, Khadija, Amna, Abdurrahman

"So what do you think?"

"Well, I didn't really expect it," replies Ibrahim.

"Well, I didn't really expect you to get all the way to the end; last I heard you were struggling in *Surah An Naba* and it might take another six weeks," replies my brother, Abdullah, who has surprised the children with a visit and two gifts, on his way home from work.[1]

"Do you really think that Amna should get one, though?" asks Ibrahim, looking over at Amna's rod.

"Ibrahim, we both know that the only way to get Amna to let you ever go fishing is for her to have her own rod, agreed?"

"*Jee haan,*" says Ibrahim. "I guess you're right; it's just Amna didn't really work that hard. She mostly distracted me."

"Ibrahim," I say, overhearing his comment from the kitchen.

"Ammi, I didn't say you didn't help, or Papa, or Sheikh Husri, or Hafidha Rabia, or Uncle Bill, or Sabir, or Nonna, or," says Ibrahim, stopping to catch his breath for a moment, then continuing he adds, "or Nani, or Yaseen, or Naeem, or… is that it?" he then asks, more to himself than anyone else.

"Don't forget your cousin, Yasmeen," adds Abdullah.

"What about Ms Suzy? Didn't she listen once or twice, and David and your Aunt Mary? And did Sheikh Husri really tutor you? I thought that he passed away in the 1980s," says Abdurrahman.

"Papa, I've heard his recording every day for eight months. He's definitely been with us," asserts a mature sounding Ibrahim. "And yes, you're right about Ms Suzy, and David and Alex and Aunt Mary and even your brother," says Ibrahim counting out each person's name on his fingers. "And, let's not forget Lieutenant Laila and Sergeant Faith, Officer Ayesha and even Private Nouman, and… our trip to the space museum," he finally concludes.

"Well, that's great, but I still think you're giving Amna short shrift," says Abdullah.

"Short what?" asks Ibrahim.

"I'm not short," bellows Amna, wanting to be included.

"No *baita*, you are definitely not short," I say to Amna, bending over, then squatting so that I am her height. I pat her gently on the back and notice that she is clutching Abdurrahman's Lenin pin, which Ibrahim has long since appropriated.

"My pin," Amna says, shaking her hand so that we take note.

"What?" says Ibrahim with some concern in his voice. He is sitting next to my brother in the living room and so is not able to see Amna but clearly has a hunch that she may be into his things.

"My pin," Amna repeats, then, "I'm not short."

"Yes you are," Ibrahim responds, getting up and approaching his sister, "and that's my pin."

"Whoa," says Abdullah, following Ibrahim. "I thought we were here to fly fish and talk about *Juz Amma*?"

"Amna, give me my pin," says Ibrahim, not taking note of his uncle's comment and shooting Amna a look of great seriousness, "or else…"

"Ibrahim," I say.

"It's my pin," Amna utters again.

"You know if neither of you is interested in these fishing rods, I can easily return them, together with my congratulations," says Abdullah, choosing a slightly different diversion tactic.

"What?" says Ibrahim, who's realized instantaneously that he cherishes the fishing rod more than the pin.

"It seems to me that we might be losing sight of the real prize," adds Abdullah.

"I'm glad they're hearing this from you," offers Abdurrahman, who's been at my side in the kitchen, washing up.

"What prize?" queries Ibrahim.

"I want a prize," says Amna.

"Don't we all," says Abdullah. Abdullah then squats next to Ibrahim and takes his hand, also strategically placing himself in between the two children so as to keep them apart. He then continues, looking at Ibrahim and all of us. "Listen, Ibrahim has just done something really wonderful; he's taken part of the Qur'aan and put it in his heart. He's memorized the whole of *Juz Amma*. I've never been able to do that, and there are a lot of other people like me who've never even attempted it. But if we memorize without actually changing our hearts then what really is the point?"[2]

161

I am surprised by Abdullah's words. Rarely have I heard my kid brother speak with such clarity or depth.

"I don't need a changed heart, just a more muscled one," says Ibrahim.

"And what would you do with a more muscular heart, Ibrahim?" asks his father.

"Love Allah," says Ibrahim, without hesitating.

"And what about Amna?" Abdullah asks.

"Well, she first has to be nice, and not take my pin, and keep to her side of life," responds Ibrahim.

"And then you'll be a good bhai jaan?" queries Abdullah. "I wouldn't wait for all that. You know you're six now. And that's pretty old. I'd imagine at six that you are old enough simply to be nice to her because you know it's the right thing to do."

"I'm not that old," responds Ibrahim. "Six is really not that old," he repeats.

"But how do you think that Amna will learn how to love and respect?" asks Abdullah.

"By Ammi and Nani teaching her and reading some books about kindness," says Ibrahim.

"What about by watching you?" says Abdullah, who is more committed to this conversation than I would have expected. I sense that he's also been struggling with many of the same issues with Yaseen and Yasmeen and he may have figured out how to get the message across.

"What do you mean, watching me? With my binoculars?" says Ibrahim.

"No, you know what I am talking about," says Abdullah.

"Well, what about the 'learning by heart' bit you were talking about before?" replies Ibrahim.

"It's a great accomplishment to memorize the Qur'aan Ibrahim, but you know the real proof is in the pudding," says Abdullah.

"Pudding?" asks Amna.

"Meaning, it's what you do with it. Are you living the Qur'aan or just reciting it? Does it change your heart, or to use your expression give you a more 'muscled' heart? And are you able to recognize, with your big heart-ed self, at the ripe age of six that your little sister actually helped you get where you are today?"

"Uncle Abdullah, Amna did not help," says Ibrahim.

"What about all the interruptions? Didn't that actually help make you concentrate more? And what about when you tried to teach her *ayaat*; didn't that help? You know your mother told me about those. She was so excited when Amna started learning from you. And what about when your little sister started reciting, totally unprompted, simply because she had heard Sheikh Husri's

162

voice and your own so many times; all that helped Ibrahim, whether you want to acknowledge it or not," says Abdullah.

Abdurrahman starts clapping softly, next to him. "*Bohaut shukria*," he then adds reaching out to shake my brother's hand. "Very well said."

"I thought I was getting the fishing rod," says Ibrahim.

"Yes, *baita*, you are, and the congratulations, but your uncle has just taught us all a thing or two," I say, looking with affection at my brother.

"And so when are we going fishing?" asks Ibrahim.

"Well, I thought I might take you the first week of August, when your cousins from Cambridge are visiting, after you all return from Austin. I especially thought your cousin David might enjoy it, based on what I've heard about him," responds Abdullah.

"Alex will also enjoy it; remember she's his twin," offers Ibrahim.

"I'm twin too," says Amna.

"Not quite, you're a little younger," says Ibrahim.

"I'm not short," says Amna again.

"Yes, you are, but that's ok; you're growing, and maybe one day, you'll be taller than Nonna," says Ibrahim, taking some of Abdullah's advice to heart.

"I'm growing," says Amna.

"Yes, and it's almost time for your bedtime and your lesson," continues Ibrahim. "If you're good and quiet and show your bhai jaan a little respect then I might just teach you the end of *Surah Al Asr*."

"And perhaps if you're good, she might even help you with the 29th *Juz inshaa Allah*," says Abdullah, smiling.[3]

"Flying?" asks Amna, somewhat out of the blue.

"No, no, first Qur'aan, then fishing," responds Ibrahim.

"Well actually, she might have understood more than you thought; I might need to upgrade your rods sooner rather than later, but, yes, I'd actually like to take you all fly fishing. It's really quite amazing…" says Abdullah, whose own mind seems to be drifting to one of his new found interests.[4]

"Fly fish… yes," confirms Amna, already on her way to the next adventure.

HIFDH TEACHING NOTE

Surah An Naba is a fitting ending to this story and the *Juz*. It is indeed a *surah* of 'Great News' and within it we hear so many of the themes that have been showcased throughout the 30th part of the Qur'aan. But hear too, Abdullah's wise words: "He's memorized the whole of *Juz Amma*. I've never been able to do that, and there are a lot of other people like me who've never even attempted it. But if we memorize without actually changing our hearts then what really is the point?" This comment is offered on the cusp of a fight between Ibrahim and Amna, which Abdullah is trying to redirect. It is an important comment, and speaks to a theme that has been articulated in many different ways, by many different characters since the beginning of the story. For those of us who are aspiring *huffadh* our work is ongoing; it does not end with an *ayah*, or a *surah*, it is rather a daily *jihad* of sorts, to preserve the words and the meaning and live the *deen* as it was intended. May *AllahSWT* make it easy *inshaa Allah* and may we be ever mindful of His*SWT* glorious and unending message.

---

[1]
Surah An Naba is the 78th *surah* in the Qur'aan and the last in *Juz Amma*. It is translated as 'The (Great) News'. As summarized by Abdullah Yusuf Ali, "It [*Surah An Naba*] sets forth Allah's loving care in a fine nature passage, and deduces from it the Promise of the Future, when Evil will be destroyed and Good will come to its own; and invites all who have the will, to seek refuge with their Lord (p.1584)."

[2]
Mu'az Juhani *RA* reports that Rasulullah *SAW* said, "Whoever reads the Qur'an and acts upon what is contained in it, his parents will be made to wear a crown on the Day of Judgment, the brightness of which will excel that of the sun, if the same were within your worldly houses. So, what do you think about the person who himself acts upon it?" (Abu Dawud Hadith Collection).

[3]
There are a variety of different approaches to *hifdh*, including starting with the 30th *Juz* and then moving on to the 29th, and 28th and then continuing from *Juz* 1. Some teachers and students prefer, after the completion of the 30th *Juz*, to continue until the 20th *Juz* and then start at the beginning of the Qur'aan. Still other approaches include starting from the first *Juz*, at inception.

[4]
Chinese proverb, accredited to Lao Tzu, the Chinese founder of Taoism, 4th Century BC, "If you give a man a fish you feed him for a day. If you teach a man to fish you feed him for a lifetime."

GLOSSARY

A Qur'aanic Odyssey is written primarily in English; however, the text also includes words from many different languages (all appearing in *italics*), including Arabic, Italian, Spanish, Russian and Urdu. The Qur'aan was revealed in Arabic; Italian is the mother tongue of Abdurrahman and his family. Nonna and Nani are learning Spanish and it is widely spoken throughout Houston, and finally, Urdu is the mother tongue of the narrator (Ammi) and her family. These pages will hopefully provide some help to readers trying to navigate the various different languages incorporated in the text.

Ababeel: bird, featured in *Surah Al Fil* (Arabic)

Abbu: father (Urdu)

Accha hae: Ok or it's good (Urdu)

Ahista, ahista: slowly, slowly (Urdu)

Al Fatihah: refers to *Surah Al Fatihah* (the Opening), the first chapter of the Qur'aan (Arabic)

Alaq: the title of the 96th *surah* (chapter) in the Qur'aan, meaning congealed blood, and refers to how humankind is created (Arabic)

Alayhis salaam: may Allah/God bless him, abbreviated as *'AS'* (Arabic)

Alhumdulilah: thanks be to Allah/God (Arabic)

Allah (Subhanahu wa-ta'ala): Allah/God, glorious and exalted is He (also abbreviated as Allah*SWT*), also sometimes referred to as Allah ta'ala (Arabic)

Amanah: it is when a person fulfills his obligations due to *AllahSWT* (Arabic)

Amore mio: my love, term of endearment (Italian)

Angel Gibreel: it is believed in Islam that the Qur'aan was communicated to Prophet Muhemmed *SAW* by Angel Gibreel (English, 'Gabriel')

Ar-Rahman Ar-Raheem: the Most Beneficent, the Most Merciful, refers to Allah/God (Arabic)

Ashura: 10th day of the month of Muharram (1st month of Islamic year) (Arabic)

Asr: the title of the 103rd *surah* in the Qur'aan and also the name of the afternoon prayers (Arabic)

Assalaamu 'alaykum: peace be upon you (Arabic), the response is *'Wa alaykum salaam'*

Authu Billahi Minishaytonir Rajeem: I seek refuge in Allah, from the accursed

Satan (Arabic)

Ayah/ayaat: line from the Qur'aan, *ayaat* is the plural (Arabic)

Bambino: child (Italian)

Bayyinah: The Clear Evidence, refers to the 98th *surah* of the Qur'aan (Arabic)

Bene: well (Italian)

Baita/baiti: boy child/girl child (Urdu)

Baita jaan: beloved/dear child (Urdu)

Bhabi: brother's wife (Urdu)

Bhai jaan: beloved brother (Urdu)

Bilcul: of course (Urdu)

Bismillah: in the name of Allah/God (Arabic)

Bohaut shukria: thank you very much (Urdu)

Buono: good (Italian)

Chai: tea (Urdu)

Chalyae: go (politely) (Urdu)

Coche: car (Spanish)

Come stai: how are you (Italian)

Day of Arafat: 9th day of *Dhul Hijja* (Islamic month) and the second day of the *Hajj* (pilgrimage). Pilgrims congregate on Mount Arafa on this day and ask for forgiveness from *AllahSWT*

Dawah: invitation to the faith, to the prayer, or to Islamic life, particularly inviting one to understand Islam, (Arabic)

Deen: religion/way of life (Arabic)

Dhur: mid-day prayer, among the five daily prayers (Arabic)

Eid al Adha: Eid/celebration at the end of *Hajj* (Arabic)

Eid ul Fitr: Eid/celebration at the end of Ramadan, month of fasting (Arabic)

Es Verdad: it's true (Spanish)

Fard: obligatory, often refers to the obligatory five daily prayers in Islam (Arabic)

Geem: sound of the 5th letter in the Arabic alphabet

Grazie: thank you (Italian)

Hafidh/a: one who has memorized the Qur'aan (Arabic)

Hadith: sayings and deeds of Prophet Muhemmed *SAW* (Arabic)

Hajj: pilgrimage (Arabic)

Hajji: an honorific title, one who has completed the *Hajj* (Arabic)

Halal: refers largely to food type and preparation, which is in accordance with Islamic belief and laws, including the exclusion of pork and wine and any by-products (Arabic)

Haq/haqqi: truth (Arabic)

Hifdh: memorization/preservation of Qur'aan (Arabic)

Huffadh: plural of hafidh, one who has memorized the Qur'aan (Arabic)

Iftari: breaking of the fast, generally consists of dates and water followed by light snacks (Arabic)

Inshaa Allah: God willing (Arabic)

Intizar: to wait (Urdu)

Isha salah: fifth prayer of the day, prayed when the sky is completely dark, after sunset/magreb (Arabic)

Jannah: heaven (Arabic)

Jee: yes (Urdu)

Jee haan: yes (more polite) (Urdu)

Jumu'ah: refers to both Friday and the congregational *dhur* prayer of Friday (Arabic)

Juz: the Qur'aan is divided into 30 *juz* (parts/sections), *Juz Amma* is the 30th and last section of the Qur'aan (Arabic)

Kaaba: cubed shaped building, in Mecca, Saudi Arabic, which Prophet Ibrahim *AS* built together with his son Ismaeel *AS*. During their requisite daily prayers, Muslims, all around the world, orient themselves facing toward the Kaaba

Kahan: where (Urdu)

Kameez shalwar: native dress of men in Pakistan, long flowing shirt and generally loose pant (Urdu)

Karabala: refers largely to the Battle of Karbala (Arabic)

Kha: sound of the 7th letter in the Arabic alphabet

Khuda Hafiz: May God be with you, farewell greeting (Urdu)

Kiya: What (Urdu)

Kiya haal hein: how are you (Urdu)

Kuch nahin: nothing (Urdu)

Laila-tul Baraa'at: the Night of Forgiveness (Arabic)

Lista/o/os: ready (Spanish)

Magreb: refers to prayers offered after sunset (Arabic)

Mamoo: mother's brother (Urdu)

Mairae dil kae qareeb hae: close to my heart (Urdu)

Masha'Allah: this is what Allah willed, used to express awe/appreciation, without any sense of covetousness (Arabic)

Masjid Al Haram: main mosque of Islam, located in Mecca, which surrounds the Kaaba

Maulvi sahib: religious teacher (Urdu)

Mein tayyaar hoon: I am ready (Urdu)

Mudood: plural of '*madd*', Arabic grammar terminology referring to the elongation of a letter (Arabic)

Mullah: teacher (Arabic)

Mushaf: "The printed text is referred to as the Mus-haf which means 'bound pages'. The orally transferred, untainted and untouched, mentally preserved, recited text is what all refer to as the 'the Qur'an'." (I. Londt, p. 23, Arabic)

Nafl: optional, often refers to the optional/*nafl* prayers in Islam (Arabic)

Nani: maternal grandmother (Urdu)

Nani jaan: beloved/dear grandmother (Urdu), see above

Niente: nothing (Italian)

Nonna: grandmother (Italian)

On y va: let's go there (French)

Pani: water (Urdu)

Phuppi jaan: dear aunt (father's sister, Urdu)

Pronto: ready (Italian)

Qalqalah: refers to an echoing sound made on any of the five letters (د, ج, ب, ط, ق) when there is a *sakiin* (stop) (Arabic)

Qari: an individual who recites Qur'aan with proper *tajweed* (Arabic)

Qur'aan khatm: completion of Qur'aan (Arabic)

Radiallahu Anhu: abbreviated as *RAA* and *RA* and translated as 'may Allah be pleased with him/her' (Arabic)

Ramadan: month of fasting (Arabic)

Rak'ah: a unit of prayer (Arabic)

Sabr: patience (Arabic)

Sahih: truly, really (Urdu)

Salaam: peace (Arabic), also used as an informal greeting

Salah: prayer, specifically referring to the five daily prayers in Islam (Arabic)

Salla Allahu 'alayhi wa sallam: May Allah bless him and grant him peace (Arabic), referring to Prophet Muhemmed, abbreviated as *SAW*

Sheer Qorma: a sweet dish made and served on Eid, popular primarily on the Subcontinent (Urdu)

Si: yes (Italian, Spanish)

Sirat al Mustaqeem: Straight path (Arabic)

SubhanAllah: Glory be to God (Arabic)

Sunnah: recommended, often refers to the recommended/*sunnah* prayers in Islam (Arabic)

Surah: chapter (Arabic) of the Qur'aan; there are 114 *surahs* in the Qur'aan; Ibrahim and Amna have started from *Surah Al Fatihah* (the first chapter) and then are making their way from the back of the Qur'aan which has the shorter *surahs*, as is common

Taqwah: being conscious of *AllahSWT* in all that one does and having respect and love for the Creator (Arabic)

Tariq: refers to *Surah At Tariq*, translated as the night star 86th *surah*, (Arabic)

Tasmia: is *Bismillahir Rahmanir Raheem*, which is translated as 'in the name of Allah, Most Gracious, Most Merciful'. It is recited before every *surah* in the Qur'aan, except *Surah At Tawbah*. It is also recited before the inception of virtually any activity

Theek hae: ok, alright (Urdu)

Thikr Allah: remembrance of Allah (Arabic)

Thunda pani: cold water (Urdu)

Tren: train (Spanish)

Vamanos: let's go (Spanish), vamanos a ver los leones (let's go see the lions)

Vsegda gotov: always ready (Russian)

Wa alaykum salaam: and upon you peace (Arabic), the response to the greeting '*Assalaamu 'alaykum*'

Wudu: ritual cleaning (Arabic)

Zabardust: great (Urdu)

Zalzalah: earthquake (Arabic), referring to the 99th *surah* of the Qur'aan

WORKS CITED

Abdullah Yusuf Ali (1989). *The Meaning of The Holy Qur'an*. Beltsville: Amna Publications.

Abdullah Yousuf Ali and S. Taha (2007). *Tajweed Qur'an*. Damascus: Dar-Al-Maarifah.

U.S. Fish & Wildlife Service (2010). 'Aransas National Wildlife Refuge'.

Araujo, F.P. (1994). *The Perfect Orange*: A Tale from Ethiopia. Windsor: Rayve Productions Inc.

Bach, R.D. (1970). *Jonathan Livingston Seagull*. New York: Avon Books.

Bemelmans, L. (1939). *Madeleine*. New York: Viking Press.

Beshir, E. & M.R. (2004). *Parenting Skills: Based on the Qur'an and Sunnah*. Beltsville: Amana Publications.

Burton, V.L. (1969). *The Little House*. New York: Houghton, Mifflin Company.

Brunhoff, J.D. (1933). *Babar the Elephant*. New York: Random House.

Curriculum Development Board/Kwa-Zulu Natal Taalimi Board (2006). Tasheelut Tajweed. Fordsburg: JUT Publishing. An online version may be accessed via: http://www.talimiboardkzn.org/Books/simple_rules_of_tajweed.pdf

Dawn (2010). "Khyber-Pakhtunkhwa," April 10.

DePaola, T. (2008). *Brava, Strega Nona!* New York: Penguin Group.

El-Magazy, R. (2000). *Amr and the Ants*. Leicester: The Islamic Foundation.

Ford, H. and Crowther, S. (1922). *My Life and Work*. Garden City: Garden City Publishing Company, Inc.

Fox, M. and Horacek, J. (2004). *Where Is the Green Sheep? Donde esta la oveja verde*. Boston: Houghton Mifflin Harcourt.

Holldobler, B. and E.O. Wilson (1990). *The Ants*. Cambridge: Harvard University Press.

Javaherbin, M. (2010). *Goal!* Somerville: Candlewick Press.

Kaiser Family Foundation (2010). Generation M2.

Khan, S. (2004). *The Miraculous Baby*. New Delhi: Goodword Books.

Lenasia Muslim Association. *Towards Reading the Qur'an: Part Two*. Lenasia.

Londt, I. (2008). *How to Memorize the Holy Qur'an*. Cape Town: Dar Ubaiy Publications.

Muth, J. J. (2002). *The Three Questions: Based on a story by Leo Tolstoy*. New York: Scholastic Press.

Omar, R. (2011). "Personal communication, June 5, re: *hifdh* programs".

Pollan, M. (2006). *The Omnivore's Dilemma*. New York: The Penguin Group.

Sendak, M. (1963). *Where the Wild Things Are*. New York: HarperCollins.

Solomon, S. (2010). *Water: The Epic Struggle for Wealth, Power, and Civilization*. New York: Harper Collins.

Solon, O. (2011). "Robot jockeys illegally equipped with stun guns in camel races," Wired, 26 January, downloaded from wired.co.uk on March 18 2011.

Taylor, J., 2010. *The Queen of Green: A Collection of Contemporary Cautionary Tales from Africa*. Cape Town: Struik Lifestyle.

The Week Online (2010). The Hajj 2010: By the Numbers, November 17, http://theweek.com/article/index/209446/the-hajj-2010-by-the-numbers , downloaded November 25, 2010.

Weatherford, C.B., 2006. *Moses: When Harriet Tubman Led Her People to Freedom*. New York: Hyperion Books for Children.

WEBSITES CITED

American Library Association: http://www.ala.org/ala/professionalresources/libfactsheets/alalibraryfactsheet01.cfm, accessed February 27, 2011

Bayyinah Institute, Talking Book: http://bayyinah.com/tajweed_book/main.html, accessed on April 28, 2011.

CIA World Factbook (2011): https://www.cia.gov/library/publications/the-world-factbook, accessed January 15, 2011.

National Aeronautics and Space Administration (NASA): www.nasa.gov, accessed June 12, 2011.

Naveq: http://corporate.navteq.com, accessed on February 27, 2011.

Pacific Institute: http://www.worldwater.org/conflict/map/, accessed on April 28 2011.

Understand Quran: http://understandquran.com, accessed on April 28, 2011.

World Health Organization: http://www.who.int/violence_injury_prevention/global_status_report/flyer_en.pdf, accessed on March 23, 2011.

HADITH COLLECTIONS

Abu Dawud Hadith Collection

Sahih Muslim Hadith Collection

Shama-il Tirmidhi Hadith Collection

SONGS/ALBUMS CITED

Bhikha, Z. (2006). 'Your mother', featured in the album by Yusuf Islam.'I Look I See'.

FILMS

History Channel (2010). Instant Expert: A Quick Guide to Egypt.

Kenner, R. director (2009). Food Inc.

One 4 Kids Productions, (2010). 'The Earth Has a Fever.'

Sound Vision (2004). 'Home Sweet Home'. Bridgeview.

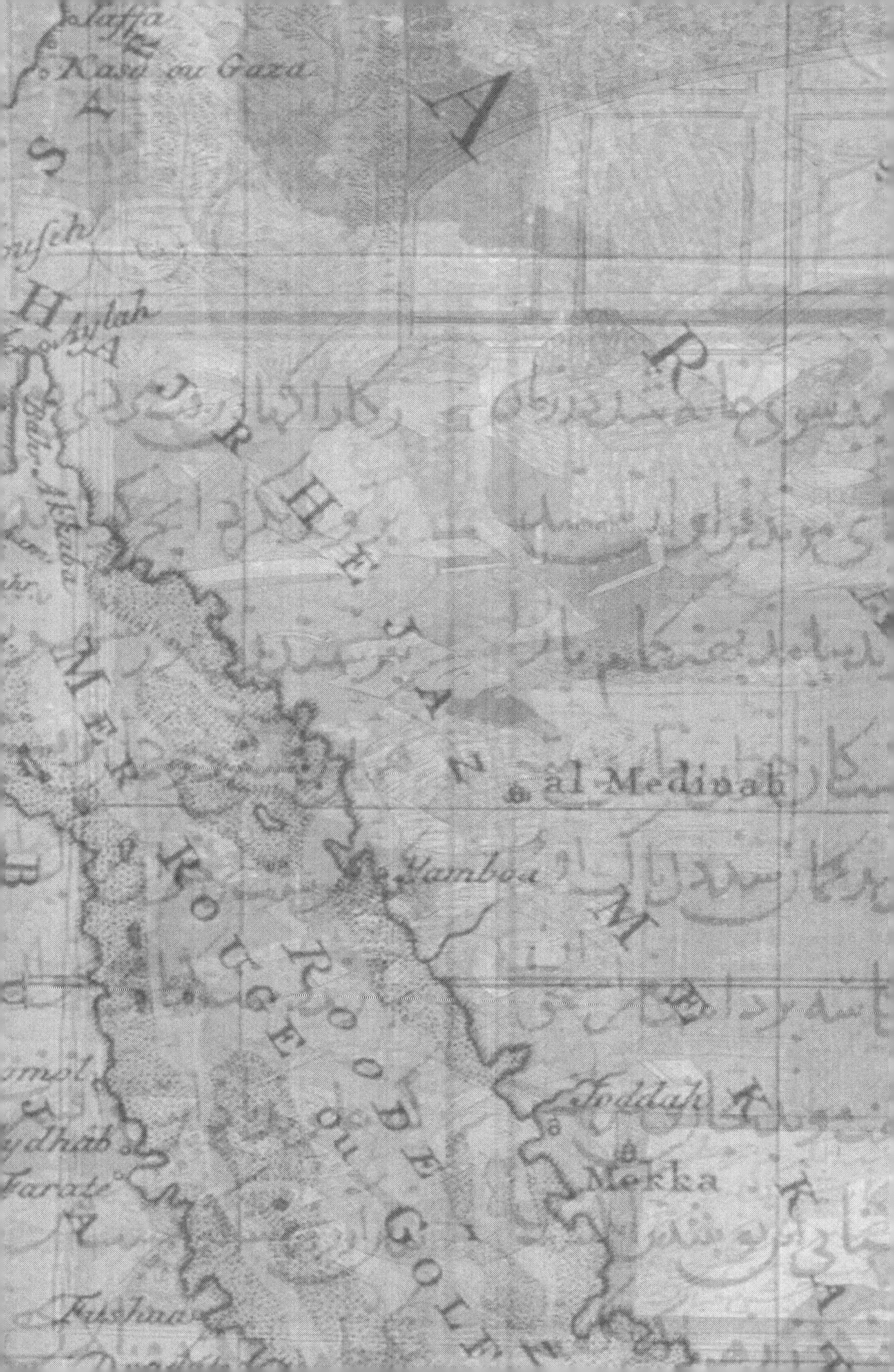

Kasu ou Gaza
Aylah
al Medinah
Yambou
Joddah
Mekka

Ahwaz

Korna

Basrah

Bandar Dilem

Bandar Rik

Karge
Karak

I. Peleche
Zesaren

Rokte

Bandar R

Anger

Che

C. Nabou

I. Lari

GOLFE van

Ghabraun

Perl Bank

de

PE

Al Katif

Kitara

Goda

B

A

H

R

A

Y

Tropicus

Cancri

I

A

Made in the USA
Lexington, KY
01 May 2012